The Detective Joanna Best Mysteries
Book 7

The Sins of the Grandfather

Cenarth Fox

The Detective Joanna Best Mysteries
Book 7
The Sins of the Grandfather

First published in 2020 by Fox Plays
www.foxplays.com
www.cenfoxbooks.com

Cover design by Oliviaprodesign

ISBN 978-0-949175-46-5

Dictionary of Australian words

Here are some of the mainly Australian words/sayings in this novel.

ABC – Australian Born Chinese
AFP – Australian Federal Police
Black stump – fictitious place in the Australian bush
Blind Freddy – fictitious unsighted person
bollocking – a severe reprimand
boot – trunk of a car
bum bag – small bag worn around your waist
Collingwood six-footer – footballer who is 5' 10" or 5' 11"
dob a sausage – dob (kick), sausage roll (goal), kick a goal
dunnies – plural of dunny, lavatory in the backyard
Forex – foreign exchange trading
hanging black crepe – telling bad news as it is, no sugar coating
Heinz 57 varieties – a dog of mixed breed
ICU – Intensive Care Unit in a hospital
Jack Dyer drop punt – kicking a football as per a famous player
kays – kilometres
Liverpool kiss – head butt to someone's face
Mummy/Mum – Mommy/Mom
nappy – diaper
nipper – male sibling
pavement – footpath, sidewalk
Pentridge – former jail in Melbourne
pit stop - toilet break, stop for food when travelling
possie – position
Redback spider – type of dangerous spider
rozzers – the police
shirtfront – front on bump to opponent in Australian football
SIO – Senior Investigating Officer
socks – sox
Soggies – Special Operations Group, specialist armed police force
The G – the MCG, the Melbourne Cricket Ground
Underbelly – TV series about organised crime in Australia
ute – utility, vehicle with tray
wog ball – soccer as first played Down Under by Greeks and Italians

For
Inge Meldgaard
Poet, Short Story Writer and Novelist

Chapter 1

Nipper ran down the driveway and opened the back door. He was all of 10. The door was unlocked. Inside in a flash, through the kitchen, along the hall and into the lounge he ran looking for lightweight items worth a bit. Money was perfect. There was a purse on the dresser. He grabbed it as the elderly woman entered.

'Oi! Who are you?'

Nipper didn't do conversation. With purse in hand he ran. The old lady tried to stop him. He punched her, hurt her, and fled. Meet child criminal, juvenile thug and tearaway, Tommy 'Nipper' Reid.

His old man, a champion pisspot, shot through when Nipper was a toddler, and how his mother kept the Social Services at bay remains a mystery. The cops could find the Reid hacienda blindfolded.

Nipper was the youngest of three boys, and as his big brothers went on the rob, naturally baby brother joined 'em. In 1950, the 10 year old larrikin was busy with his break and enter routine, nicking anything not nailed down. It was time for the cops—again.

'What's he done this time?' groaned Nipper's frustrated Mum.

'Where is he, Mrs Reid?' they asked.

'Dunno,' became her standard reply.

As a teen, Nipper ran errands for crims, graduated to serious deeds, and fell into organised crime. Later, he set up his own empire although became more a Mr Medium than a Mr Big.

By middle age, Nipper dabbled in drugs, money laundering and "insurance". The cops had his number on speed dial but a far bigger threat came from younger criminals who fancied his operation.

Of course Nipper defended his patch and when a rival mobster, sporting six bullet holes, was found in a South Morang paddock, the cops went hunting for T. Reid Esquire. Nipper fled to Broadford.

At his son's place, he explained. 'It's nothing to do with me, son. I need to keep me head down. When they find whoever knocked Mr Invincible, I'll bugger off home.'

Back in the 1990s, the Victoria Police Homicide Squad was run by DCI John Robbo Robertson whose six-year old granddaughter was Joanna Best. Nearing retirement, Robbo wanted to bow out with a 100% homicide clear-up record.

To solve what appeared to be a gang-related murder, Robbo wanted all Melbourne mobsters dragged in for a chat with Nipper definitely on the list. Getting crooks to talk would be harder than numbering the grains of sand on St Kilda beach but doing nothing wasn't an option.

Robbo and his team arrived to find Nipper not home. Mrs Nipper was fluent in two languages—*No Comment* and *I Don't Know*.

Back in their car, Robbo's DS Tuck reported. 'Boss, the next-door neighbour heard Nipper say he was off to his boy's place.' Robbo knew Nipper's son's address in Broadford, about 100 kms from Melbourne.

Nipper's toddler grandson, also Tommy, loved Grandpa but Nipper's daughter-in-law, Rosa, wanted shot of her father-in-law yesterday. Of kisses and hugs were there none. Nipper kept out of Rosa's way in the downstairs spare room and played with his grandson.

Tommy the toddler and Tommy the grandpa were a fantastic team, their love overflowing. They were having a ball when, without warning, the cops came calling. Nipper's son, Cain, yelled.

'Dad, it's the cops.'

Nipper was out the door in a flash. His son's property had road access at both ends. Nipper's car was parked at the rear. It took him no time to reach the vehicle but he lost precious seconds getting the damn key in the ignition. He wished he'd reversed into the property so he could race straight out. Finally the engine roared into life, Nipper threw the gear shift into reverse and floored it. Clunk.

His stomach lurched, bile erupted; he stopped and died inside. The cops came running. Cain and Rosa came running. Nipper froze.

His gorgeous wee grandson, the apple of his Pop's eye, had raced after his Pa and run behind the vehicle to reach the driver's door.

Why didn't the kid run straight at the car? Why didn't the ignition key slip into place sooner? Why didn't God prevent this gut-wrenching tragedy? These and other questions would haunt Nipper forever.

Forget being nabbed by the Homicide Squad. Forget being arrested on suspicion of murder. But never, ever forget the death of a child.

No-one could. Every year on little Tommy's birthday, and on the anniversary of his death, Nipper and family suffered agony; even seeing a little tacker in the street kick-started their misery. Nipper would never knowingly drive past kindergartens. If he could turn back the clock, he would; gladly. To undo what he did, he'd pay any price.

Was the fatality inevitable? I mean, if Nipper had obeyed the law, would the police have been there? Was his lawless childhood the root cause of the tragedy? Was he an accident waiting to happen?

It's scary for a driver when they hit something but don't know what. Nipper threw open his door, and it was the kid's silence that screamed the loudest. If only the child had cried; a scream would've been lovely.

Could the hardened criminal ever feel worse? Please explain what could be worse. Nipper's son and daughter-in-law were hysterical. The cops gave first aid—a waste of time. Nipper was beyond distraught. It was a tragedy with a capital T, and Will Shakespeare, who lost his son when the boy was young, later wrote from first-hand experience.

> *Grief fills the room up of my absent child,*
> *Lies in his bed, walks up and down with me,*
> *Puts on his pretty look, repeats his words.*

Of course Nipper didn't mean to do it but knowing and hearing that only made it worse. He suffered every day and especially at night when trying to sleep. He never again had a good night's rest. Nipper Reid accidentally killed his adored and adorable toddler grandson. In desperation, he blamed the police and Detective Chief Inspector Robbo Robertson in particular. His time would come. Revenge is a dish best served cold.

As Nipper accidentally did the unthinkable, a 16 year-old girl joined him in the everlasting suffering stakes. Vicki (Not her real name) lived in Burwood with her parents and two younger brothers. They were in the middle of middle-class. Dad worked in a hardware store and what he didn't know about paint wasn't worth mixing. Mum worked four days in a bakery. They were law-abiding folk with a black, six year-old Labrador called Buster. He didn't care about being middle-class.

Every January the family holidayed at Blairgowrie, about 90 kms from the Melbourne CBD. Blairgowrie sits on Port Phillip Bay close to the tip of the Mornington Peninsular. The waters of the bay are usually calm and shallow and ideal for young families. The sand at Blairgowrie is clean and plentiful and great for sandcastles.

The brothers had a ball camping there; their older sister not so. Vicki was in Year 11 with hormonal energy to burn. To help maintain her sanity, Vicki was allowed to bring her first best friend, Madison (Maddie) who prevented her teenage girlfriend going potty. The girls wandered to the shops with strict instructions to avoid strangers and particularly those of the male sex; fat chance that'd work.

With their ice-cream, the girls would find a shady spot to watch the world go by. The world in this case consisted of boys. The girls would amuse themselves by labelling each passing male as a great lover, lousy lover, or complete dork. It produced many a laugh; for the girls.

The problem with this so-called game was it kept putting sex at the front of their brains, and we all know we should be careful about what we dwell on and wish for. Both girls were virgins although had dabbled in the preliminaries at parties and school socials.

Thus the scene was set. After the evening meal and as darkness grabbed its pyjamas, Vicki asked if the girls could stroll to the shops.

'One hour only,' said Vicki's Mum, and the girls were genuinely grateful. There was no upmarket club for trendy teens. There was no club full stop. They bought a coffee, sat on a bench and watched the water. They didn't see the three young men until they were upon them.

'Good evening, ladies,' said the first. He was mid-twenties, tall, fit, athletic and full of it. Vicki and Madison were both thrilled and wary. Vicki could hear her mother's warnings playing full volume on a loop.

'Hi,' said the girls.

The spokesman stood close to Vicki, and the other two males were less talkative and stood close to Madison. She turned to the duo who did their best to impress. Simply being there was most of the routine for the males, and looking half decent topped up the requirement. To the girls, these weren't pimply, callow fellows, their classmates. These boys were men with cigarettes and not a trace of bum fluff.

Brody, the one who fancied Vicki, had done this before. He could smell willing female flesh from afar, and played his would-be beau on a string. The offer was simple. Let's take a short drive to the surf beach, have a drink and watch the sun go down over Bass Strait.

The girls looked at one another. *Should we? Could we?*

Vicki laid down the rules. 'We have to be back in an hour,' she said.

'No problems,' grinned Brody. He indicated. 'Your chariot awaits.'

It was a Holden Commodore in good nick. Brody opened the front passenger door for Vicki while the other two gents hopped in either side of Madison in the back. In case of an emergency, she had nowhere to go. Brody drove sensibly and kept up his line of friendly banter. From St John's Road, they reached the car park. Then it was not far to the surf beach. Brody opened Vicki's door, took her hand and headed off along the sandy path. It was getting dark and the area was unlit.

Madison found her two escorts equally obliging. They seemed less pushy but alone and outnumbered, her nerves began chatting. One of the males had a box with cans of full-strength beer. They walked slowly as the sand was deep. Brody and his babe were out of sight.

He'd picked up chicks before. His life in the touring car industry gave him regular opportunities to mix with nubile females. His sex life was busy. He rarely had to exert pressure on many of his conquests with 'willing' and 'up for it' being listed on their CVs.

Brody stopped and pointed into the gathering gloom. 'There's a short cut to the beach down there.' He stepped over the fence and stretched his arms towards Vicki. She didn't have time to think. He picked her up and lifted her off the sandy path and into the sand dunes. She squealed, not with delight, but nervous excitement. He put her down so she stood facing him. She looked up at him. Using his teasing system, he paused, bent and gently kissed her mouth.

She loved the sensation and wanted more. He had plans, grabbed her hand and led her into the dunes. He knew the exact spot.

The other three struggled. Gathering gloom, a sandy pathway, grog carrying, and an unwilling female didn't help; or rather did for the girl. Madison stopped. 'I don't want to go on,' she said.

'Come on, babe, we're nearly there,' said the guy not carrying the beer. 'You'll love the surf.'

'No,' she said. 'I want to go back.'

The males exchanged glances. One made a face; "it's a no-show".

'Okay,' said the drink waiter. 'I'll take you back.' He spoke to his mate. 'You join the others. I'll catch you up.' He winked.

They split with Madison escorted back to the car. The male put the box of booze in the boot. 'Wait here,' he said and left. She was too scared to ask him to unlock the door. The car park was dimly lit, and a few vehicles were parked at discreet locations. She waited and worried.

Brody drew Vicki deeper into the sand dunes. They could hear the surf but dropping down into a valley, he stopped and drew her towards him. His method was simple; flatter, use patter, never batter. With someone new, and in this case inexperienced, it was important to make her feel wanted. He whispered. 'You are amazing.' He kissed her with gentle passion. She responded in kind. He turned up the passion. She responded in kind. The tried and tested routine was on schedule.

He dropped to the grass, out of the wind. He held up a hand and helped her to join him. He eased her on to her back and kissed her again. They lay side by side. In the darkness, Brody caressed her body. She tensed then relaxed. The kissing turned passionate and Brody's free hand expertly undid Vicki's belt. She was pre-occupied with his mouth, and only when his hand slid inside her jeans did she freeze.

Shit thought Brody, *too fast*. He withdrew his hand and returned to the smooth chat lines.

'I don't want to,' said Vicki who, as if in the sea, floundered in the surf. It was literally over the next dune.

'Relax,' whispered Brody. 'I'll take care of everything.'

She stood but her feet couldn't get a footing in the shifting sand. 'I want to go,' she said breathing faster and harder.

He grabbed her arm to try and calm her. She panicked and tried to pull away. He held her tight. 'Don't be a silly bitch,' he said, pulling her back to the grass. Instinctively she slapped his face. It stung. He returned fire and his slap to her face stunned her. A struggle began, unfair because he was bigger, stronger, and angrier and could never face his mates if he failed to conquer. Male pride is a kicker, and being defeated by a woman an eternal disgrace to any rapist. Besides, his mates were having a threesome with Madison.

He held her down, and her panic exploded. The more she struggled, the more he attacked. To her it was a nightmare in slow motion. With his strong hand around her throat pinning her to the ground, she couldn't breathe. She froze making his task easier. He tore at her jeans and all she could think of were her parents and what her mother would say. And worse, how could she ever tell her mother.

She didn't want to die or be bashed. She didn't want sex.

Vicki found her first sexual experience to be filled with pain, fear and confusion. He was the one making the noise. He finished, withdrew and stood adjusting his clothing. Someone called.

'Oi, where are you?'

Brody looked up at his mate standing on top of the dune.

'What are you doing here?' snarled the rapist.

'We drew a blank. What happened?'

Brody dressed. 'Silly bitch did the tease and freeze routine.'

'But you did yourself proud, mate.'

The two men looked at the teenager lying on her back. She was in shock and unable to move. In the darkness she looked at the two mates who stared at her half-naked body.

'Where's Woofer?' asked Brody.

'Here,' called the third male bouncing in and surveying the scene and especially the girl. 'Ah, bullseye,' he said. 'We drew a blank.'

Brody climbed up the dune. 'Where's the other bitch?'

'I left her at the car.'

'Outside?' growled Brody.

'Of course.'

Brody beckoned to his mates. 'Right,' he said, 'she's primed and ready to go. Get stuck in.'

Vicki couldn't think straight. She thought her nightmare was over. Wrong. As Brody's pals filled their boots, Vicki rose above the sand and watched herself in an out-of-body experience, unable to move, speak or react. It was half a Dickensian opening sentence—it was the worst of times. Brody stood watching the crime. When the third rapist climaxed to the cheers of the onlookers, the trio indulged in a spot of backslapping and headed home.

But no, the ignominy continued as Brody returned, dropped beside the motionless female and ripped away her panties. 'It's trophy time, lads!' Their laughter faded as they headed to the carpark.

Vicki wept, her mind a mess and her body worse. Time meant nothing. Her pain had teeth and bit hard. Everything ached—her face, breasts, genitals, even her right big toe which was crushed by someone's boot.

Leaning against the slope of the sand dune, Vicki managed to dress. She lifted a hand to her face and smelt and saw blood. With streaming tears, she staggered up the dunes to the fence. Falling over it, she turned left hoping to head towards the car park. She stumbled and fell. Through the pain she went, turned a corner and nearly died. Someone headed towards her. Oh no, they were back for more.

'Vicki?' said Madison, and the friends hugged with emotion.

The victim couldn't speak and her friend quickly knew what happened. To allay her friend's fear, Madison explained how the three males had driven off. The girls struggled back to the carpark and collapsed. They sat on the ground and wept together. A couple got out of the back seat of the only remaining car. The woman went to get in the front seat but stopped when she saw the two teens.

'Are you all right?' she called.

'Come on,' said the boyfriend.

'Shhh,' said the terrified and ashamed Vicki. Madison ignored her and called. 'No. My friend's been attacked.'

The girlfriend arrived in a hurry. 'Jesus,' she said bending to look at the victim. She called to her boyfriend who arrived with far less speed.

'Can you help us, please?' begged Madison.

'Sure,' said the girlfriend. 'We'll drive you to the hospital.'

'No!' snapped Vicki as the women helped her to the car with Vicki and Madison in the back. The smell of the lovemaking made Vicki dry retch—surely love had nothing to do with it.

They drove. 'Please take us back to Blairgowrie,' said Vicki.

'If you've been attacked,' said the girl, 'you need to go to hospital and tell them what happened. They'll call the cops.'

Vicki shouted. 'No police! My family is camping at Blairgowrie.'

Madison looked at her friend and then at the girlfriend in the front. Madison nodded. The girlfriend addressed the driver. 'Did you hear her?' He looked at his girlfriend, nodded and drove to Blairgowrie.

At the shops, the teens thanked the couple then hurried to the public toilets. Madison helped her friend restore her face and hair to something approaching normality. Getting the blood off her jeans was hopeless. When done, they headed back to the campsite.

'Tell nobody, Maddie,' said the victim. 'This didn't happen.'

'I can't do that,' said Madison. 'We have to tell someone.'

The threat came quickly. 'You tell my Mum, anyone, and I'll never speak to you again.' Madison looked at her friend and nodded. 'Now let's get our story straight. We got trapped by the tide and had to take the long way home.'

Vicki and Nipper were peas in a pod; both were shattered.

About 30 years after the Blairgowrie rape incident, Madison was half watching the evening news. An item grabbed her attention. Former racing driver Brody Miller was dead, killed in a car crash on a country road. The man was a dual Bathurst winner, three times Targa Tasmania champion, and poster boy for touring car racing around Australia. Many racing fans mourned his death. Many couldn't believe he survived all those hair-raising crashes, only to die in a bog standard sedan on a suburban road travelling within the speed limit. Bloody trees on the side of the road are often unforgiving. Wearing a seatbelt would have helped. Was he drunk? Suicidal?

Footage and photos online, on TV and in the papers showed the dashing young man as he was 30 odd years ago. Many a female heart had been jumpstarted by the dashing Brody. He'd finish a race then, that night, start horizontal dancing with a willing female; sometimes two. But not all his conquests were consensual and not all were of age.

Madison Wright, now Braintree, saw the news item and instantly recognised the man. She thought immediately of her schoolgirl friend, Vicki (Not her real name) and that holiday in Blairgowrie. Would Vicki see the publicity about the man who raped her all those years ago in the sand dunes at Koonya Beach? If she did, what would she think? Madison hadn't seen or heard from Vicki in decades. There were no phone calls, Christmas cards or text messages as the girls, now middle-aged women, didn't even know where the other lived.

Chapter 2

Jo Best couldn't sleep. Two weeks ago, here in her flat, a madwoman pressed a loaded gun against her right temple and was a heartbeat away from rearranging the detective's brain. Messy didn't come close. Who'd be a cop? And who would have thought she'd be saved by a drug runner from Miami, and an overweight pathologist? Jo thought she now knew how soldiers felt having returned from war with trauma attacking their mental health. Fitful best described her sleep.

To add to her near-death experience was the fact her colleague and lover, DI Pierre Richelieu, was lying in an ICU fighting for life having been run down by his estranged wife and unknown step-sister; two armed madwomen. To generate even more grief or bewilderment for Jo, days before his near fatal attack, Richelieu had changed his will making Jo a beneficiary to the tune of a minor royal's ransom.

What the hell is happening in my life, she thought?

Her boss, DI Elly Rose had told Jo to take leave. 'Go and see medicos, take their advice, prescription drugs too if necessary, but don't return to Homicide, if at all, until you're fit and raring to go.'

Jo kept replaying those words—*don't return to Homicide, if at all.* That was hard. She'd endured scary experiences as a homicide detective; been shot at, assaulted, kidnapped and almost arrested. She once hid in a priest's bolthole to escape two randy aristocrats. Through all those experiences, two things remained; her love for the job, and her medicine for any post-traumatic stress—running. Her healthy diet, her father's bone structure, and a pair of expensive running shoes meant she would pass any pinch test with ease. What body fat? Her mental health survived thanks to her physical health. Pavement and park pacing kept her sane.

She saw her local GP, a woman in her 40s who juggled a growing family with a busy practice. 'Jo,' said the GP, 'I could refer you to some terrific therapists but, and at the risk of being reported for unprofessional behaviour, you'd be wasting your money. You are the most sane and stable person I know, which I find amazing considering the scrapes and adventures I read about. How many of them are true?'

Jo laughed. 'Which ones are we talking about?'

'And when are they making a TV series about your life?'

Jo laughed again. A visit to Stephanie was a tonic in itself.

Back in her darkened bedroom, Jo pondered sleeping pills. She'd asked Stephanie about that issue. 'Not for you, officer,' said the GP. 'What you need is a healthy sex life.' More laughter from patient and doctor leaving those outside in Reception wondering what the heck was going on. Mind you, Jo's laughter had a hollow ring to it. *What sex life*, she thought?

Her bedside clock showed the bewitching hour was next in line. She willed herself to sleep but failed when her phone rang.

'Sarge?' she said.

'That was quick,' said DS Deborah "Billy" Hughes. 'Good to know you're ready to roll.'

'But Sarge, DI Rose said I was to take leave.'

'What, forever? It's time to climb back on the horse; yes or no?'

Jo hesitated. She hated doing nothing. She loved a challenge. 'That's a "yes", Sarge. What's happened and where?'

'You can walk there. Body found in the Heidelberg Rovers Soccer Club in Simpson Road. Ten minutes.' Click.

Jo knew she had a heart as it slipped into overdrive. She dressed, donned a cap to hide her unruly locks and ran to her car. Billy didn't have her geography right. From Clifton Hill she could easily get to the football ground in Heidelberg in ten minutes but by car.

Driving to the crime scene, she tingled. She was back on the job.

Dieter Fischer gave his life to football. Living in Melbourne, Australia, meant he often had to explain that, to him, football meant soccer and not the Aussie Rules game worshipped by millions of Melburnians. Dieter had been a promising soccer player as a teen. Many professional clubs had him on their radar until injury cruelled his pitch. The surgeons got him walking but never would those dancing feet sprint, dribble and shoot again. Coaching youngsters became his life which he now did at the Heidelberg Rovers Football Club.

Not any more though as he lay on the floor of the committee room, dead as the proverbial. On the wall hung a photo of the premiership team he coached two seasons ago; the cup, the kids and the coach. He was smiling in the photo but not now.

Jo parked and headed for the building. Uniformed officers had strung tape, and stood guard against the public and the press. Jo approached displaying her ID. The constable nodded and lifted the tape. She entered the clubroom and heard a familiar voice.

'Well look what the cat dragged in.' Jo smiled at Detective Senior Constable Charley Baldwin. She liked him when they met on her first day at Homicide. She still liked him and wanted the hug he gave her. 'How are ya?' he asked stepping back to look at her. 'You look terrific.'

'Don't answer without your solicitor and union rep present,' said Billy Hughes from the doorway to the crime scene. 'This way, Senior.'

Baldwin and Jo exchanged glances before she headed to the committee room. Inside with DS Hughes were DI Elly Rose, the boss of Homicide, and DS Justin Fletcher. Jo nodded at her colleagues. Billy held out her hand and Jo shook it. It was like old home week.

'Nice to see you, Detective,' said the boss who wasn't bursting with enthusiasm. 'Are you fit for active service?'

'I am, ma'am.'

Rose trusted her youngest and best detective. 'Meet the late Dieter Paul Fischer, CEO and coach of the Heidelberg Rovers Football Club.'

She paused and the others looked at Jo. *What? Are they expecting me to solve the case just by looking at the body?* She broke the silence. 'Who discovered him?'

'Anonymous call,' said DS Fletcher. 'It could have been a late night dog-walker who saw the lights on and came in to investigate.'

Jo nodded at the photos on the wall. 'That's him in happier times.'

The others looked at the wall and saw how quickly Senior Constable Best could take in a crime scene. She had a reputation for observation and particularly with photos.

Baldwin appeared in the doorway. He was about to announce the arrival of the pathologist but his words were unnecessary.

'Soccer?' she queried. 'I know nothing about bloody wog ball.' The officers smiled and moved back to give Dr Gabrielle Strange easy access to the body. She stood in the doorway. 'Good evening officers, or should that be good morning?'

Charlie Baldwin tried to help her finish adjusting her protective garments. She hobbled, wobbled and protested. Once dressed, she saw the word *Committee* on the door then moved to inspect the body. 'Never join committees; they're the perfect place to get stabbed in the back.' She looked at the nearest detective who happened to be Jo. 'Jesus Joyce, it's the deranged detective. How are you, girlie?'

'Well, thank you, Doctor. And your good self?'

'All the better for seeing you. And listen, I need another drug run this week.'

Jo knew this meant expensive chocolates, and was both delighted and embarrassed. DI Rose was annoyed. 'Ladies if we could turn our attention to the deceased.'

Strange looked at the Homicide boss. Being close to retirement, the pathologist was tempted to say what she thought but instead gave a forced smile and knelt, with creaking joints, to examine the former footballer. The others watched. DI Rose wanted something, anything. She should have waited.

'What does your initial examination tell you, Doctor?' asked Rose.

'He's dead,' said Strange without looking up. Rose grimaced. 'Facial bruising suggests a fight, wound to the back of the head suggests a fall, and stab wound to the heart suggests first-degree murder. Although in what order these events occurred and which one or ones pushed him into eternity, I'm unable to say until I get him back to my place for an intimate tête-à-tête.' She grinned then carried on examining.

Rose headed to the corridor, silently ordering her team to follow.

'We have his name and address. DS Hughes you've drawn the short straw to tell the family.'

'Ma'am,' said Billy. 'Jo, you're with me.' There was a pause with Billy looking like she'd taken over. 'That's if it's okay with you, ma'am.'

Rose nodded. 'Justin, take Charley and talk to anyone nearby who saw or heard anything.'

'At this hour, ma'am?' asked DS Fletcher.

The sarcasm was thick. 'No, wait till they've all had a good night's kip.' Fletcher got the message. 'Check for CCTV and collect details of anyone associated with the club. There'll be stationery in offices and contacts on their web site. Obviously don't release any victim ID until

the family are informed and we're positive he is who we think he is.'
Fletcher didn't like being treated like a novice.

The detectives parted as forensic officers arrived along with a vehicle for the former soccer coach, now definitely off-side.

'The victim lives, lived in Doncaster,' said Billy. 'That's my neck of the woods, so you can follow to save me driving back here.'

Jo followed and pulled up behind Billy's car in affluent Doncaster. No cars sat in the street as most of the homes with bowling-pin balustrades and manicured lawns had two-car garages; some had three. Jo caught up with her sergeant who explained the plan.

'I'll break the news while you do your thing.'

'Sarge?' whispered Jo as they walked down the drive.

'The photo thing,' replied Billy in a soft voice, 'where you solve the crime by peering at pics.' Jo felt good but worried. *No pressure then.*

The doorbell sounded. Who was home? Children? What does anyone think if someone rocks up to your house at 0045 hours? The detectives waited. A light came on in the hallway and above the front door. The detectives heard someone. An adult female voice spoke from behind the closed door.

'Who is it?'

Billy spoke. 'Is this the home of Mr Dieter Fischer?'

'Why? What's happened?' The woman became more anxious. 'Who are you?'

'We're police officers. Are you Mrs Fischer?'

The main door opened but the locked security door remained shut.

Both detectives held up their ID. 'May we come in, Mrs Fischer?'

She unlocked the security door. Two other people appeared with all three in their night clothes. 'This is my daughter and grandson.'

The detectives nodded but wanted the family in the lounge and seated. Telling terrible news could bring on a fainting fit, horrendous screams or mind-numbing silence. 'May we sit down?' asked Billy. The tension kept building. The Fischer family knew this had to be bad news but didn't want to hear it, or believe it. Everyone sat, the daughter and grandson either side of the widow. Billy did what had to be done.

'There's been an incident at the soccer club, Mrs Fischer, and I'm very sorry to tell you your husband has passed away.'

Jo disliked *passed away* preferring to say *dead* or *died*. *Killed* or *murdered* she wouldn't use, at least not at first.

As if to support Jo's thinking, the recently widowed Mrs Fischer asked for clarity. Shock sometimes throws clear thinking out the window. 'Is he dead?' she asked.

'I'm afraid so, yes. Please accept our sincere condolences.'

Mrs Fischer's reaction was no reaction. She felt numb and became dumb. Her daughter and teenage grandson sat closer offering their loved one what comfort they could.

'We're very sorry for your loss, Mrs Fischer,' said Billy, hating these situations even after 26 years in the Force.

Silence took over and pauses dominated the conversation.

'What happened?' asked Mrs Fischer. 'How did he die?'

'We're not sure,' said Billy maintaining the same flat voice and volume. 'He may have been in a fight. He had injuries to his face and head.' Jo noted the stab to the heart didn't get a mention.

After another pause, Mrs Fischer made a simple declaration. 'It was Barry Clunes.'

'Mum,' protested her daughter. 'You don't know that.'

Mrs Fischer looked at her family. 'You two go back to bed. I'll come and see you when the police have gone.'

'Are you sure, Nan?' asked the grandson. She nodded and her daughter and grandson left.

Mrs Fischer stood. 'I'm sorry. Would you like tea or coffee?'

'We're fine,' said Billy only to be overruled by Jo.

'I'll make it. Is the kitchen through there?' Mrs Fischer nodded. Jo held out her hand. 'I'm Senior Constable Jo Best.'

'Elizabeth,' said Mrs Fischer, 'Liz.'

'Detective Sergeant Billy Hughes,' said the senior officer admiring the excellent people skills displayed by her junior colleague. 'May we call you Liz?'

'Please do,' said the bereaved woman.

'Tea or coffee, Liz?' asked Jo.

'Tea please; milk no sugar, but you have whatever you want.' Jo left, and Billy and Liz sat.

'Is your name really Billie, as in Billie Holiday?'

The detective explained the spelling with a *y* and the link to former Prime Minister Billy Hughes, glad to be able to talk about something, anything other than the brutal murder.

'When can I see my husband?'

'Later today and we'll need you to identify him. He's being well cared for but with any suspicious death, there are certain procedures we have to follow.'

'By suspicious, do you mean murder?'

Billy paused then nodded. 'Senior Constable Best and I are Homicide detectives.' The widow said nothing. 'May I have details about your husband, please; his full name, date of birth and such?'

Liz gave Billy the details and Jo returned with the tea and the women settled.

Before the detectives could begin questioning, Liz asked. 'Did my husband suffer?'

Tricky. 'I would say not, Liz. Once we obtain the results of the post-mortem, we'll be able to explain things in more detail.'

'You'll save yourself a lot of time if you arrest Barry Clunes.'

The detectives exchanged a glance. 'We've never heard of Mr Clunes. What's his connection to your late husband?'

The widow spoke uninterrupted. 'Clunes is the builder sacked when he failed to complete the construction of the new grandstand. Before the sacking, my husband and Clunes argued often and with anger. Dieter poured his heart and soul into the football club, and this new facility was to be his crowning achievement. With Clunes producing slipshod work and falling way behind, he was sacked leaving Dieter's project in ruins.'

Jo took notes and Billy again took pride in the way the youngest detective in the squad conducted herself. As the interview came to an end, Billy looked at Jo giving her the chance to ask a question.

'Apart from Barry Clunes, did your husband have any enemies?'

Liz paused. 'He hated the President but my Hero is much more a coward than a killer.'

'My Hero?' asked Jo still taking notes.

'It was Dieter's nickname for Alex Hero, the president of the club. He's heavily involved with Clunes and my husband.'

Jo took the details and looked at Billy. She nodded and was about to stand. 'One more question, Liz. Have you been home all night?'

The temperature dropped and fast. The friendly, sympathetic detectives seemingly became cold and calculating coppers. They weren't but Jo wanted the grieving widow to account for her movements in the hours when her husband was bashed and stabbed. Billy felt her guts shrink.

'I was here all night,' said the widow.

Jo wanted to say, "And can anyone confirm that?"

Liz jumped in first. 'My daughter and grandson were with me, and so was my elderly mother who is upstairs, and I'd rather we didn't wake her as she's frail and has a bad heart.'

Jo felt rotten. Billy took over, thanked the widow, promised to keep her informed of all developments, and politely shoved Jo out the door. They said nothing until they reached the street. 'My car, now,' said Billy and Jo sensed a rocket. Inside Billy's vehicle, the rocket arrived.

'That was brilliant work, Detective Senior Constable, until the last two minutes. What the hell are you doing suggesting a grieving widow has knocked her old man? We may need her help tomorrow. That was straight out of the DI Steele playbook.' Jo remembered her first boss who hated the young detective, and had zero tact when dealing with people. Pause. Silence replete with heavy breathing. 'Well?'

Jo kept her cool then stood up to her colleague. 'What happened to my first Homicide sergeant who taught me to trust no-one, and to keep the pressure on all possible persons of interest?' Billy sighed. Jo nailed her again. 'And let's face it, Sarge, of widow's tears came there none. We've both seen wives fall to pieces when told their husband was dead. Liz Fischer was calm and lucid throughout. What if she stands to cash in an enormous insurance policy? What if she's the brains behind the hit, and plans to run away with Mr Hero?'

'All right, all right,' snapped Billy. She took deep breaths. 'You may be damn clever but don't follow the likes of DIs Steele and Blunt. Humanity can help the bereaved and not everyone's a killer.' Jo didn't know what to say. 'Go on, piss off,' said Billy, and Jo got out.

'Goodnight Sarge,' she said.

'Goodnight, Senior.' The door began to close. 'Oh and Jo.' The door didn't close. 'It's good to have you back.'

Hughes started her car and Jo closed the door.

Chapter 3

A few hours later, Homicide squad members gathered in the Incident Room. Those who attended the Heidelberg homicide discussed their findings. Those who didn't wanted news. The boss entered with an unknown male. The hubbub ceased and DI Rose spoke.

'Good morning.' The squad replied as one. 'The most important matter first. The latest on DI Richelieu is he remains in ICU and is holding his own. If nothing else, the DI is a fighter.' There were murmurs of support. 'We all know Detective Senior Constable Best was framed for the attempt murder on our colleague, and I'm delighted to welcome her back.'

Most agreed and strong applause lingered. Rose tried to resume speaking but had to wait for the heartfelt reaction from Jo's colleagues. Not all of them mind. DI Blunt offered limp-wristed support.

Rose turned to the person standing to one side. 'And I'm pleased to welcome a new member of the squad fresh from a study year in the United States; Detective Sergeant Rick Melody joins us from today.' Rose indicated the new man who nodded. Members murmured their welcome. Baldwin whispered to Jo. 'Does he sing?' Rose continued. 'Take a seat, Detective,' and Melody followed orders.

Because of DI Richelieu's absence, almost certainly permanent, and as the now senior officer after DI Rose, DI Blunt was waiting to be told he would be the Senior Investigating Officer on the soccer coach homicide. Alas, he was to be disappointed—again. Rose explained.

'I've asked DS Hughes to be SIO on this latest investigation, and those thinking we're top heavy in the DS department and light on when it comes to Detective Inspectors, will be pleased to hear of the appointment of Acting Detective *Senior* Sergeant Billy Hughes.' Blunt chewed glass. Hughes accepted the congratulations. She'd been after promotion but didn't want to leave Homicide to get it.

It wasn't exactly a hoopin' and a hollerin' but most members were thrilled to see an old hand rewarded, and the applause was stronger and longer than for Jo who became a cheerleader for her favourite DS now Senior DS.

Okay, Acting Senior DS but what the heck do I call you?

DI Blunt forced a plastic smile and provided the softest applause since the Sheriff of Nottingham acknowledged Robin Hood's superior archery skills.

'And as the SIO, Acting Detective Senior Sergeant Hughes can explain the latest with our homicide in Doncaster.'

Billy stood in front of the display board. 'It was actually in Heidelberg, ma'am although the victim lived in Doncaster.' She referred to three photos; headshots of the victim and others involved. 'We're waiting for reports from Dr Strange and Forensics but as of this morning we have two persons of interest.' She pointed to pictures. 'This is the victim, Dieter Fischer, aged 62, a fit and healthy football coach and the club CEO. This is Barry Clunes, alleged cowboy builder who made a mess of the new and incomplete grandstand for the soccer club run by the victim. He and the victim hated one another, and Clunes is looking at bankruptcy thanks to the victim taking legal action.'

'Have we spoken to Clunes?' asked DI Blunt desperate to play a role in the investigation.

'Planned for this morning, Inspector,' replied Billy making no mention of who might lead such an interview. Billy pointed to the third photo again taken from the soccer club's web site. 'Current president of the soccer club is the aptly named Alex Hero. The murdered man's widow named him as someone else mired in the building fiasco.'

'Not being picky, *Acting* Detective Senior Sergeant Hughes,' said Baldwin adding flavour to her new title, 'but being there and hearing Doc Strange give her preliminary report, are we sure it's a homicide?'

'Meaning?' asked Billy.

'Well if he was punched and fell, could it be manslaughter, and could the perp have been acting in self-defence?'

'He was stabbed in the heart, Senior Constable and, in my limited experience,'—her sarcasm sloshed around the floor—'I think shoving a knife between someone's ribs tends to fall into the homicide camp.'

'Sarge,' continued Baldwin, 'no, sorry *ma'am*.' Hughes glared at him. He was confused. 'Well what *should* we call you?'

'Lucky,' said Blunt in a low voice heard by a few.

Everyone hung on Billy's reply. 'Stick with Sarge unless given special permission in which case it'll be Boss.'

'Thank you Acting Detective Senior Sergeant Boss,' said Baldwin. Members laughed and Rose was pleased with the banter. She wanted results but encouraged a relaxed feeling between detectives.

Billy continued. 'Now, what do we know so far? DS Fletcher?'

Fletcher reported on the interviews he and Baldwin conducted. 'Charley and I went door-knocking and generated any number of complaints.'

'Not *every*one complained, Sarge,' said Baldwin.

'We got nothing; nobody heard raised voices or speeding vehicles, and neighbours are not overlooking the clubrooms. Many complained about builders with the unfinished grandstand.'

'CCTV?' asked Billy.

'Nothing in the immediate area, not even in the club carpark.'

Billy looked at Jo. 'Senior Constable Best and I broke the news to the family. Jo?'

Surprised she was asked to report; Jo reckoned Billy was trying to ease her back into the routine. 'The wife of the deceased, Liz Fischer, her daughter and grandson, about 15, were woken and shocked although the family, and particularly the widow, showed little emotion. She didn't cry or collapse. She sent her daughter and grandson to bed and discussed her husband in what I thought was more a businesslike rather than personal way. As Senior Sergeant Hughes indicated, the widow was keen to push the builder and president as suspects.'

Jo looked at Billy and sat.

'Thanks, Senior. So, tasks; interview Clunes the builder, and Hero the president. Chase up pathology and forensics. And investigate the soccer community here in Melbourne. Who knows anything about the local soccer scene?'

DI Blunt wanted in. A few weeks ago he stuffed up an arrest of a returned serviceman in a wheelchair. Blunt was lucky. The bungled arrest could have been far worse. But since that incident, he'd been ignored or given crap jobs. Now he was desperate.

Years ago he was taken to a soccer game by a mate who was mad on Melbourne Victory FC which, Blunt reckoned, qualified him to investigate Melbourne's soccer community.

'I'm a soccer fan,' he lied. Billy seized on the offer believing it was a dead end job but someone needed to do it.

'Thank you, DI Blunt.' She looked around. 'Senior Constable Payne, you're the sporting type.' He groaned and others laughed. 'You can assist DI Blunt.' Payne said nothing. 'DS Melody, we'll throw you in at the deep end. Barry Clunes is a person of interest. You and Senior Constable Best can have a chat with Clunes and, if necessary, arrest him.' Jo tried to look at Melody without looking. He looked straight ahead. He'd heard about Ms Best. Her reputation had legs. She did as well although they were not on show today.

'Boss,' said Melody having learnt the jargon.

'DS Fletcher and Senior Constable Baldwin will interview the club president, Alex Hero.'

'Boss,' said both men as one. Billy looked at them thinking they were taking the mick but their faces gave away nothing.

'And DI Rose and I will follow up with Dr Strange and Forensics. Questions?' Silence. 'Right, be gone.'

Jo knew she should introduce herself to the new DS but wanted a private chat with DI Rose. 'Ma'am, may I have a quick word?'

Rose led her to one side. 'Well?'

'Are you okay with me continuing to visit DI Richelieu?'

Rose paused. She knew the history between Jo and Pierre. Since the attempt to murder Richelieu, Rose knew the love goalposts for Jo and Pierre had not so much been shifted as moved to Mars. She wanted Richelieu to survive and Jo to have her mind on the job. The pause between Jo's request and Rose's answer seemed never to end.

'No problem,' said Rose, 'but two things, Senior. Nothing you do must hinder Pierre's recovery, and remember you've had more than your fair share of luck since joining Homicide; don't push it.'

'Ma'am,' said Jo then looked to one side because a new colleague appeared and Rose introduced them.

'DS Rick Melody; Detective Senior Constable Jo Best.'

They shook hands.

Chapter 4

Kylie Bowman walked into the Dandenong Police Station. 'Yes, madam?' asked the fresh-faced female constable, Jan Katter.

'My husband is missing.'

Constable Katter encountered her first misper. She found the paperwork. 'How long has he been missing?'

'Two days.'

The constable looked at Kylie. 'Two days?' Kylie nodded. 'Why haven't you reported this before?'

Hubby Max hated cops, and overstaying on a camping trip would never be a reason to report him missing. 'He sometimes stays away longer but he hasn't rung to say he'll be late.'

'And that's unusual?'

'Yes.'

'And obviously you tried his mobile?'

'I can't because there's no reception in the high country.'

'Well if he's in the high country how could he ring you?'

'There's a landline in Licola. He's got a fishing spot by the Macalister River.'

'What, in a camping ground?'

'No, he parks his 4WD and walks into the bush. It's private land but he never damages anything and always cleans up afterwards.'

'And he goes camping alone?'

'No, he takes our dog, Bluey.'

'So where is this spot?'

'It's about 3 kays along Tamborine Road.' Kylie meant Tamboritha Road although the names meant nothing to either woman.

The officer took details, including a description of Bluey, the beloved Australian Cattle Dog. 'Okay,' she said. 'We'll contact the local police to get the search started. If your husband gets in touch or comes home, call us immediately. It's a huge area and we don't want to even start looking for someone who's safe and well.' She handed Kylie a card.

'Thank you,' said Kylie.

'Don't worry. He's probably got a flat battery and will turn up soon.' Kylie left and the constable took the form inside to her sergeant.

He knew Gippsland well but didn't like the vague description of the misper's possible location. 'Get on to Heyfield,' he said.

Victoria's high country is glorious with a good sprinkling of mountains. The area is great for bushwalking and climbing, offers stunning views, can be horrendously difficult for firefighters in the bushfire season, and includes lovely waterways such as the Macalister River with camping spots offering swimming, fishing and kayaking.

Two young uni students, in love, were enjoying a few days based in the caravan park at Licola. They enjoyed plenty of activity by day and plenty of a different type by night.

Kayaking on the Macalister River, the female heard a dog barking and saw an Aussie cattle dog pacing the bank, seemingly distressed.

Without thinking, Isabella changed direction. Boyfriend Simon saw her and followed. The dog was glad to have their attention and told them to get a move on.

Isabella dragged her kayak out of the river and patted the dog. It took off and the woman followed. When she reached the camp site, she called. 'Simon!'

It was a voice rich in panic and fear. Simon raced towards her. The dog ran in circles around a tent which lay flat beneath a hefty branch from a nearby eucalypt.

'Jesus,' said Simon.

'There's someone under there,' said Isabella, stating the bleeding obvious as bleeding had literally seeped from the tent. Simon moved close to the carnage. The dog became more excited. 'Hello,' called Simon. 'Can you hear me?'

Human replies, none; canine replies, many.

'They might be alive but unconscious,' said Isabella.

'We'll never move that branch,' said Simon.

'We have to get help. I'll stay with the dog. You go to Licola and call the cops.'

'You sure?'

'Use the landline. Get going.'

Simon headed back to their kayaks but stopped when she called.

'No, go via the road.' He was uncertain. 'You can run on the road, and if there's a car, flag it down. It'll be quicker than paddling.'

'Okay.'

'Hang on,' cried Isabella as she grabbed the dog's collar. 'His name is Bluey and there's a phone number.' She yelled the number which Simon wrote on a pad in his bum bag. 'Go,' she cried and he did.

Dandenong police rang Heyfield police with news of a missing camper. Two local uniformed officers set off driving the 50 odd kilometres to a vaguely described camping spot near Licola. As they were driving, their station in Heyfield got a landline call from Simon, the jogging kayaker. Found: one body. It seemed the lost husband had turned up.

Simon was told the police were on their way, and to wait outside the massive shopping emporium known as the Licola General Store. He did and was picked up and driven to the tent, to Bluey and Isabella.

The travelling cops from Heyfield carried a description of the camper including his tatts. The cops at Heyfield rang Dandenong with news of the phone number on the dog's collar. It was the number provided by Kylie Bowman. The Dandenong cops decided to wait until the en route Heyfield cops reached the camp site, and laid eyes on the body before ringing the wife, now likely widow. Another few minutes wouldn't make much difference, and you don't want to tell someone their family member is dead when they ain't.

At the Macalister camp site, Isabella found dog food in the 4WD parked in the bush, and Bluey got stuck in. Perhaps his anxiety stimulated his appetite. He knew his master was in the tent and couldn't understand why he didn't appear and give him a pat. Simon was pleased his bandana placed under a rock helped him direct the Heyfield police to the correct location. Bluey barked excitedly when the police and Simon arrived. Isabella met the cops.

The police, Sergeant Pepper and Constable Leigh, surveyed the scene, looked with difficulty inside the tent, checked for a pulse, found none, and knew they had to remove the branch.

'You can give us a hand, Simon,' said the sergeant.

'What about *me?*' asked Isabella who didn't want to help because of what they found but didn't like being rejected because of her sex.

'You could do us a big favour, Isabella,' said the sergeant, 'and control the dog.' She'd formed a bond with Bluey and led him aside.

Moving the branch was tricky. It was heavy with another branch off the main limb. The constable had an idea, and the three men took their positions.

'Remember,' said the sergeant, 'we need to try and preserve what's under there so for Christ's sake, don't drop the bloody thing.'

'He's not going to be in mint condition anyway, Sarge,' said the constable, and Simon made a mental note to never join the police.

Pepper gave the count of three, and all lifters heaved. Nothing moved until, at last, there was movement at the station. Hearts pumped and the sergeant screamed, 'This way, this way!'

The plan worked until Simon tripped on a tent peg, pushed too hard, sending the sergeant flying backwards. He roared as the branch settled a millimetre from his foot. Simon found himself lying on the lumpy tent, and Bluey broke free snapping at the canvas.

Isabella ran to restrain the hound. The constable went to help his boss wondering if an injury to his senior officer meant the constable's career was irreparably damaged. At least the branch was no longer on the tent. The sergeant's biggest injury was to his pride. He hobbled for show, and ordered the lovers and the dog to step back.

It wasn't a pretty sight. The flattened tent had bloodstains where the sleeper's head and upper body now lay.

Lying flat beside the tent, Sergeant Pepper opened the flap and peered inside. He'd attended many road accidents. This was worse.

'Is he dead, Sarge?' asked the constable.

'Well if he's not, I hope he's got good dental cover.' He pointed at his colleague. 'Get the contact details of this lady and gentleman, then get on the radio and tell Heyfield we need detectives from the CIU in Sale, and a doctor. Tell them 2.3 clicks north of the Licola Store. Look for the police tape. Oh and we need an undertaker.'

'Right, Sarge.'

'What about Bluey?' asked Isabella.

'We can't take him,' said Simon, and Isabella felt a surge of mistrust towards her boyfriend. 'We've got the kayaks.'

He was right but Isabella still felt sad.

'We'll take the dog,' said the sergeant. 'He won't leave here without his master anyway.'

The kayakers gave their details and, with a pat and a hug for Bluey from Isabella, the lovers left the crime scene. If only Bluey could talk.

There wasn't much the uniforms could do. Put tape on a tree beside the road for the medico, detectives and undertaker; secure the area, check the surrounds and wait. Then Sergeant Pepper remembered.

'Rufus Goodes,' he said although the name meant nothing to Leigh.

'Sarge?'

'He moved to Licola last year.'

'Who is Rufus Goodes?'

'He worked at the Heyfield mill when Adam was a boy. He'll know about this tree.' He headed back to the road. 'Stay here while I fetch him. Keep one eye on the stiff and another eye out for the suits.'

Rufus had kept his weekender up past Licola for years but once he quit the mill, he left Heyfield for good. Pepper found the shack and pulled up in what was jokingly called the front yard.

'Well bugger me,' said the old timber cutter coming out on his front porch. 'It's Pepper Pig.'

'G'day Rufus. How y'goin', mate?'

'I was fine till you showed up. So who died?'

'I need to pick y'brains.'

'Too late, mate; went to mush years ago.'

'Listen, there's a tree down the road I want you to have a look at.'

'A tree?'

'Yeah, I'm thinking of arresting it.'

'Why that one? There are millions of the buggers in me back yard.'

Pepper walked around and opened the passenger door. 'Won't take long, the taxi's free and I'll shout you a beer when we're done.'

Rufus took off. His Heinz 57 varieties mutt followed, hopped in and off they went. Seatbelts? Rufus had a beard doubling as an air-bag.

'Now listen, Officer, I can't afford to be seen in a police car in Licola. I have my good reputation to protect.'

Pepper laughed. 'You'll be the talk of the town, Rufus. What's the current population here?'

'I think the permanents are pushin' 30.'

They joked on the trip into and then out of Licola to the crime scene. Bluey barked then went all quiet when a fellow canine appeared. Rufus met the constable and the crime scene.

'Now, Rufus,' said Pepper, 'inside this squashed tent is a squashed body caused, we reckon, by that fallen branch.'

'That'd kill anyone,' said Rufus moving for a closer look.

'But don't touch anything, mate.'

'So you've had a look inside the tent?'

'We have and want your expert advice. You've felled more trees than anyone this side of the black stump.' Pepper pointed to the tree with the missing branch. 'Did the branch fall from that tree, and if so, can we blame God?'

Rufus wandered to look at the tree and then the fallen branch. 'Blind Freddy can see the branch came from that tree but what made it fall, bit hard to tell.'

Pepper pointed. 'Is the tree on its last legs?'

'Yep, it's a bit like me.'

'We want details, Rufus, your expert knowledge please, mate.'

'All right, look here.' He pointed to the end of the fallen branch, the part which had been attached to the trunk. 'That's dead or as good as. This branch was gunna fall any time; yesterday, today, t'morra.'

'Thanks, mate,' said Pepper, 'and now the big one. Did it fall from old age, did God give it a tap or did someone use it as a trampoline?'

'It wouldn't take much of a storm to snap that branch.'

'You reckon?'

'I know.'

'Have you had any storms here this week?'

Rufus shook his head. 'Nah, it's been pretty still.'

'Okay, I think we're done, Rufus, so thanks a lot, mate.'

'No problem. Bit of bad luck he had to die on his first camping trip.'

The cops froze. 'How do you know that?'

'Come off it, only a city slicker with no bush smarts would camp under a rotten tree.' The cops looked at Rufus who pointed at Sergeant Pepper. 'Now me and Tangles needs a lift and don't forget that beer.'

The sergeant addressed his colleague. 'Right, I'll take Bluey to that girl, Isabella. Rufus, please get your mutt and Bluey in my truck.'

And so Bluey got to stay in Licola with Isabella.

Chapter 5

'He's not here, I don't know where he is, he's moved, and if I ever see him again it'll be too soon.'

DS Rick Melody, on his first interview for Homicide, and Jo Best, stood outside the front door of a suburban, cream-brick-vanilla three-bedroom house in Nunawading. It had a front garden which had been allowed to play outside on its own with no parental care whatsoever. The woman who answered the door was not dressed for a wedding.

'Are you saying, Mrs Clunes, your husband no longer lives at this address?'

'Didn't I just say that?'

'And what's his forwarding address?' Both women sighed although Jo tried to hide hers.

'Don't know, don't care.' She guided a toddler and a cat back inside and closed the door.

'Right,' said the new boy on the block. He didn't look like a goose and was too houseproud to admit mistakes; besides, he knew his good looks would nearly always get him out of tight corners. He smiled at Jo and she liked what she saw. They walked to the car.

'Was it something I said, Senior?'

'One door closes, Sarge, and another one opens,' replied Jo.

'Okay, Ms Philosophy; where's the other door?'

'We could try the neighbours, the Master Builders Institute or even the Heidelberg Rovers Football Club. Someone'll know where he is.'

They were lucky and Melody was impressed with Jo's practical suggestions as well as her figure. The third neighbour told them about Barry's brother, Gavin, who was an electrician with a van advertising his services. It didn't take them long to track down his website which included his home address. There they met another Mrs Clunes.

She told them where her husband was working and that his brother, Barry, was helping at the same site.

'Mr Barry Clunes?' asked Melody as he and Jo held up their ID announcing their Homicide credentials.

The embattled builder oozed despair and defeat. *Not the cops. Why me?* In recent times he'd lost everything—his home, kids, marriage, business and wealth. He was broke, bust and bewildered and about to be questioned about murder. Not his best day.

Melody led and Jo noted that her role in this team, unlike with Billy Hughes and Justin Fletcher, was not discussed. 'Mr Clunes, we're investigating the death of Mr Dieter Fischer.' Clunes' face registered a mix of shock and fear.

'Fischer's dead?' he said.

'You didn't know?'

'Why would I?'

'We've been told you and Mr Fischer didn't see eye to eye.'

Barry's sarcasm started dancing. 'Oh, so any disagreement with a dead person solves the case. You cops are unbelievable.'

Melody ignored him. 'Where were you last night, Mr Clunes?'

'Do I have to answer these questions?'

'No,' said Melody without any emphasis.

'Then I've got work to do.'

He set off and Melody grabbed his arm. He was shocked and Jo worried. 'Barry Clunes I'm arresting you on suspicion of murder.'

Clunes stopped and raised his hands, breaking from the detective's grasp. 'Whoa, whoa, whoa; let's not get too hasty.' He paused. 'What do you want to know?'

'Where were you last night from 6 pm?'

'I went to see Fischer at about 9. We had words, there was a scuffle and I pissed off. He kept shouting threats as I walked to my truck. I had a flat tyre so fixed it and left. And no, I didn't kill him.'

The comments seemed to throw Melody and Jo. They weren't expecting him to admit what he did. If he killed Fischer, why confess he was at the crime scene at all? The DS didn't have an immediate follow-up question and in the pause, Jo took over.

'Tell us about the scuffle, Mr Clunes. Who did what?'

Clunes was thrown by the emergence of the female, and Melody could see why people warned him about a certain Senior Constable.

'We've been at each other's throat for weeks. I told him what I thought of him. He went ballistic, swore in a foreign language then shoved me in the chest. I stumbled backwards, got mad and threw a punch. It hurt me so it must have hurt him. He went down and whacked his head. I spat on the floor next to him then walked out. In the car park, I could still hear him swearing. Then he went quiet.'

Melody didn't make eye contact with Jo but jumped in as if it was his interview. 'So you admit striking the victim and causing him to hit his head on the floor?'

Clunes nodded. 'Yeah and I'm sorry I didn't hit him harder. The prick ruined my life and now he's dead, my life might even improve.' Again Melody was stuck for a reply. Jo refused to bail him out. Clunes glared at the cops. 'So if we're finished, I've got concrete to pour.'

Melody hesitated so Clunes went back to his building work. The DS didn't look at Jo but walked away leaving her to follow.

'What do you know about the new DS with the musical moniker?' asked Charley Baldwin as he drove DS Fletcher to the crime scene.

'Bugger all. Been on a study junket in the US, and what he did and where before, I don't know.'

They discussed Billy Hughes becoming an Acting Detective Senior Sergeant, and the fallout from DI Richelieu's injuries, and then how they would tackle their person of interest. They arrived at the Heidelberg Rovers clubroom and saw the place in daylight. The police tape was gone but there were bunches of flowers propped against the front of the building. The detectives knelt to read the cards. Many were in a child's writing expressing sympathy for their late coach.

The main door was unlocked. They stepped inside and a man heard them and came out of an office. The police recognised the president from his photo at Homicide.

'No press,' said Alex Hero. 'Please leave.'

'Police, Mr Hero,' said DS Fletcher as the detectives raised their ID.

He was shocked and lost his bluster. 'How do you know my name?'

'You're an important man, Mr President,' said Fletcher, and Baldwin thought his colleague's choice of language was smart.

Hero hesitated then indicated his office. 'In here, officers.'

They sat and the questioning started. The difference with these detectives, as opposed to Melody and Best, was in their preparation. Fletcher and Baldwin knew who would lead and what they would ask.

'How long have you been the president, sir?' asked Fletcher showing deference to the status of the office.

Hero liked the respect in the question. 'Six years, and I was on the committee for three before that.'

'So you've known the deceased for many years?'

'I have.'

Then Baldwin joined in and threw the interviewee, not only because he was a new player, but because of his question.

'How would you describe your relationship with the deceased?'

This was not a question with a yes or no answer. Now he had to explain what could be a tricky situation. 'We had our moments.'

Fletcher jumped back in. 'What's that in English, sir?'

Hero didn't like the question and worse, the possible sarcasm. 'I must say, Detective Sergeant …'

'Fletcher, sir, DS Justin Fletcher, and we asked for an explanation of your answer which was, "We had our moments".'

Hero took his time. 'You probably know or will soon enough, we've had a major scandal over the building of our new grandstand. It's a huge investment for a suburban club but we were lucky to obtain grants, and because we promised a number of community groups access to the facilities, we had high hopes this would be a fantastic asset for many people, and not just the Heidelberg Rovers. Dieter Fischer was the person behind the project, and he agreed to employ then fell out with the builder leaving the club facing ruin. Naturally I was angry, still am, and told Mr Fischer I held him responsible. We argued many times and, I regret to say, we threatened one another.'

'What sort of threats?' asked Fletcher.

Hero tried to make light of it. 'Oh, you know, things you say in the heat of the moment but would never actually do.'

'What did you say to Mr Fischer when you threatened him?' pressed Fletcher.

Hero lost his temper. 'Oh all right, I threatened to hurt him.'

'Hurt him? How?'

'Something like "rip your bloody head off", and he said as much or worse to me.'

Baldwin got the look from his superior. 'Where were you last night, Mr Hero, from 6 pm?'

The question didn't appeal to the president. His nose twitched and his heart changed gears. 'I was at home.'

'All night?'

'Yes.'

'Can anyone confirm that? asked Fletcher.

'Confirm it?' snapped Hero. 'Isn't my word good enough? I'm the president of the club for God's sake.'

'It's a simple question, sir.'

'My wife; is she good enough?'

'And her name, Mr Hero?'

'Oh, this is ridiculous. It's Elena.'

Baldwin made notes as he spoke. 'And your home address and phone number, sir?'

The president could see he would never win. He gave the information through clenched teeth and quietly seethed.

'Do you know if Mr Fischer had any enemies, inside or outside the club?' asked Fletcher.

'Barry Clunes.'

'And who is he?' asked the DS already knowing the answer.

'He's the man who destroyed our building project, and who hated Dieter Fischer more than anyone else in the world.'

'Well I am honoured,' said Dr Gabrielle Strange when DI Rose and Acting Detective Senior Sergeant Hughes entered her workspace. 'It's the boss lady and her number one lackey.'

'Good morning, Doctor,' said Rose. 'Have you met the recently promoted number one lackey?'

'What?'

'Meet Acting Detective *Senior* Sergeant Hughes.'

Strange sniffed. 'You lot are all acting. I suppose you're here for my pearls of wisdom re the wogball winger.' The women were pleased this was not a public place. 'Walk this way.'

Strange withdrew the covering sheet revealing the late Dieter Fischer's face and chest.

'What's the cause of death, Doctor?' asked Hughes.

'Not the punch to the face, not the crack to the back of the skull when he fell, but definitely the stab wound to the heart.' She pointed and the female detectives peered at the wound. 'Just the one mind, as I've said a million times when offered a drink, but, and imperceptible as it may be, there's a second but not fatal knife wound here in the eyebrow.'

'The eyebrow?' both detectives asked as one, fascinated.

The DI bent to get a better view. 'I have a pic, ladies.' She flicked a switch and a close up of the victim's right eyebrow dominated a screen. 'Can you see it?'

Both detectives nodded. 'Unusual,' said Rose.

'What's it mean?' asked Billy.

'Ah,' replied Strange, 'psychological analysis is extra. Would you like a quote for my additional services, officers?'

The detectives smiled. Sometimes the wit alone of the pathologist was worth the visit.

'Anything else, Doctor?' asked Hughes.

'For the moment, no, but if there is, you'll read about it in my superbly crafted PM.'

'Thank you, Doctor,' said Rose and turned to go.

Strange made them stop. 'So how is my favourite detective settling back into her day job?' she asked.

Of course the cops knew she referred to Jo Best.

'I think she'll be all right, Gabrielle,' said Rose switching to the personal approach. 'And she swears blind you alone saved her life.' Strange scoffed. 'If we both keep an eye on her, between us, we can guide her back to doing what she does so well.'

'You were about to say what she does *best*,' teased the pathologist. The detectives smiled. 'And what about her love life?'

The detectives stopped smiling. That question produced silence.

Detective Senior Constable Stephen Payne stood out as someone who didn't stand out. He won zero awards for bravery, although falling through a skylight one night, and saving the life of his colleague Jo Best was down to stupidity rather than courage. He may have wanted promotion but lacked the skills and ambition to ever achieve such success. He would make an excellent bagman. He wasn't corrupt, simply an average copper wearing an average suit.

Being teamed with DI Callum Blunt didn't faze Payne. He preferred working with males, and Jo Best was never going to be his best buddy. 'Where to, sir?' he asked of his DI.

'The HQ of Melbourne Victory over the road from the G.'

Payne knew the Melbourne Cricket Ground well and, as a Melbourne FC supporter, spent many an afternoon in the Members' Stand supporting his beloved Demons. However, of the round-ball code played across the road, he knew zip. He headed for Olympic Boulevard driving too slow for the impatient DI.

Blunt's black mood grew darker as he pondered his move to Homicide. He thought it would be a powerful stepping stone for promotion with Assistant Commissioner his eventual goal. To date he'd stuffed up one case, been ignored for future assignments, and instead been allocated insignificant and useless tasks like talking to soccer administrators on a wild goose chase investigation. The fact he volunteered for this gig only made his misery worse.

They parked and entered the stadium. A receptionist greeted them.

'Police,' said Blunt flashing his ID, and living up to his name. 'Who's the senior person here?'

'Do you mean the CEO, sir?'

'I do and need to see him now.'

The receptionist made a call and the CEO appeared looking worried. Which of the team's players had done something to warrant the attendance of the police? Drunk driving, under-age sex, what?

Introductions were made and the trio settled in the CEO's office. Blunt had his spiel down pat and, although showing bluster, was in fact talking bullshit, a habit of his. The CEO knocked him flat.

'I think, officer, you need to speak with the people at Football Victoria. They would certainly know the deceased. We're a professional football team and I'm afraid whoever directed you to us has a limited knowledge of the game here in Australia and, specifically, in Victoria.'

Ouch.

Payne looked sideways at his DI. He thought he saw steam seeping from Blunt's noggin. The person who gave Blunt the lead was Blunt himself, Mr Know-All; another stuff-up by Callum.

Following directions they found themselves in St Kilda Road in another CEO's office. Dominic Greene not only knew Dieter Fischer, he knew the man died the night before and wanted to help the police in any way possible. Dominic called in his 2IC, Mario Rossi, believing two experienced heads were better than one. Blunt was quietly pleased. *If these guys know anything, I'll get a jump on my colleagues.*

'Gentlemen,' he began, and mispronounced the victim's first name. 'I'm investigating the suspicious death of Mr Dieter Fischer.'

'Dee-ter,' said the CEO. It's spelt *Die* but pronounced *Dee*.'

Payne wondered about the DI. *He said I'm investigating the case, and then couldn't pronounce the victim's name even after Billy Hughes had mentioned it several times at the morning briefing.*

'Whatever,' said Blunt. 'What can you tell me about the man and why do you think he was killed?'

'So it is murder?' asked Mario, genuinely curious.

'Sorry, gentlemen' said Blunt who wasn't. 'I'm the detective. I ask the questions which I would encourage you to answer.'

Payne winced, and the two football administrators wondered how such a moron ever got his job, let alone rank.

'Sorry,' said the soccer official who, like Blunt, wasn't.

The CEO tried to help. 'Dieter was a well-known, popular and highly-regarded figure in Victorian soccer. If you're asking about enemies he might have had, I'd say none.' The CEO looked at his colleague.

'I agree,' said Mario. 'He was a top bloke and will be sadly missed.'

'What about the failed building project?' asked Blunt. 'What's the inside story there?'

The soccer chiefs held back. 'It's unfortunate,' said the CEO.

'Unfortunate?' queried Blunt. 'A multi-million dollar project goes tits up and the man in charge is dead. I'd call that a tad more than unfortunate.' Silence. 'Well?' demanded Blunt.

'We hear all sorts of gossip and rumours but there always are when things go pear-shaped.'

'What rumours?' asked Blunt like a dog with a bone. The CEO looked at his colleague. 'Don't look at him. Tell me.'

'One rumour we heard was that Dieter reckoned the builder was being heavied.'

'What, extortion?'

'It was one of the explanations as to why the builder messed up.'

'So a criminal moves in on the builder demanding a cut of his fee or forces the builder to buy materials from the crim, or both? Is that it?'

Mario despaired. 'We honestly don't know. We have no evidence and the only person who may is Dieter and he's dead.'

Blunt stewed. He wanted details. He looked at the officials but not at his colleague. Payne worried. Being associated with DI Blunt could be dangerous to one's career.

'So who would know about this extortion?' demanded Blunt.

'We don't know there *was* any extortion,' replied the CEO.

Blunt barely disguised his threat. 'If I find the criminals behind this building collapse, and discover you know them or anything about them, I'll be back.'

He stood, glared at them, and left causing Payne to apologise. 'Thank you, gentlemen,' he said then scurried after the DI.

The CEO looked at his colleague. 'What a tosser.'

Chapter 6

The body in the tent was Max Bowman. Not yet identified by someone who knew him but with the dog and its collar with phone number, the tatts on the mangled man's arms matching the description given, the 4WD nearby, and the location as listed by his wife, now widow, spot on, the cops were pretty darn sure they'd found the missing camper.

The Heyfield cops radioed their base, and they rang Dandenong who rang Kylie with the bad news. She sounded shocked and sad.

Her first call was to brother-in-law, Graeme. 'He's dead,' she said.

'What did they tell you?' asked Max's brother.

'There was an accident at his camp site.'

'And he's dead?'

'Yes, and the cops want me to identify the body.'

'When?'

'Not sure. I guess they'll bring him back to Melbourne.'

'We got lucky.'

'Shhhh,' whispered Kylie.

The brother-in-law paused. 'And did they find Bluey?'

'He's okay. The cops took him to Heyfield. I can pick him up.'

'I'll drive you.'

'Thanks.' There was a long pause with a heavy silence.

The brother-in-law re-started the conversation. 'I'll come round tonight.' Kylie said nothing. 'I love you,' he said then ended the call.

The Licola crime scene came alive. Two detectives from the CIU in Sale arrived with a GP. The Heyfield uniformed cops fetched a tarp from their vehicle as the weather threatened. It wouldn't do to have detectives and forensics examining a scene where any evidence had been washed away.

The doctor declared the victim to be dead. The detectives discussed the possibility of foul play.

'What have we got?' asked the first. 'Is it accident, suicide or murder?'

The second turned to the medico. 'Wotcha reckon, Doc?'

'You Sherlock, me Watson,' he said. 'But if it's a suicide, the method has to be written up in *The Lancet* and the *Guinness Book of Records*.'

'I fancy accidental death,' said the second. 'What goes on the death certificate, Doc, the cause of death I mean?'

'Stupidity.'

'I agree,' said the uniformed sergeant. 'What idiot camps under a tree with a branch ready to fall if a baby magpie winks at it?'

'Any marks on the body, Doc, to suggest foul play?'

The medico shook his head. 'It's impossible to tell. The weight of the branch has obliterated any prior wounds, fight marks or ID on most of his upper body. I wouldn't fancy doing a PM on this bloke.'

'And we're sure it's the missing camper?' asked the first detective.

His colleague nodded. 'The tatts, the dog and the 4WD make him easy to ID.'

'You finished, Doc?' asked the first detective. The medico nodded. 'Well how about we record it as a death by misadventure but to cover are arses, we send a report to Homicide?'

'Sounds good,' said the second detective, and left the two uniforms to wait for the undertaker.

'Can you do us a favour?' called the sergeant. 'The victim's dog is back at the Caravan Park. Can you drop it off for us at Heyfield?'

And so Bluey scored a free ride with the cops and the GP back to Heyfield. It was the least he deserved. If only that pooch could talk.

The undertaker arrived, and the body was removed, off to the big smoke.

Finn Ruby had been Max's best mate forever. When Kylie rang him to say his pal had been killed in the High Country, he went straight to see her. She wasn't surprised he came immediately. He wasn't surprised to see her not crying. Over instant coffee she told Finn what she knew of the accident.

'Hit by a falling tree branch?' he asked, thinking his mate was so unlucky. 'Was he walking past when it broke off in a storm?'

'No, he was in his tent.'

Finn thought. *It can't be true. She has to be lying.* 'Who told you?'

'The cops.'

'They're lying.'

Kylie shrugged. 'They found him in his tent when they got there.'

'Who found him?'

'A couple of uni students kayaking on the Macalister.'

'What, they saw him from the river?'

'No, they saw Bluey going mad.'

'Bluey's alive?'

'Yes. He's been taken to a country cop shop, and Graeme said he'd drive me to collect him.'

Finn's mind buzzed. Something didn't add up. Lots of things didn't add up. 'What can I do?'

Kylie shrugged. 'Dunno. Speak at his funeral.'

Finn studied her. He had questions but decided, for now, to stay schtum. He stood. 'Sing out if you need anything.'

She followed him to the back door. 'Thanks, I will.'

Finn glanced at a large pair of boots on the verandah and an oversized shirt on the line.

Bloody Shorty, he thought and drove straight to his local cop shop.

DI Rose and Billy Hughes arrived back at HQ. Billy went to her old desk and saw an email. It was from a uniformed sergeant in the burbs, a bloke she worked with before joining Homicide. His email intrigued.

> *G'day Billy, how y'going?*
> *I had a bloke in today about his mate who died in the High Country. Local uniforms and detectives reckon it's death by misadventure. The mate was killed by a falling branch while camping. The bloke says a few things don't fit.*
> *1. His mate was an experienced bushman and would never camp under a tree.*
> *2. His mate's dog always slept with his master in the same tent but was found barking like mad outside the tent.*

Billy smiled. She'd enjoyed working with her former colleague and knew he had a great nose for spotting a crime. She picked up her phone to call him when DI Rose approached holding an email. Snap.

'This is interesting,' said Rose. Billy read the email but stopped after a couple of lines and pointed to her monitor. Both women read the other's information. Rose had received a report from the Gippsland detectives giving details of their finding. They'd decided it was an accident but would wait for the PM and the Coroner's reports.

'They're covering their backs,' said the Acting Detective Senior Sergeant.

'They are,' said Rose, 'but was the victim drunk or on drugs, and how many would be needed to pick up and drop a massive branch?'

'And why was the dog not harmed?'

Rose looked at Billy. 'Fancy a trip to the sticks?'

'You do realise I'm SIO on the soccer coach killing?'

'And?'

'You wouldn't?'

'Why not?' asked Rose with a straight face. 'Blunt becomes SIO on the soccer guy, you run the suspicious death in Gippsland. You choose.'

'Callum can't be trusted to run a cake stall, and you want to make him SIO?'

Rose shrugged. 'I can't keep *not* using him. He's gotta be given responsibility at some stage. We'll do a swap.'

Billy was unsure. She thought about it and worried about Blunt.

Rose didn't believe what she was about to say. 'He'll be fine.'

Chapter 7

That afternoon the squad met and as SIO, Billy Hughes ran the show. 'Right, who's first?' No-one volunteered. 'Great. I hope that's not a sign of your lack of progress.' She paused, waiting for someone to speak. Nothing. 'Okay, DI Rose and I went to see Dr Strange. We await her PM report but two interesting facts. The cause of death was a stab wound to the heart, and hidden in the victim's left eyebrow ...'

'Right,' said Rose.

Billy accepted the correction. 'Thank you, ma'am; hidden in the victim's right eyebrow was a tiny knife wound.'

'Significance?' asked DS Fletcher.

'It's unknown at this stage. Forensics are yet to report and there was a lot of traffic in the club house. Now, who's next? DS Melody?'

The new recruit gave his first report. 'Senior Constable Best and I tracked down Barry Clunes, the failed builder of the grandstand. The poor guy's on his uppers. He's broke, lost his business, marriage, kids and self-respect. He admitted having fallen out big time with the CEO, and admits he went to see the victim about 9 pm last night.'

'He said that?' asked Billy, shocked.

Melody grabbed everyone's attention. 'He admitted fighting with Fischer. Clunes reckons the victim pushed him so he punched Fischer. Clunes reckons the victim fell and hit his head but swears Fischer was alive when our person of interest left.'

'And?' asked Billy. Melody looked at Jo. 'Senior?'

'That's it, Sarge. But he didn't hesitate in telling his story.'

'Why wasn't he arrested?' asked Blunt.

Melody shrugged. 'We wanted to hear from the rest of the team, and his confession expressly denied having killed the man.'

Blunt pushed it. 'What about the assault?'

'Again, we were glad he said he was at the crime scene and fought with the victim. But there were no witnesses so I thought it better to get details from others to make an arrest more likely to get the truth.'

'Good decision, Sergeant,' said Rose, and Blunt backed off.

Billy stepped in not wanting a debate on whether Clunes should have been arrested. 'What about the club president? Justin?'

'Mr Cagey,' said DS Fletcher. 'If evasive and anger equals guilt, Alex Hero is our man. He was pissed to even be interviewed. He too confessed to having ding-dong arguments with the victim but offered an alibi for the time in question.'

'You don't buy it?' asked Billy.

'He claimed he was home all night with his wife able to verify same but we tried calling and visiting, and Mrs Hero has vanished.'

'Okay,' said Billy. 'There's plenty to chase up there. Now, DI Blunt, any joy with the soccer community?'

Blunt seemed smug, which was his default position, but now his smugness overflowed. 'Spoke with two heavyweights at Soccer Victoria. Our victim is well-known and well-liked. But I reckon the key to the murder is the contract to build the grandstand, with a possible link to corruption involving organised crime.'

A bomb went off in the incident room knocking detectives sideways. DI Rose felt her stomach lurch downwards. If Blunt was trying to big-note himself and flatten the others, he was off to a flyer.

'Say again,' said Billy.

'There's big money in construction and we all know it attracts serious villains. The reason the project collapsed could well be because the local Mafia got their claws into the supply chain. Fischer's the guy in the white hat. He discovered the corruption, and to keep him quiet, they knocked him.'

DI Blunt was not a regular contributor but now he had the floor, he gave it both barrels. Billy looked at DI Rose who looked bilious. If these claims were true, this case could become a media frenzy.

'Senior Constable Payne, anything to add to DI Blunt's comments?' asked the SIO.

Blunt didn't care about any doubting of his report. He believed he was on a winner. Payne's colour matched that of the Homicide boss. 'No, Sarge, err ma'am, err Senior, *Boss!*' He spoke louder with each new moniker and if that was a ringing endorsement of Blunt's assessment, God help us all.

'Right,' said Billy, 'anyone else?' Silence reigned. Billy was worried about giving out follow-up tasks knowing she would be off the case in the morning to be replaced by the blundering Blunt.

She looked at Rose who gave an imperceptible nod.

'Okay,' said Billy, 'tomorrow we bring in Mr Clunes for a chat. We find the president's wife and confirm his alibi. And we scrutinize the grandstand building contract looking at every deal, purchase order, supplier, contractor and worker. Clear?'

'Clear,' came the massed reply.

'So who does what, Boss?' asked Baldwin.

Billy paused. 'I'll tell you in the morning.'

A buzz began as Billy and DI Rose left the incident room.

Jo headed home taking a detour to Fitzroy North. She made sure her bag contained quality Haigh's chocolate. The pathologist was at home preparing one of her delicious pasta dishes. The aromas tugged you into the kitchen. The women enjoyed a coffee and chocolate; hardly the ideal starter but then this was never a calorie-free zone.

'So, back on the horse already, hey? Fallen off yet?'

'No and I don't intend to.'

'Good for you. And how's your love life?'

Typical Gabrielle. No mucking around. No gentle warm up. Just dive straight in. Besides she knew why Jo had called to see her.

'I value your opinion, Dr Lifesaver.'

Strange scoffed. 'Ask your questions, girlie, and I'll tell you no lies.'

Jo had many questions, took a deep breath and jumped in. 'How should I handle Pierre?'

Gabrielle scowled. 'What sort of a dumb question is that? Go and see him; now, tomorrow, often. You're all he has, woman. He's been shafted by his so-called mates in Paris, and attacked by his so-called family here and abroad. All he has is the love of his life—you. Go as soon as you finish your bloody coffee; just leave my chocolates.

She grinned and Jo felt better.

'What do I say if he asks me to marry him?'

'Don't.'

Jo's face collapsed. 'Don't? Why not?'

'Because it'll look like you're marrying him for his money.'

Jo's nostrils flared. 'What happened to love?'

'What indeed? Peggy Lee asked the right question.'

Jo wasn't up on song lyrics and didn't follow. She wanted guidance. 'Gabrielle, he's named me as the main beneficiary in his will.'

'So?'

'If Pierre dies, I'll never have to work again.'

'And is that what you want?'

Jo's hackles stood tall. She wanted to start punching. 'No, and I don't want Pierre to die. What do you take me for?'

'Does he know his family tried to kill him and then tried to kill you?'

Jo's face fell apart. 'I don't know.' The pause lingered. 'If he doesn't know and asks what happened, what do I say?'

'Aren't you lot trained in delivering death notices?'

Jo's face shouted disappointment. 'Thanks for nothing, Doctor.'

They looked at one another. 'You're a big girl, Detective. You're old and wise enough to make your own decisions. Take control, Missy.'

Jo paused. 'I've run out of questions.'

'No you haven't.' Jo knew what was coming. 'Do you want kids?'

Boy, typical Dr Strange; hit 'em between the eyes.

'With the right man, yes.'

'Well he's not the right man. Erectile dysfunction is the least of his worries. His body is not fit for purpose. And you know Monsieur Richelieu will never work as a cop again.'

'Never?' gasped Jo knowing that was the likely outcome but hearing it from a medico made it so final.

'I can't see him sitting in a wheelchair sorting traffic reports. Besides, he's loaded. He doesn't need to work.'

Jo fell silent and then began to silently weep. Strange came around the kitchen island and hugged her.

'You're lovely and he's gorgeous but you must know sometimes life is a right proper bitch, and besides, Jane Eyre is fictitious. It would be wrong for both of you to marry; each other I mean. He would know you were making a huge sacrifice and that would break his heart. You would always feel you were doing him a favour putting you on the defensive. It's a classic case my girl—life sucks.'

Strange kissed Jo's forehead then went back to cooking.

Jo recovered and whispered. 'Thank you.'

'Go on, piss off, before you make me cry as well.'

She turned her back on Jo and did cry, too proud to be seen. Jo clenched her fists then turned and quietly walked along the hallway closing the door on her way out.

'Can I help you?' asked a nurse.

'Yes, is it possible to visit Detective Inspector Pierre Richelieu?'

'Are you Jo Best?'

Jo stopped, tongue-tied. *How did she know?* 'Yes, I am.'

'Monsieur Richelieu is always talking about you. He described you to a tee. I'm glad you're here. He needs someone to cheer him up. I'll see if he's awake.'

She left and Jo felt awful. A second nurse entered the station. 'Can I help?' she asked.

'Thanks, I'm being looked after.'

'You're the police detective, Jo Best.'

Bloody hell, talk about a quiet visit. 'I am; guilty as charged.'

The first nurse appeared. 'You can go in but please remember he's still weak so not too much excitement.'

Bloody hell again. What will I find? She entered expecting the worst but was wrong. It was worse than the worst. Pierre was a trim, fit good-looking 42 year old man. When someone fit and lean loses weight they look frightening. His hair had been cut, badly, and Jo knew he would hate that. His shoulder bones protruded above his hospital gown. Again, in another life, a man of his taste would wear expensive slumber attire.

How do I hide my shock? She moved to the side of his bed. He was half sitting up with all manner of medical equipment attached to his body. Apart from looking strange and wounded, he smiled. That he couldn't disguise or stop. His voice was soft and husky.

'Ma fille chérie, bonjour, bonjour.' He offered a hand which saved Jo's worry. *How can I kiss him? Where will I kiss him?* She took his hand, squeezed and kissed it, once, twice and then again.

'Bonjour, Inspector, it's lovely to see you.' That was a lie because he wasn't lovely, and she couldn't stop the tears.

He became anxious. 'No, no, no, Joanna.' Too late. The shock, the sadness, the truth behind his situation all propelled her tears. Pierre reached for a button and a nurse appeared.

'Monsieur?' she asked looking at Pierre. He nodded and the nurse looked at Jo now feeling even worse. Giving comfort to grieving relatives was a regular requirement for nurses dealing with seriously ill patients. 'Have a seat, Jo,' said the nurse pulling a chair forward.

'Thank you,' said Jo fumbling for a tissue. She looked at the nurse. 'Thanks, I'm fine.'

The nurse left, speaking at the door. 'Now you behave, Monsieur.'

It was a lovely quip and Richelieu found his smile still worked.

'I apologise for giving you such a shock, Mademoiselle. But forget my feeble appearance. My 'eart, it is fine and still my feelings for my favourite detective, they burn as bright as ever. So, 'ow are you? What are you doing? Tell me everything, *everything*, s'il vous plait.'

Jo stopped crying only to suffer pain. Her chest felt tight, squashed. *What can I say? What does he know?*

'I'm fine, Pierre, and busy. I'm so sorry for not visiting. I promise I'll come every day if I can, and if I can't I'll call you.'

Now it was his turn to cry which made Jo feel another type of pain. She stood and bent to wipe his eyes. He grabbed her wrist and clung on for dear life. What could Jo do? Then an alarm sounded on a device beside his bed and two nurses appeared. One adjusted a tube beside his bed and the other gently pushed in between Jo and Pierre.

'You should go,' whispered the nurse.

Jo left. At the door she turned but Pierre wasn't looking. He was fighting for his life.

Ever since she was attacked by thugs, Jo took a wider path to her front door once she parked around the back. She kept thinking of Pierre lying helpless as the nurses battled, she assumed, to save his life. She turned the corner and someone was sitting on her doorstep.

'Out all night?' asked Billy Hughes.

'Sarge,' she said. 'Oh sorry, Acting *Senior* Sarge.'

'Shut up and let me in. I need the loo.'

Jo put the kettle on and when Billy entered the kitchen she saw the face that had been crying all the way home from the hospital.

'What's happened?' asked Billy, concerned.

Jo took a deep breath. 'I've been to see DI Richelieu.'

'Good for you.' Jo was surprised at her comment. 'It's obviously bloody awful.' Jo nodded. 'Even worse when you love the guy.' Wow.

Jo stood still so Billy guided her to the lounge. 'I'll make the tea. You sit and concentrate on crying.'

Over a cuppa, Billy let Jo explain her hospital visit. 'But Sarge, I still don't know what, if anything, he knows about the attack or the gunfight here at the O.K. Corral.' Billy listened. 'And whose job is it to tell him? Not his family; they're dead or in jail. The police? And if so, who? Me? It seems only yesterday I was suspected of his attempt murder.'

Billy waited till Jo ran out of words. 'I'll ask DI Rose about what Pierre's been told which'll give you a clue.'

'Thanks.' She sipped. 'So may I ask what you're doing here?'

'I thought you'd never ask. How do you fancy a trip to the bush?'

'What?'

Billy explained the suspicious death in the high country, and how she planned to investigate. Jo was more than keen but hesitated when told the name of the other team member.

'It's you, me and DS Melody,' said Billy.

Jo didn't smile or feel glad. 'Oh?'

'He comes with good refs and you've already worked with him. So keep it under your hat but pack a bag as we may have an overnighter.'

Billy left and Jo fell back into sadness. Her bathroom mirror told no lies, and red was the colour of my true love's eyes. She grabbed her trainers when her phone rang and the caller ID gave her a lift.

'Michael Chan; I thought you and Alan had run away.'

'Ah no, we remain the dull and boring couple living the dream here in downtown Northcote. So how are you? I bet you're back at work.'

'I started yesterday.'

'And Pierre; how is the French superstar?'

Jo paused and Michael noted the silence. 'I saw him tonight, Michael, and I'm still in shock.'

His voice dropped. 'Oh God, I'm sorry.' His sadness was genuine.

'I'm about to go for a run. We must catch up, Michael. We have one, possibly two homicides I'd like to discuss.'

'For my usual fee,' he said and laughed.

She laughed. 'Of course. Talk soon, and thanks for the call.'

'Bye,' he said then spoke to his cat. 'The detective said "Hi, Alan".'

Chapter 8

Jason Lilliput was a laidback dude, 52, amateur musician, pot smoker and married to Chelsea. No kids, at least none living. Jason hadn't paid a barber since milkshakes were 1/6. His facial hair had longevity and decorated itself with pepper and salt tips and streaks. Their married abode in the not-so-posh part of Drouin, 90 kms east of Melbourne, needed repairs, renovations, and ideally removal.

Jason worked as a truckie for ages until the accident, and now lived on his disability pension. Chelsea worked in the local supermarket three days a week. They were a rung and a half above poverty.

It was a marriage of convenience. Neither loved or hated the other and as two can live cheaper than one, staying together had its benefits. Their only real disagreement was on photos. Their long deceased and much loved child, who would now be pushing 30, was not displayed anywhere. Jason wanted their son's pictures around the house. Chelsea didn't. She could never forget the agony of the boy's suffering, and seeing his photo set off her depression. The young lad drowned in a next-door neighbours' swimming pool when he went walkabout and got through the unlocked child-proof gate. Chelsea's screams were recorded in jet aircraft decibels, and Jason and Chelsea never recovered.

Whenever Chelsea stayed with her cousin in Melbourne, Jason pulled out the photos of the boy, and of the three of them as a family, and placed them around the house. They were always put away before Chelsea came home.

She opened the appropriate drawer once and found them face up—that was so against their rules—and knew Jason had placed them around the house. She wanted to scream at him but found her sadness stronger than her anger.

The couple's mundane existence sat well in this quiet country town. They had little money, little joy and little future. Roll another joint, Jason.

Next morning at Homicide, Billy called the meeting to order. 'As promised, we have tasks to allocate although, and I'm sure you'll be thrilled to know this, it'll not be by me.' The squad was hooked.

What's going on? Billy gets promoted, made SIO then dumped.

'Say that again, Sarge,' said a bewildered Baldwin speaking for everyone except DIs Rose and Blunt.

'There's a suspicious death in the sticks and I'm taking two officers to Gippsland to confirm it's a homicide.' More babble from the masses. 'DS Melody and Senior Constable Best will accompany me, and your new SIO on the Dieter Fischer murder enquiry is DI Blunt.' She looked at him. 'Sir.' Callum strode to the front barely able to contain his glee.

Billy indicated to Melody and Jo and the three left the room. A few called after them such things as, 'Send us a postcard,' 'Behave,' and 'Redbacks live in dunnies!' The catcalls died and DI Blunt glared.

'Right, DS Fletcher with Senior Constable Baldwin will continue interviewing the president, Mr Nero. It's his alibi you need sorting.'

'That's Hero not Nero, sir,' added Baldwin. Blunt ignored him.

'DI Rose with Senior Constable Payne will interview our builder friend, Mr Clunes, who seems keen to confess to everything except the actual killing, and I will work with admin officers and investigate the building contract which fell over. Anyone not with a specific task, see me and I'll give you more than enough to keep busy. Let's rendezvous at 1400 hours, and don't come back without solid evidence. Questions?' Nobody spoke. Blunt looked at the head of Homicide. 'DI Rose, anything to add?' She shook her head. 'Right, let's go.'

DI Rose had major concerns about her decision to make Blunt the SIO, and to help allay her fears, she crossed her fingers *and* her toes.

Fletcher and Baldwin sat in their car. 'We must let our fingers do the walking, Charley,' said the DS. 'Let's not race to the soccer club only to have the president tell us his wife's on holiday.'

'Agreed, sir,' said Baldwin, 'so what's the plan?'

'Let's locate the woman in question from where we sit right now.'

'Sure but how?' Fletcher looked at Baldwin. 'Is this a test, Sarge?'

He laughed. 'Trust me, I don't want to front a meeting to tell our new SIO we couldn't find Mr *Nero's* Mrs.'

Charley laughed. 'I bet he'd kick off if we called the SIO, DI Runt.'

'So, how can we flush out Mrs President?'

Charley had an idea. 'I'm guessing Mr President has given his wife strict instructions to provide him with a rock solid alibi.'

'Agreed,' said Fletcher.

'And he's told her to lie low somewhere and not answer the phone.'

'Correct again.'

'So if we tell Mr Prez we can't locate his wife and therefore will have to take him into custody as a suspect in the murder of his CEO, he might be encouraged to help us locate his good lady.'

'You're not just a pretty face, Senior,' said Fletcher, and rang the President of the Heidelberg Rovers. Within five minutes, the detectives were driving to an address in Templestowe where Elena Hero waited. She kept the officers on the doorstep.

Unsurprisingly, Mrs Hero was no heroine and meekly agreed her darling husband had been at home by her side all evening when the unfortunate "accident" happened at the clubhouse.

Not wanting to draw a complete blank, the officers tried different ways to extract information from the loyal wife. If she had gossip or dirt on her old man, she kept it to herself. At this stage, the president was in the clear. They thanked the obsequious wife, and left.

In the driveway, they stopped when a voice whispered from the garden. A woman, who looked like the one they'd recently interviewed, approached. 'I must speak to you.' The detectives moved to the woman. 'Come closer,' she said, 'so she cannot see you.'

'Can we help you, madam?' asked DS Fletcher.

'I am her sister.'

'Elena's sister?'

'Yes. She is afraid of her husband. He treats her badly. He tells my sister what to say.' She paused. 'And he has a woman.' The sister stopped and looked terrified. 'You are the police, yes?'

'Yes,' said Fletcher, and the woman's relief was palpable.

'She will only tell you what her husband tells her to say.' She looked back towards the house. 'No more; I must go now,' and she did.

Fletcher and Baldwin looked at one another and both felt good.

DI Rose drove and Senior Constable Payne worried. Working with DI Blunt was frightening; working with DI Rose merely intimidating. 'We'll start at the building site, Stephen. Do you know if our Mr Clunes resembles the proverbial brick shithouse?'

'Ah, no Ma'am, I believe he's of average height but muscular.'

'Good. I'll do the talking and, if necessary, you can cuff him.'

'Ma'am,' said Payne and spent the rest of the journey looking out his window.

They pulled up near the building site and Payne, using a photo they carried, spotted their quarry. 'That's him, unloading the ute, ma'am.'

'Thanks,' said Rose and they headed for Barry Clunes. He saw them coming and wondered about the woman.

'What now?' he said suggesting he would object, run or at best, say nothing.

'Good morning, Mr Clunes. I'm DI Rose from Homicide and this is my colleague, Detective Senior Constable Payne.'

'I've told your other lot what happened.'

'You did and we're grateful but there are more questions, and as you've admitted being at the scene on the night in question, and to assaulting Mr Fischer, we'd like to conduct a formal interview back at the station.'

'And what if I don't want to be part of any formal interview?'

'Then I'll arrest you and you'll be taken by force if necessary.' She indicated. 'Our car's over there.'

'And how will I get back here?'

Rose didn't mince her words. 'If you get to go home, we'll drive you, but it will depend on the answers you provide.'

Clunes wanted to swear and tell the cops where to go. Once he would have done so. Now, as a broken and bitter man, he lacked fight.

'Can I tell my brother?'

'Of course, and Senior Constable Payne will accompany you.'

He glared at her then walked away with Payne in close pursuit.

DS Melody drove, Acting Senior Sergeant Hughes sat beside him and Detective Senior Constable Best had the back seat to herself. Billy gave the others as much information as she knew. They chatted about the possibilities of the suspicious death but as the ever-expanding south-eastern suburbs of Melbourne whizzed by, conversation lagged and silence became the norm. It was about 200 kms from Melbourne to Heyfield, and they'd be stuck in the vehicle for more than two hours.

Through Warragul and Moe they went and, at Traralgon, turned towards the high country along the road to Maffra. In the run into Heyfield, Billy told her colleagues they were to offer nothing of their facts leaving the talking to the locals. And at the camp site, they would offer nothing until they'd examined the scene. 'Keep your powder dry and let the others do the talking.' Jo reckoned she would never stop learning from DS now Acting Senior Sergeant Billy Hughes.

They arrived at the Heyfield police station where stiff limbs were stretched and the real work began.

The local constabulary were expecting the suits from Homicide. After a coffee—tea for Billy—Sergeant Pepper took the trio to where the 4WD vehicle, tent and camping gear were stored. 'No forensics yet, Sergeant?'

'We're still waiting for them, ma'am.'

'And this is all secure?'

'It is.'

In the station, Bluey was there pining for his master so examined all the new arrivals hoping to find a human he knew. His master was chilling out in a local funeral parlour awaiting a trip to Melbourne and a meeting with Dr Gabrielle Strange. The visitors were about to be driven to Licola when Jo asked a question.

'Is there a vet in Heyfield, Sergeant?'

Everyone looked surprised. 'No, the nearest is in Maffra.'

Billy was curious. 'What's up, Senior?'

Constable Leigh remembered. 'Old Nobby Wainwright's here in town, Sarge.'

'He's retired.'

Billy wanted answers. 'Jo, what's going on?'

'If the dog was at the scene when the victim died, a blood sample might be handy down the track.'

Billy again admired the thinking of her junior colleague. 'Good thinking, Senior.' Billy turned to the locals. 'Could the retired vet take a blood sample?'

'He was a vet for over 40 years,' said Pepper.

'Right,' said Billy. 'Can you, Constable ...'

'Leigh, ma'am, Dennis Leigh.'

'Can you, Constable Leigh, take the dog to this retired vet? We want a sample of Bluey's blood and a letter from the gentleman confirming his action, and when the sample was taken.'

'Old Nobby could do it blindfolded and I reckon he'll be tickled pink to be asked,' said the uniformed constable.

'Good man,' said Billy who turned to Pepper. 'And your radio works at Licola?'

'It works pretty much everywhere, ma'am.'

Billy and her colleagues were led to the local police vehicle. She sat beside the driver with Melody and Jo in the back. It was large, a 4WD for off-road policing with an aerial so tall it tickled low clouds.

En route to the camp site, Jo made conversation. 'Am I right, Sergeant, in guessing with a name like Pepper, you get the occasional smart-alec remark?'

He smiled. 'Once or twice,' he said. 'My first name's Peter so for years on cold Winter nights I copped *Peter Piper picked a peck of pickled peppers*, and the older guys used to sing that well-known song by the Beatles. So yes, Senior Constable, your guess is correct.'

'No mention of a certain pig?' asked Jo who remembered what her niece and nephew used to read.

'One birthday, some smart-alec constable gave me a book which I promptly gave to my granddaughter.'

The resultant jocularity helped pass the time. Yesterday, Sergeant Pepper placed tape in a discreet way beside the murder scene, making it easy to locate the spot. They inspected the site.

Everything was gone. The camper was meticulous and little of the bush, apart from the tent location, had been touched.

The massive branch, the killing machine, lay to one side. Billy began questioning. 'So who's been here, Sergeant?'

'We've had the two kayakers who found the body, me and Constable Leigh, a GP and two CIU detectives from Sale, and the undertaker and his assistant. Oh and an old timber worker who told us the tree was rotten and the branch could have dropped any time.'

'Where did he come from?'

Pepper explained how he knew Rufus and sought him out. Billy realised they were working with a good country copper who knew things and more importantly, people.

'Rufus reckoned the victim must have been a first-time camper to set up where he did.'

Billy absorbed the facts. 'Thanks Sergeant.'

'And as you saw, ma'am, we have the vehicle, tent and camping gear back at Heyfield.'

'Good. And you conducted a sweep of the area?'

'We did, Ma'am,' said Pepper.

Billy looked at her colleagues. 'We'll try another. Look for footprints approaching from another direction, anything dropped or caught in the bush, another campsite.' Jo and Melody agreed areas and set off.

'We had a good drop of rain overnight, ma'am,' said Pepper. 'It won't help any forensic search.'

'Tell me again about the kayakers; were they genuine, nothing to do with the incident, or what?'

'Genuine, and if they hadn't spotted the dog, the victim might still be here.'

'You have their details?'

'We do, ma'am.'

Billy went for a walk towards the river. It was a beautiful spot, personally chose by Mother Nature, with flora and fauna loving the locale. The comments from the victim's mate and local police echoed in Billy's head. *Why would an experienced bushie sleep under a tree and give his beloved dog the flick?*

The others came back. Melody found nothing. Jo wasn't sure. 'The footprints around where the 4WD was parked are not all the same.' The other three looked at her.

'Meaning?' asked Billy.

'You remember the double murder in Elsternwick, Sarge?'

'Your first homicide, Senior Constable, is seared on my memory.'

Jo wanted to say homicides, plural, but explained. 'The footprints had different pressure points as if a smaller foot wore bigger shoes or, in this case, boots.'

'Take photos.'

'Already done, ma'am.' Billy glared at Jo who grimaced. On their first day, Billy had warned Jo about never calling her ma'am.

Billy turned to Sergeant Pepper. 'Right Sergeant, let's have a quick chat with the Lord Mayor of Licola.'

The bloke running the general store knew Max, and confirmed his knowledge of bushcraft and camping were second to none. But now Max Bowman would never camp under any tree, let alone a rotten one.

Blunt made no attempt to talk with admin staff at Homicide. He worked solo. If his theory proved correct, the publicity for this investigation would be massive—even a TV series—and guess who would be front and centre on the Awards' Night? Unprepared, and like a bull at a gate, he blundered off in search of a scoop. You'd think after his Melbourne Victory FC stuff-up he'd have learnt his lesson. He hadn't, and his first port of call was the Master Builders Institute.

He was shown into a senior executive's office who joined by two other senior officers. Blunt blinked. They were all women. He had the notion master builders would be blokes with a carpenter's pencil behind their ear, and wood shavings on their hairy arms. Three impeccably dressed women killed that prejudice.

Being a limelight lover and supercharged with self-confidence, his strategy was his alone. Again his lack of preparation meant he tempted fate. Will he ever learn? As soon as he raised the issue of the new grandstand at the Heidelberg Rovers ground, the MBI put him right.

'Not every builder is a Master Builder, Inspector,' said the CEO. 'If you as a client want a reliable and professional builder, choosing someone registered with our Institute is your guarantee of quality work on time and on budget.'

Blunt moved back to square one, and copped more bad news when another female executive finished studying her tablet and announced.

'The project was awarded to Clunes Construction which is not a member of the Master Builders Institute of Victoria.'

"Shit,' mouthed Blunt sans audio.

'May we ask why you have come to us, sir?' asked the CEO.

'I'm investigating a homicide at the Heidelberg location and been given information the construction work may have been compromised by criminals.'

Good answer, Callum, although the problem now was what to say next; especially when he heard the reply.

'I repeat, Inspector, if that *is* the case, why come to us? We're a professional Institute promoting the highest standards in construction, which we combine with a range of activities supporting worthwhile charities.' She handed him a brochure. 'This provides more details.'

Blunt looked at the brochure listing several good causes all of which benefitted from the largesse and expertise of the Institute. Oops. Then he looked at the three women who said nothing. It's your move, Sunshine. He tried desperately to slither away grabbing at even a fragment of the moral high ground. He failed and his next question meant the hole he dug became even deeper.

'So would there be an association of builders who do not belong to your group?' he asked.

One woman looked at her colleagues. 'Do the cowboys have one?'

Another maintained the aura of sarcasm. 'I've never heard of it.'

'I don't think there *is* such an association,' added the CEO. She turned to Blunt. 'I'm sorry, Inspector ...' She hesitated.

He hated her all the more for making him repeat his name. 'Blunt,' he said and stood. 'Thank you, I'll see myself out.'

For the DI, it was the longest walk from any office, and Callum's mission to destroy the Mafia Down Under was stuck on that rickety rockety road.

Chapter 9

The failed builder, Barry Clunes, waited in the interview room at Homicide. He was given the option of having a solicitor but had recently taken a vow of poverty to spend nothing ever again. 'You can apply for Legal Aid,' said DI Rose. Clunes snorted. His wife reckoned he took a vow of poverty when it came to paying child support. DI Rose told Payne she would lead thus pleasing the Senior Constable who hoped for zero responsibility. The detectives entered, the preliminaries were completed and the recording commenced.

'How did you win the contract for the Rovers job?' asked Rose.

Clunes felt no pressure. 'My company tendered and won.'

'What's your experience in constructing sporting club buildings?'

Clunes shrugged. 'None, but a building's a building. We've built factories, houses, extensions, more. Construction's the same; you read the plan, get the best subbies, and Bob's y'uncle.'

'Have you ever made a mess of any previous project?'

'Never.'

'So why did you fail with this job?'

'I told the other cops why.'

'Well now you can tell us.'

Clunes sighed. 'My business partner quit. My married partner quit. The final payment I was owed for two previous jobs, one a biggie, didn't come through. Cash flow problems meant I couldn't pay people. Subbies quit. I was working 15 hours a day, seven days a week. There were penalties in the contract for missing KPIs. The club withheld payments. That crazy weather weekend meant a wall had to be demolished. It was the perfect storm, a template for failure.' He looked at them. 'I could go on.'

'Do you own a knife?' His mood changed. He hesitated. 'Come on, Barry, it's a pretty simple question.'

'Yes.'

'Where do you keep it?'

'In the toolbox in my ute.'

'And where it is now?'

'In the toolbox in my ute.'

'You're sure?'

'Why are you asking? What's a knife ...' He stopped. 'Oh, so the coach was knifed.'

'Tell us about your fight with Mr Fischer.'

'It was hardly a fight. We both swore and made threats. He pushed, I punched; he lost his balance and fell backwards. I left to the sound of his threats.' Clunes spoke with emphasis. 'He was still alive.'

'What did he say?'

'Over weeks that he'd take me to court and bankrupt and ruin me— and I'll say this for him, he's kept his word.'

'Would you say revenge is a good motive?'

Clunes thought. 'Does having a good motive prove I killed him?'

Payne was impressed, and Rose now knew her suspect was no pushover. She kept switching her approach and the next question stymied Clunes. 'Describe the relationship between Fischer and Hero.'

Clunes sniffed. He didn't care what he said. 'They're both bastards.'

'Okay, we know why you hated Fischer. But why hate Hero?'

Clunes looked surprised. 'Is that your best trick question?'

'Sorry?'

'I hear stories about cops being thick but this is the first time I've seen it in action.'

The detectives looked at one another. 'Senior Constable, have you any idea what Mr Clunes is talking about?'

'He's lost me, ma'am.'

Clunes shook his head. 'God, I can't believe it. You don't know.'

'Know what?'

'If you don't know why Hero pissed me off then you really are thick. And you call yourself detectives. You couldn't detect a hammer in a box of nails.'

'Humour me, Barry. What did President Hero do?'

'Not a lot; just took a cut of my contract.'

It was time for the detectives to be surprised. 'What?'

'I was lucky. Originally, he wanted 10% but I got him down to 5.' The police thought he was joking. 'Oh come on, how do you think I got the contract in the first place? He knew I wasn't in the Master Builders Institute and glossed over that. And when things went bad, his thieving was the straw that broke the camel's back and sent me broke.'

'Hero got you the contract?'

'Of course. He convinced the committee I was the best man for the job because he knew he could screw me. And my low quote meant they could use part of the grant money on other things.'

'You're accusing him of fraud.'

'Only because it's true. Look, Fischer never wanted me to get the job. We were enemies from the off. Then he told me he was close to proving Hero was on the take, and when he found the evidence he was going to report Hero to the club committee and the cops. That's why Fischer was killed by Hero or one of his mates. If you reckon I had a motive, take a gander at Mr President, our wonderful Hero.'

This was major news and Rose felt stupid not having done more research to be better prepared. She didn't know if the accusations by Clunes were true but if they were, she had a hell of a lot more investigating to do, and now, at least two persons of interest.

She ended the interview, took Payne outside and ordered him to take Clunes to his ute, look for his knife, have Forensics meet them there and, if the knife was found, have it seized by Forensics. Mr Clunes was going nowhere until that knife was sorted.

Rose rang DS Fletcher. 'Where are you, Justin?'

'I could say in a meeting but we're having a coffee, ma'am.'

She became annoyed. 'What happened with Hero's alibi?'

'Good and bad news, ma'am. The wife backed him but the wife's sister said he's a rat. The sister won't speak until she's alone.'

Rose explained how, according to Clunes, Hero was allegedly on the take. 'Find the president and put the issues to him. You've met the sister-in-law, and now know about the dodgy bookkeeping. Don't reveal your sources but let him think you might know more than you're letting on. If necessary, bring him in and interview under caution.'

'Will do, ma'am.'

'And we need a forensic accountant to go through the building contract and the club accounts. Questions?'

'Only one, ma'am. Should I be running this through the new SIO?'

'No, and I'll take responsibility. Ciao.' The call ended and Fletcher gave Baldwin the news.

They discussed tactics en route to the Heidelberg Rovers clubrooms. They had no evidence—yet—of Hero's mistress, his supposed false alibi, and the alleged fraud. The key was to let him know they knew certain facts and see how he responded.

They were lucky. Mr President was in his office on the phone. His door was open and the detectives appeared.

'Knock, knock,' said Fletcher and Hero's face went from black and white to technicolour.

'I'll call you back,' he said to the voice on the phone and ended the call. 'Gentlemen, what now?'

Fletcher played a straight bat. 'Sorry to interrupt Mr Hero but there are a few points we need to clear up.'

He indicated the chairs and the detectives sat. 'Have you found the guy who killed Dieter?'

'You think it was a man, sir?' asked Baldwin.

The question threw Hero as did the fact the cops shared the role of asking questions. He wasn't sure who would fire the next bullet.

'Ah, figure of speech, I have no idea.'

Fletcher tried the softening up approach. 'We went to interview your wife, sir, and she was most co-operative.' Hero had a sinking feeling. He was sure the next sentence would start with *but* or *however*. 'She confirmed your alibi for the night of the murder.'

Hero produced a miserable smile. 'Good.'

Fletcher changed gears and, if this scene were in a movie, spooky music would now be heard. 'We also met your sister-in-law, sir.'

Hero smelt fear. *Where is this going? What did the bitch say?*

Baldwin attacked from a different angle. 'Who does the accountancy work at your club?'

'I do,' said Hero too quickly. 'I'm experienced in bookkeeping and this saves the club a lot of money.'

'And what about the auditing of the books?' More fear for Hero.

'We use a local firm. A father of one of the junior lads is a qualified auditor.'

'Did this same gentleman audit the contract for the grandstand?'

Sweat beads started pushing their way to the surface of the president's forehead.

'No, because of the catastrophic building failure, and the future court action, we're waiting to see how things pan out. It might be a while before we get to the bottom of the fiasco, if we ever do.'

The detectives fell silent. Hero was under mounting pressure and saying nothing is often a way to ramp up the stress for the interviewee.

When he did speak, Fletcher took the approach of asking for help. Naturally this appealed to Hero. But the question was loaded. More like packed with explosives, and the slightest wrong move by the president would have him dangling from a window on the 22nd floor holding a super thin rope. Oh, and with the wind gusting.

'We would be grateful, sir, if you could help us verify an allegation we've heard.'

'If I can,' he said hiding his trepidation.

'We're looking into an allegation Mr Fischer was murdered to stop him going to the police.'

'The police? You?'

'No, we're Homicide, sir; I mean to detectives who investigate fraud.' Hero swallowed. 'We've been told Mr Fischer discovered possible corruption with the building contract, and was about to blow the whistle when he was killed.'

'Incredible,' said Hero feeling sick, 'absolutely incredible.'

He needed to produce saliva to speak.

'Can you help us, Mr President? What have you heard about fraud or corruption regarding the grandstand building project?'

Hero looked serious and shook his head. 'I'm sorry, officers, but all I've heard is one sob story after another as the incompetent builder made a dog's breakfast of what was a straightforward construction.'

'How did Barry Clunes win the contract in the first place?' asked Baldwin.

'Committee decision and supported by Dieter Fischer.'

The detectives went for the silent response again and Hero's comments lingered as if on a loop. The cops exchanged glances then thanked the president and left. He wanted to throw up.

Blunt fumed. Not only did the Master Builders Institute give him nothing in his quest to pin Fischer's murder on organised crime, he came away looking a proper tool. *Thank God I'm working alone.* Having a partner would have seen his embarrassment broadcast all around the squad. He stopped for a coffee to plan his latest raid.

Trying a new approach, he entered the office of the United Construction Workers Union. Their reputation was well-known as far as outer space. *Up the bosses* and *Take no prisoners* were in the opening paragraph of their constitution. If the Master Builders Institute didn't have burly builders running their show, the UCWU did. It had more strict rules about membership than the Melbourne Club. Blunt entered the foyer, and wearing a suit made him an immediate target. Snipers took aim while in their foxholes, aka, offices.

'G'day,' said Blunt trying to appear cool and non-threatening. He showed his ID without any flashy movement. 'Police,' he said producing a zero reaction. Had he announced he was the head of the SAS and the building was surrounded by hundreds of heavily armed crack troops, he would have received the same reaction.

What the fuck do you want? thought the tattooed receptionist with Blunt clearly able to read the man's mind.

'I'd like a word with your boss, please. It's about corruption in the construction industry and how your members are getting screwed.'

Blunt had loosened his tie, chewed gum and spoke in as uneducated voice as he could. If this was an audition, most directors would have called, "Next".

'Wait here,' said the pretty receptionist in a fetching singlet with a beer gut doubling as a dam wall. Blunt looked at the other "gentlemen" in the foyer all of whom graduated from the School of No Expression. The receptionist returned and beckoned with his head; not a word.

Blunt entered the boss's office. He didn't stand or offer Blunt a seat. A Mexican standoff began, a tactic used by the union boss on all his enemies which, at last count, numbered in the billions.

Blunt dived in. 'DI Blunt, Homicide,' he said and the boss sniffed. 'I reckon there's a possibility some of your members are getting screwed on a building site in Heidelberg. It's a grandstand at a soccer club. Do you know the project?'

The boss cleared his throat then stood in a quick movement. Blunt felt a flicker of fear noting the boss had more tatts then teeth and his dentures were nigh on perfect.

'We fight our own wars, officer,' were the boss's first words.

'Fair enough,' replied Blunt wondering if jumping through a window would be his best move.

'And we don't appreciate the law coming in here under some bullshit excuse about caring for our members.'

'It's not bullshit.' Blunt tried not to sound desperate but failed.

'Now we don't want you to leave empty-handed, officer. Do we boys?'

There were now three other receptionists in the boss's office. They luckled; a union member's cross between a laugh and a chuckle.

'Okay,' said the back-pedalling detective. 'I'll sort this out m'self.'

He turned to leave and, as if having been choreographed, the three receptionists slid—glided would be an exaggeration—into position across the only door, the only exit apart from the window, in the room.

Bother, gosh and *damn* were a few of the words Blunt wanted to utter. Instead he went for the serious threat routine. 'Gentlemen, hindering a police officer in the pursuit of his duties is a criminal offence. Now, kindly step aside and we'll forget all about it.'

Nobody moved. Blunt was reasonably fit and could handle himself but four gorillas in the mist was a bridge too far. The boss nodded and three construction workers grabbed the detective, frogmarched him out of the room and down a flight of stairs.

Blunt knew threatening to arrest his companions would be useless. His only hope was to leave the building alive and in one piece.

They stumbled into a courtyard, a suntrap for ten minutes a day with all four sides the walls of the old and rock-solid building. The cement floor had a soft carpet of discarded cigarette butts. A weather-beaten wooden chair appeared, and Blunt sat by force thereon. This was the first time since arriving he'd been invited to sit.

He tried so hard to not appear scared despite shitting himself. Two men held him down, one using his thumb to press on one of Blunt's shoulders. God it hurt. Two wooden, square boxes appeared. They had a bottom and sides but no top with each side about 6 inches tall. Blunt's ankles were grabbed and his feet lifted. The boxes slid forward and his shoes landed, one foot per box.

Two buckets appeared and fresh concrete sloshed into each box.

'Hey!' yelled Blunt but stopped when the pain in his shoulder turned exquisite.

A bricklayer's trowel pushed the concrete to the top of each box. All of Blunt's shoes were covered and the exposed bits of his socks just above his ankles were now a new colour. He wanted to scream and his mind played terrible tricks.

I'm a good swimmer but who can swim wearing concrete shoes? This is gangster stuff. Is Marlon Brando a member of this union?

It got worse. His hands were pulled behind his back and tied. Gaffer tape went under the chair and over his upper legs, twice. He was in another version of the stocks.

His captors left without a backward glance. They didn't care. Ridicule was their trump card. Alone, the detective had time to reflect. In a way, he wanted to be killed. For him to survive and for this situation to become public, he could never enter a police station again. His embarrassment would become the stuff of legends.

Traffic sounds wafted in from the nearby outside world. *Should I call out?* He decided against it thinking it might bring the lads back to help him remain silent. Then his luck changed. His phone rang.

The lift this sound gave his spirits is hard to describe. From despair came hope but, as in all good yarns with their black spots and barriers, another bobbed up to smash our hero. Hero?

The phone buzzed in Blunt's side jacket pocket but no matter how hard he squirmed and struggled, he couldn't reach it. He figured one digit, well stretched, might just hit the Speak button. He would shout his request. His finger extended like Pinocchio's nose. He arched his body, stretched, strained and squirmed. Tantalisingly close he came when the caller rang off. 'Ahhh,' screamed Blunt and collapsed into a new position called Hunched 101.

He didn't know how long he'd been in this restrained predicament when he heard footsteps. The lads returned. He looked down and saw nothing but concrete, solid concrete. He could wiggle his toes but his shoes and feet were locked. The boss and his three secretaries entered the courtyard. One knelt, tested the concrete and gave a thumbs up. Another knelt and, using a hammer, whacked away freeing the boxes. Blunt now wore unusual rectangular footwear. No laces mind but his concrete shoes came in a lighter shade of grey.

The boss moved and stood a couple of metres in front of Blunt. His staff moved aside. The boss held up a swish camera and snapped away.

He stepped forward and showed Blunt the back of the camera. A selection of shots appeared.

'Now get this, detective,' said the boss. 'If you ever come near us again or even mention this little visit, someone's ugly mug and fancy footwear will saturate the internet with an emailed attachment to every cop shop in town.' He glared at Blunt. 'Are we clear, Constable?'

Blunt felt fantastic. *Forget embarrassment, humiliation and mockery, I'm alive.* He nodded. 'No problem ... and thanks.' He hoped his gratitude would get him out sooner.

The gaffer tape was removed and his hands untied. Then, still sitting on the chair, three labourers, with difficulty, picked him up and tipped it backwards to make Blunt easier to transport. His arms did the helicopter crash routine, as he was carried through another door, along a dark and ghost-ridden corridor. The sounds of traffic became louder. The boss pulled back old bolts on an old door in the old building. Daylight flooded in.

Blunt was lifted off the chair and couldn't move. Three helpers pushed him onto a small area above four steps leading down to the footpath. People, cars and the rest of the world hurried by. He heard the door thud shut and the bolts rammed back into place.

Well done, Callum. We'll have to call you Sancho as you go about enjoying your windmill-tilting adventure.

And so ended another unsuccessful excursion in Blunt's quest to expose the Melbourne Mafia.

Idiot.

Chapter 10

Beside the Macalister River, Billy Hughes, DS Melody, Jo Best and the Heyfield sergeant reviewed the situation. Billy ran the show.

'Okay, we're agreed it's an unusual death. Is it accidental due to bad luck and/or stupidity, murder or suicide?'

'Far too tricky for suicide,' said Melody. 'And no dog lover would ever put his best friend through what that dog endured.'

'Is still enduring,' added Pepper.

'I agree,' said Jo, 'although if it's murder, only Tarzan could have done it.'

'What, someone with super strength?' asked Hughes.

'Has to be at least two killers,' said Melody; 'could be more.'

Billy needed to make decisions. 'Sergeant Pepper, we need Forensics to examine the 4WD, the tent and camping equipment.'

'All materials ready for inspection.'

'What about this crime scene?' asked Melody.

Jo shook her head. 'Little value, Sarge; it'll be three, possibly four days after the event when someone turns up, and we've had solid rain. We've got plenty of pics. Let's stick with the body, vehicle, tent and its contents.'

'Agreed,' said Billy.

'Who'll do the PM?' asked Melody.

Billy decided some time ago. 'If there are clues, Gabrielle Strange will find them and the sooner the better.' She looked at her colleagues. 'Right you two, homeski, unless you want to spend a night in Licola.'

They were driven back to Heyfield. There they collected the dog's blood sample. 'Old Nobby was delighted to get back in the saddle,' said Constable Leigh.

Jo patted the dog who still kept looking for his master to walk in. 'What's happening about Bluey?'

'Should be collected soon,' said Leigh. 'The victim's wife and his brother are on their way.'

The Melbourne detectives thanked their bush colleagues, and pointed their chariot towards the Big Smoke; next stop Melbourne.

As they did, DI Blunt crouched on the landing upon which he'd been dumped, trying to find cover from the passing traffic. He couldn't walk due to his size 10 shoes becoming size 24, each weighing what seemed like a tonne. He refused to call any fellow officers. If even one discovered his plight, he knew the story would flood the Victoria Police grapevine, and Blunt would be diagnosed with a fatal dose of ignominy. He grabbed his phone and called.

'Brother-in-law,' said a surprised voice. 'Where's the fire?'

'Listen,' said Blunt. 'I'm in a spot and need help. Where are you?'

'I'm in a backyard in Collingwood unblocking a drain. Where are you? And what the hell are you doing ringing me?'

'I'm trapped.'

'What, in a drain?'

'I need you to come and rescue me.'

'Is this a wind-up?'

'No. I'm dead-set serious.'

'Call the cops. You know; the blokes with guns and flashing lights.'

'I can't.'

'What, you've lost their number? Try Triple Oh.'

Blunt began to lose it for the second time today, only this time worse because he was so close to escaping his latest nightmare with a minimum of damage.

'All right,' he said, surrendering. 'Bring me those parking tickets and I'll have them sorted.'

'Shit, you really *are* in a jam.'

'I'm in Carlton off Lygon. When you get near the Trades Hall, call me and I'll guide you in.'

'And you want me to bring those parking tickets I told you about?'

'Yes,' snapped a frustrated detective, 'oh, and a hammer.'

'A hammer?'

Blunt hissed with spittle. 'Make sure you bring a fucking hammer.'

After an hour or so, the travelling Homicide detectives stopped in Warragul for a bite to eat. Fed and watered they returned to their car. 'Fancy driving, Senior?' asked Billy, and threw the keys to Jo. 'I need a kip. All this promotion malarkey has done me in.'

So Jo drove with DS Melody alongside her, and the sometimes snoring Acting Detective Senior Sergeant in the back. They hadn't been going long when Jo's phone rang. 'Bugger,' she said.

'Do you want me to answer it?' asked DS Melody.

'Please,' said Jo. He did.

'Detective Senior Constable Jo Best's phone, DS Rick Melody speaking.' Melody covered the phone and spoke to Jo. 'Michael Chan.'

'Oh put him on Speaker.' Melody hit Speaker. 'Hi, Michael.'

'And hi to you, Detective. Am I interrupting a major crime raid?'

'No, I'm driving two fellow detectives back from Gippsland. We've had a suspicious death in the sticks. What's news?'

'No news. I wanted to firm up our date.'

'Michael, what's with the lingo? *Firm up* sounds like it came from a dictionary for pretentious bright young things.'

He sounded pleased. 'How did you know? That's exactly where I read it. Does this mean I'm now officially cool?'

Melody looked at the driver. *Who is this woman?* Billy slept.

Jo laughed. 'You're an idiot.'

'Thanks, I've always loved your compliments.'

'I'll call you tomorrow, Michael, and please dust off your homicide solution handbook.'

He laughed. 'I'm excited. Drive carefully, Detective. Bye.'

Melody replaced Jo's phone. 'Is he uniform or plain clothes?'

'He's not a cop, he's a friend who helps us out on a few cases.'

Billy was awake. 'He's not my friend and there's no us. He works solo with our driver, and between them they've solved a ridiculously serious number of tricky homicides.'

Melody looked impressed. 'I'd like to meet him.'

'Sorry, Sarge,' said Jo, 'but the good Doctor is *my* snout.'

'And he's a quack?' asked Melody.

'Doctor of Philosophy in some obscure field of computer science.'

'Fair enough. So are you Starsky or Hutch?'

Jo laughed and they drove west with the sun disappearing before them. Billy dozed but woke when Jo's phone rang again.

'Bloody hell, Senior,' she complained, 'can't you switch it off?'

Melody looked at Jo who nodded.

'Detective Senior Constable Jo Best's phone, DS Rick Melody speaking.' Melody covered the phone and spoke to Jo. 'Jack Carr.'

'Speaker again, please,' said Jo. Melody hit Speaker. 'Doctor Carr, what a pleasant surprise.'

'G'day Detective and my apologies if this is a bad time.'

'It's never a bad time to talk to my favourite GP.' Her fellow travellers became eavesdroppers. 'How are the kids and your folks?'

'We're fine and over the moon to hear you've come through that terrible spot of trouble you had.'

'No trouble, Jack, just a minor misunderstanding.'

'Bullshit,' whispered Billy Hughes.

'And how are you? Busy as ever?' asked Jo ignoring her boss.

'We were pretty upset when you had to leave the party. Michael Chan gave us some background, and the kids and my folks have been asking about you so they'll be thrilled to hear you're back on the job. Do you ever stop?'

'I'm like you, Doctor, a workaholic.'

He laughed. 'Touché. Well I won't keep you. And I've been ordered to tell you to look after yourself.'

'Thanks Jack and my love to all the family.'

'Bye Jo, bye.'

Another call ended and Melody spoke to himself. 'How did you enjoy your latest case with Homicide, Detective Melody? Oh it was great, especially acting as Detective Senior Constable Best's secretary.'

All three laughed only for their mirth to morph into a groan as Jo's phone rang yet again. 'Right, no more,' said an irritated Billy; 'time to switch to message bank.'

Melody held up a hand as he reached for the phone. 'Last one, boss.' He answered. 'Detective Senior Constable Jo Best's phone, DS Rick Melody speaking.' Melody covered the phone and spoke to Jo. He wasn't sure he caught the name. 'Pierre?'

Jo hesitated. Billy leant forward and extended a hand. 'I'll take it.'

Melody was thrown. He looked at Jo who looked at him and nodded. Billy took the phone.

'Hello Inspector, it's DS Billy Hughes. How are you?'

He replied with only Billy able to hear. There was no way she was going to make this call public.

'Senior Constable Best and DS Melody, who is new to Homicide, are with me driving back to Melbourne after a day in Gippsland. Jo's driving.' More words from Richelieu. 'There's no problem, Inspector. I'll tell Jo, while you concentrate on getting better and back home ASAP.' He thanked her and said goodbye. 'Au revoir, Monsieur.'

Billy switched off Jo's phone and handed it to Melody.

'Pierre says hi, Jo.'

'Great,' said the driver hoping like hell she wouldn't cry.

'I'm feeling better after my siesta,' said Billy. 'Pull over, Senior when it's safe and we'll swap possies.' Jo did so, willingly.

DI Blunt was dying, not from a fatal disease but a condition called embarrassment. He crouched on the veranda hard against the metal railing and as far out of sight as possible. His calves were killing him because his feet were flat on the tiled surface while his legs were bent to help him avoid being seen. His unfashionable footwear caused serious pain and stress as the detective squatted in agony. Then relief came when his phone rang. At last his brother-in-law drew near and soon, soon Blunt's disastrous day would be over.

He snatched his phone. 'Where are you?' There was no answer so he quickly looked at caller ID. It read DI Rose. Shit!

'DI Blunt?' asked the head of Homicide.

'Oh hello, ma'am. How are things?'

'Fine with me but you sound as if you're between a rock and a hard place.' *Is she psychic?* That was pretty darn accurate as the cold stone of the old union building proved as comforting as an abusive bully.

'No, it's all good here.'

'Where are you?'

'I'm following a lead in Carlton. I think we may be on to something with this organised crime angle.'

'Really?'

'Indeed.'

'Well as SIO I think the sooner you get back here the better.'

'Absolutely. I'm waiting for an important lead who I think will unlock two important blocks on my investigation.'

Rose thought he was a loose cannon and this latest conversation simply reinforced her theory. *What blocks?*

'Right, I'll see you soon.'

'Will do,' said Blunt, hit *End* and swore. Two minutes later his brother-in-law rang, and was told the address. He found a park in another hemisphere, and stood on the footpath in front of the building. No sign of his copper relative. Then a sound was heard amidst the traffic. 'Psst,' was the best the Inspector could do. When the plumber, complete with hammer bounded up the steps, he could not stop laughing. Blunt grabbed the hammer and attacked his new shoes.

Finally the brother-in-law ran out of hilarity and took the tool. That's the one made of wood and metal. 'I'll do it, you idiot.' The plumber had smashed a few floors to get at broken pipes in his time, and soon the concrete was broken and pieces pushed aside. 'I hope you get a shoe allowance, Callum.'

The Inspector stood without thanking his saviour. He stamped his feet to get rid of small bits of remaining concrete and restart his circulation. 'Now listen, mate.' The word *mate* was used in the context of the word *bastard* which was used in the context of the word *rat*. 'You breathe a word of this and I'll have every traffic cop in Melbourne personally following you with traffic ticket in hand.'

'Speaking of which,' said the brother-in-law, 'here's your invoice for today's service call.' He handed Blunt a collection of parking tickets. 'Some are overdue so don't muck around.' Then the plumber, with his hammer, smiled at the cop and took off back to his vehicle, laughing uproariously causing pedestrians to stop and look.

Blunt could not bring himself to try and influence Traffic so finished up paying the hefty fines out of his own pocket. Seriously, DI Blunt could genuinely say he'd had a shocker of a day.

Barry Clunes didn't seem nervous. Detective Senior Constable Payne with a uniformed officer took the suspect back to the building site where Clunes and his ute were based. An officer from Forensics arrived and all four headed to the ute and its now important toolbox.

'Open it,' said Payne, 'then step back.'

Clunes maintained his casual approach and opened the unlocked toolbox. The officer from Forensics examined the contents and, after a short search produced a knife.

'Is this it?' asked Payne. Clunes nodded. The knife was secured. 'Barry Clunes, I'm arresting you on suspicion of the murder of Dieter Fischer.'

'Oh why?' moaned the suspect.

'You do not have to say anything ...'

Clunes was cuffed and returned to Homicide. For a man who admitted he confronted the victim on the night and at the time the murder took place, and who took police to his knife which may have been used in the killing, this approach was unusual. Was he bluffing? Was he guilty but didn't care because his life was such a mess?

The report from Forensics might be the final nail in Barry's coffin.

Blunt fumed. In front of his Homicide colleagues, he'd talked up his theory about organised crime being in some way involved in the murder of Dieter Fischer. If true, and he could prove it, he'd cop elephant stamps galore. Headlines leapt out at him. *On his own, brilliant DI solves case and smashes organised crime.*

But so far, his great ideas, goals and tactics all came to nothing. And worse, he came within a whisker of being the biggest loser in town. Thank God his disasters went unrecorded.

No, hang on. He despaired. *That schmuck of a union boss took photos, not of me taking a bung or carousing with prostitutes but worse, sitting in a chair, trussed up like a Christmas turkey wearing; what are those things on my feet?* Callum Blunt is wearing concrete shoes. And they're last season's fashion to boot; or rather, to shoe.

The only way to save his career and make his gamble pay off was to tackle the last remaining sector of his plan—the organised crims.

What? Is he mad? Mad, probably; desperate, definitely.

Chapter 11

In his Cremorne townhouse, Callum showered, dressed and changed his shoes and socks. His old underwear and socks went in the bin.

He called his pal, the former boss of Homicide, DI Grant Steele, now at the AFP. Steele listened to Blunt's idea about organised crime as the link to the Fischer homicide and gave up one name.

'Ernie "Lockjaw" Maginnis is your man,' said Steel.

'Lockjaw?'

'Yeah, he never opened his mouth to shout anyone a drink. I'll send you his number. He was a crime reporter back in the bad old days. He knew every crim worth knowing. He's on the piss now and past it but if you catch him when he's only half-cut, he'll give you the gen.'

'Thanks mate. I'll keep you posted.'

'I see that bitch Best walked away scot free again. Must be a cat, she's got nine lives. What's she doing now?'

'Back at Homicide.'

'Unbelievable.'

'She won't last. When her French boyfriend carks it, she'll fall in a screaming heap.'

'I wish. Keep me in the loop, mate.'

'Will do.'

Wearing concrete free shoes and socks, Blunt rang Lockjaw. Dropping DI Steele's name helped and Blunt made his offer.

'Listen mate, how about I buy you a beer, and we have a yarn.'

'Make it two beers and a whisky chaser and you're on.'

They met in Lockjaw's local. Blunt was rapt. He knew no-one with inside information on Melbourne's gangsters, and specifically those with their fingers in the construction industry. Now he'd found what he hoped was a genuine lead. Lockjaw wasn't his best hope; he was his *only* hope. Blunt cut to the chase.

'So who's got their fingers in the construction industry?'

'Not sure now I'm an ambassador for AA, but I know who would know.'

'Yeah but which major crim would talk to a homicide cop, any cop? I can't believe they'd even spit on me.'

'This bloke will. He's retired and like me, is fading fast. You need to talk to Lenny the Mower. Just make sure you take the best Scotch.'

'You're kidding me,' scoffed Blunt. 'A retired crim will talk to a cop?' Lockjaw had a look suggesting Blunt was calling him a liar or loser. Blunt apologised. 'Sorry mate, and thanks. Another beer before I go?'

Lenny "The Mower" Pearson started growing dope, 50, no 60 years ago. He grew and sold so much grass they called him The Mower. He was a lot like Nipper Reid, both now ex-crooks, both served time, and now in their 80s, both doing bugger all. Their paths never crossed, even in Pentridge. Both hated the police, and the former DCI John Robbo Robertson was one ex-pig they both hoped got cancer.

Lenny, like a lot of old lags, never forgot. He hated cops but hated certain crims even more. Now too old to settle scores, he never stopped imagining getting even with the pricks who screwed him years ago. Elephantine memories are not just for pollies from rival ALP factions. Crims too crave payback.

So when a Homicide cop rang, recommended by Lockjaw Maginnis, Lenny agreed to meet the cop in The Mower's impressive Strathmore home. The suburb suited the retired crook. He had the poshest house in postcode 3041 without the publicity copped by villains in upmarket, old-money Toorak.

Callum was beside himself. Thanks to Lockjaw, he scored an invitation to pop in for tea with Lenny the Mower. 'Did you hear me, Lenny?' asked Blunt. 'I'm a Homicide cop.'

'I heard ya the first time. I'm old not deaf.' They laughed. 'Look, to be honest, mate, I'm bored shitless, and to show how desperate I am, I'll even have the filth in here. Don't be late. Punctuality is a virtue.'

The visitor placed a bottle of Upshot whisky on Lenny's dining room table. 'I hope you like the local brew,' said Blunt wondering if he should have gone Scottish.

'It'll do.'

Billy dropped DS Melody in East Melbourne. He had an apartment in Docklands so had the choice of train or tram. He hated public transport so hollered for an Uber and was home in ten. Jo remained in the back seat as Billy headed for Clifton Hill along Powlett Street. The driver forgot she would have to drive past Pierre Richelieu's fabulous apartment in Hotham Street, the one mentioned in a recent re-write of Pierre's will. The major beneficiary of Pierre's new will sat in the back seat feeling miserable.

'Good trip, Senior. You did well,' said Billy.

'Good trip, Senior. You did well,' mimicked Jo, remembering Billy was now an Acting Detective *Senior* Sergeant.

'Ha, ha.'

They approached Pierre's apartment building. Jo couldn't hold back. 'Are you going to tell me what Pierre said on my phone in the car?' she asked with a mix of fear and anger.

'Yeah sorry, Jo. I took the call because I didn't think you'd want me, and certainly not DS Melody, listening to your private conversation.'

Jo glanced at the wonderful place where she'd spent time with a wonderful man. 'Thanks,' she said. 'And?'

'And yes I wanted to hear how he was and if there was anything I could do.' Jo didn't reply. 'He sounded okay and, being the gentleman he is, didn't want to interrupt anyone working on a case.'

They headed north and crossed Albert Street. Jo blurted a request. 'Can you drop me here please, Sarge?'

'What?'

Jo spoke faster. 'Here, please, right here.'

Billy pulled over close to Victoria Parade. She turned to face Jo. 'What's up?'

'Nothing. I've been sitting in cars for five hours. I need a walk.'

Billy had a hunch. 'You mean you want to visit DI Richelieu.'

'I do and anyway, I need to stretch my legs.'

'How will you get home?'

'Oh Sarge, you're starting to even sound like my bloody mother.' She opened her door. 'Thanks for the lift. I'll see you in the morning.'

'Give the DI my love,' said Billy. Jo nodded, closed the door and waited till the car turned into Victoria Parade.

It was an uphill walk of 500 plus metres to the hospital and she needed the exercise. The ICU ward was relatively small with about 20 beds, and stepping into reception meant you were easily spotted.

'Detective Best,' said the nurse who greeted Jo last time.

'Jo, please call me Jo.'

'I'm Katrina, and Pierre has been much better today. I'll go and tell him you're here.' She disappeared and a male came into reception.

'Hi,' he said. 'Who have you come to see?'

'DI Richelieu.'

He smiled. 'You must be Detective Jo Best.' He held out his hand. 'I'm Dr Grant Buchanan.'

Jo shook her head. 'I'm not sure why but everyone here seems to know me. As a detective I'm struggling to solve the mystery.'

The doctor laughed. 'Too easy,' he said. 'First you've made the news with your spectacular cases. Second you called our patient DI and not Mr or Monsieur Richelieu. Third, Pierre talks about you non-stop. And finally, I happen to be good friends with a fellow medico, Dr Jack Carr, who too is forever singing your praises.' Jo grinned. 'So, does that help with your mystery?'

'Yes, it does,' she said and they both smiled.

Nurse Katrina appeared. 'You can come in, Jo. Monsieur Richelieu demands your presence.'

Thanking the doctor and the nurse, Jo took a deep breath. Her atheistic soul uttered a prayer. *Please God, don't let me cry.*

Blunt glowed inside. Here he was sitting in an ex-crim's lounge about to get tips on the underworld, even one of which might help Callum nail the murderer of Dieter Fischer and, better still, break up an organised crime gang. He was purring.

Finding Lenny Pearson made up for Callum's almighty stuff-ups with the builders and the union. The workers screwed him big time with humiliation to spare. Now Callum believed in third time lucky. This time he would crack the case. Or would he?

The Mower, you see, had an ulterior motive. Decades ago, he was stitched up by a Young Turk, a fellow crim, and today, Lenny still craved revenge. Enter the DI who would do the old lag a favour.

Callum asked Lenny about crooks involved in corruption in the construction industry, and up popped the name of Lenny's hated former enemy. The Mower set up Callum to give the rival a smack. Is it possible to actually feel sorry for DI Blunt?

'Listen mate,' said Lenny. You wanna take a squiz at Miguel Spaniell, known as Mickey Spillane to his mates and as *Mister* Spaniell to the likes of me and you. He never meets no-one at home. His office is part of upmarket Brunswick off Sydney Road. He owns the building and frequents the trendy wine bar and café on the ground floor. Only the best Colombian coffee is good enough for Miguel Spaniell. He runs a legit labour hire firm which is how he gets his claws into builders. He still calls it insurance when in fact it's good old protection.'

'That's fantastic, Lenny,' said Callum. 'You've done me a big favour. What can I do in return?'

'Sadly, nothing son; I haven't even got a parking ticket you can fix.'

Blunt laughed while his guts ached. Paying his brother-in-law's parking fines burnt a whopping hole in his pocket. 'Listen mate, I'll be back with more of your favourite tipple once this bastard is banged up.'

'Great, but one final tip, son,' said Lenny.

'Which is?' asked Callum, his ears twitching with anticipation.

'Don't go nowhere near them pricks in the Construction Workers' Union.' Blunt felt a shiver tap-dancing on his spine. 'They'll have you fitted for a pair of concrete shoes before you can spit. Stick to them traditional crims and Miguel Spaniell in particular.'

'Gotcha,' said Callum, feeling sick as he topped up Lenny's Scotch.

Chapter 12

Jo entered Pierre's room. The tubes and machines were there as was his ordinary haircut and unfashionable night attire. But now she was prepared for his weight loss and shrunken features, having seen them before through moist eyes. Now their shock value was less dramatic. Pierre was upright, almost sitting straight and tall. As always, his smile was downstage front and centre. It was his most powerful weapon, melting the heart of any warm-blooded female with at least 5% of her bone structure interested in romance. His eyes were the engine room of his smile and were on full power. Energy flooded his lips. His pearly whites were pearly white. Jo's heart opened a song-sheet.

'Bonjour Detective. You look more beautiful every time I see you.' He had the script and delivery down pat. He was the antithesis of a creep, and the personification of a man who could capture a woman's soul, and make her mother feel content and happy.

Jo moved to him and without thinking leant in and kissed his lips. 'Bonjour Inspector. It is so lovely to see you looking so well.'

She brought a chair forward and sat by his side. She couldn't ignore the tubes or the machines showing results but found it easy to chat. He wanted to know all about her cases, and not because he missed being a detective. He wanted to know because he felt a part of her life. He wanted to know if she was safe, happy and likely to succeed.

Jo explained the Gippsland trip, the body in the bush, and her idea about how the dog might provide a clue.

'Not only beautiful but always so clever,' he said. 'And tell me about this new Detective Sergeant. Tell me if 'e 'as already fallen in love with you as any normal man would.'

Jo laughed off his question and switched back to DS Hughes being promoted albeit in an acting capacity.

Time flew by with Jo impressed with the Inspector's improvement. Both were disappointed when nurse Katrina arrived. 'Sorry to break up the party, officers, but somebody needs their equipment checked.'

As the nurse moved to Pierre, Jo prepared to leave. 'It's lovely to see you, Monsieur. I will tell the squad about your brilliant progress.'

'Merci, Mademoiselle.' He blew her a kiss. Jo hesitated.

Katrina interrupted. 'I'm sorry, Jo, but even close family are advised to step outside on certain occasions.'

Jo smiled with embarrassment and left, waving as she departed.

'Au revoir,' she heard as she headed for the stairs.

Outside in Victoria Parade she thought about getting home. She checked her phone. It was about 4 kms. She could run it easily in 15 to 20 minutes wearing her top of the range trainers. *What the heck, I'll walk anyway. Plenty to think about.*

Turning into Brunswick Street, she set a cracking pace when someone tooted. Not unusual for this busy part of Melbourne. The horn tooted again. Jo looked and saw the car she spent several hours in earlier today. The passenger front window was down.

'Get in,' ordered Acting Detective Senior Sergeant Deborah Hughes.

Jo sat and did up her seatbelt. 'There's a law against stalking.'

'So how is the Inspector?'

'How did you know I'd even go to the hospital?'

'I thought I trained you to never answer a question with a question.'

They looked at one another. 'Thanks,' said Jo, 'and yes, Pierre looked miles better than the other day although I left because he was about to receive treatment which required a little privacy.'

'Poor bloke.'

'Could it be a type of organ support?'

'You're asking me?' Billy chose her words carefully. 'Look Jo, I want Pierre to get better and be out of hospital as soon as possible. But I think we both know he'll never work as a detective again.'

'From what I've seen, he'll never work again full stop.'

Billy was glad to hear Jo say that, to face facts. 'What I'm concerned about is your reaction to his recovery.' Jo looked at Billy. They stopped at a set of lights so Billy looked at Jo. 'Don't take this the wrong way. Sometimes giving up somebody is seriously hard.' The women lost interest in their journey until an impatient driver tooted because the lights had changed. The detectives barely spoke for the rest of the trip.

Billy dropped Jo at her flat in Clifton Hill. 'Thanks for the lift, Sarge, and I promise I won't mention your stalking to anyone.'

The senior officer laughed and drove home. Jo stood on her doorstep. *What a day.*

Nipper Reid's son, Cain, was 54 and his wife, Rosa, 53. They'd lived in the same Broadford house, 48 kms north of Melbourne, for ages. When a tragedy such as the one they suffered—their toddler, Tommy, was accidentally killed by his grandfather, also Tommy—the strain of such an event can and does wreck a marriage. It was tough for Cain and Rosa, and horribly so on Tommy's birthday and on the anniversary of his death. But here they were, grandparents themselves, and still married; not that they were all that happy.

Cain was on the phone. He walked out of the lounge because Rosa was watching her favourite soap, and the world could end before she'd give up being glued to the set.

Cain came back and watched what was left of the latest episode. Then he spoke. 'That was the old man.' Rosa never initiated a conversation about her father-in-law. She accepted the fact Nipper didn't deliberately kill her boy but could never forget the fact that if Nipper had not been a criminal, her boy would still be alive.

'He reckons Mum is not good.' There was still no response from Rosa although she tolerated her mother-in-law. 'The quack says she should go into care in what they call respite. It's like a short time in the nursing home where ...'

'I know what respite care is,' she said, her anger on a slow burn. Any time her father-in-law's name crept into the conversation, Rosa's default position was one of depression and resentment with a dash of smouldering rage. Cain explained.

'It'll help Nipper because, having a break from caring for Mum, gives his heart a rest as well.'

Rosa knew what was coming and had the word "No" in her armoury and ready to fire.

'You know what it's like with elderly parents,' said Cain laying the foundation for his request.'

Here we go, she thought. *Bring up my parents and how we had to look after both of them in their dying days.*

Cain kept building his case. 'Your Mum cared for your Dad when she didn't have the strength to lift a pillow. We agreed to put your Dad in care, and because we had the spare bedroom, your Mum came to live with us. She had her independence yet had us on call if needed.'

Rosa should have said what she thought ages ago. It was cruel to let Cain continue building a case for the request she would always veto. It was time to come clean. She gave her husband both barrels.

'You know my decision. Nipper's never coming here even for a visit let alone a bloody stay.'

Cain despaired. 'Aw come on, Rosa. He's an old man, he's dying. Every day he thinks about his grandson and what he did. He adored Tommy and the kid adored his Pop. That day lives on in Nipper's mind and will never go away. It gets worse. And we both know he's gunna die a depressed and lonely old man.'

'No,' was all she said; two letters with each weighing a ton. *Immovable* would be an accurate description of Rosa's position.

Cain switched tactics. 'Can you not see how your hatred of Nipper is affecting you? He might be a shell, a walking bloody zombie but you, Rosa, you're a wizened and spiteful witch. You're old before your time.'

Rosa felt as if her face copped a slap. She and Cain had rarely discussed their mental health as affected by the death of their son. Raising the subject now was shocking. And more so for Rosa because she knew Cain spoke the truth. She *was* old before her time, and spite dominated her thinking.

Her heart was padlocked, and every morning she ate resentment and anger for breakfast. She hated the world as much as she hated her father-in-law. The death of her little Tommy savaged her soul. She looked like she thought, and avoided mirrors; hating her image.

But there was something far worse. She knew to save her soul or conscience or spirit, she would have to back down and dump her bitterness towards her father-in-law. And if ever an impossible task existed, that was it. Rosa back down? Pigs flying over a frozen hell would come first.

She knew she didn't have to forgive Nipper, embrace him, tell him she was sorry for her behaviour—none of that. All she had to do was not oppose him. Simple? More like unbelievably difficult.

She left the room, left the house, slammed the door and set off, where, she didn't know. Cain went to the fridge and grabbed a beer. 'Shit,' was all he said.

In Drouin, Jason Lilliput strummed his guitar seeking the right chord. He found it, scribbling its name. He couldn't read music but had perfect pitch, and an ear for lyrics and chord progressions. He wrote songs he liked and which appealed to a small but dedicated fan base. Doing gigs in pubs was his fun time, his release from boredom and a marriage which was neither one thing nor the other. His phone rang.

'Jason,' he said not keen on his surname.

'G'day Jason, it's Keith Ballantyne. How ya going?'

'What's happened?'

Keith was the manager of the local supermarket where Jason's partner, Chelsea, worked a checkout three days a week. She was at work right now. Jason never had a call from Chelsea's work unless something was wrong.

'Nothing, mate but I wanted to have a chat about Chelsea.'

'Something's happened.'

'No, we're all good. But she's been behaving a little strangely of late and I wondered if you've noticed.'

Jason had. He said nothing to Chelsea and played it cool with her boss. 'What have you noticed?'

'Not a lot.'

Jason fumed. He wanted the truth. 'What have you noticed?'

'She gets annoyed with people for no good reason. She had a go at a customer the other day. It's not on. And for someone who never swears, she swore at me.'

'You're nothing special, mate; she swears at me.'

'Is she crook, going through the change of life, got money troubles or something?'

'She'll have money troubles if you sack her.'

'No, no she's a good worker.'

More silence. 'What do you want me to do?'

'Have a word perhaps.'

'Me?' Jason failed Counselling 101. 'No way, mate.'

'Has she got a friend who could talk to her?'

Jason spoke the truth. 'She doesn't do friends.'

'What about family apart from you?'

'She has a cousin in Melbourne.'

Back came the silence. 'Well I think she needs help, mate. I don't want to let her go.'

'Let her go? Why don't you say the word? You mean *sack*.'

Keith paused. 'I hope we don't get to that.' Both men fell silent. After a pause, Keith continued. 'I'll see ya.'

The line went dead and Jason looked for his weed. He didn't need an excuse for a joint but one right now was all he had to calm his shaking hands.

Chapter 13

It was the morning after the day in Gippsland, and detectives had plenty to say. Rose, Hughes and Blunt entered, with SIO Blunt in charge. He displayed his usual expression of no expression while relishing the opportunity to run the show.

'Thank you; now I know there are facts to deliver so let's tackle each homicide in chreno ... chronow ... no, let's do them in date order.'

Everyone sat stunned. DI Blunt delivered a joke, well his idea of humour. Blunt, a comedian? *That's* the joke. It was so obviously contrived. Even the world's worst comic would have groaned aloud at Callum's calamity. Was the DI trying to become "one of the boys"? Surely, that's mission impossible. Members reacted with silence as Blunt fought to escape his humiliation.

'With Dieter Fischer, late of the Heidelberg Rovers, we have at least two persons of interest; the president, Alex Hero, and the failed builder, Barry Clunes. So, who's first?' DI Rose stood and Blunt crept away to hide.

'Senior Constable Payne and I brought Clunes in for questioning. He declined a solicitor and again proved co-operative. He confirmed his presence at the clubrooms on the night Fischer was murdered.'

Blunt grew bold. 'Have we established it *is* a homicide, ma'am?'

'Dr Strange reports he died from a stab wound to the heart. Of course with the punch to his face, and the blow to the back of his head when he fell, he might have become disorientated or depressed, snatched the knife from Clunes, and died in a fight but current thinking is homicide by lethal stab wound to the heart.'

Blunt inwardly fumed at being put back in his box, and swore to beat these bastards at their own game. DI Rose continued.

'Clunes again admitted punching Fischer and said the victim fell and struck his head. Clunes claimed he heard Fischer swearing as the builder returned to his ute. Senior Constable Payne took Clunes back to his workplace where, from his toolbox, a knife was retrieved, again confirmed as his by the suspect, and said knife is now at Forensics and we await their analysis.'

'Thank you, DI Rose. Any questions?'

DS Melody asked, 'How did Clunes behave, ma'am?'

'He's either a brilliant actor or not guilty. He didn't over talk, his voice didn't go up at the end of sentences, and his body language was unremarkable.' She turned to Payne. 'Do you agree, Senior?'

'Absolutely, ma'am.'

'Now I understand it's unusual for an obvious suspect to admit to so much other than the stabbing, but if the knife contains Fischer's DNA, perhaps Clunes is trying a double bluff and is our man. He has motive and opportunity, there are his confessions to time and place, and it's possible, even likely the murder weapon has the victim's blood and owner's prints.'

The difference between Billy Hughes and Callum Blunt as SIO was that while Billy encouraged comments, Blunt inspired no-one. He didn't even thank DI Rose after her report. No manners that man.

'Okay,' said the struggling SIO, 'what do we know about the President?'

DS Fletcher reported. 'Senior Constable Baldwin and I set out to check Mr Hero's alibi. He claimed he was at home that night. We finally located his wife at her sister's house and Mrs Hero unconvincingly supported her husband's alibi. We were stopped in the garden by Hero's sister-in-law who said her sister did as ordered by hubby, and he had a mistress, as yet name and address unknown.'

'Well done Detective Sergeant,' said Blunt wanting to move on to his report.

'There's more to come, sir,' said Baldwin enjoying the opportunity to correct a senior officer and especially a prick. Blunt scowled.

Fletcher gave Blunt a nothing look and continued. 'DI Rose learnt from Clunes that his company won the grandstand job thanks to President Hero who, by return favour, copped a backhander and was being paid 5% of the contract price by the builder.'

That prompted a reaction. 'Charley and I then popped in on Mr Hero and told him we'd spoken to his sister-in-law, and asked about the auditing of the club's books. He became a body language expert's dream. I reckon he thinks his sister-in-law grassed him up on the alibi and the mistress, and when we asked about the club's books being audited, as well as the building contract, he developed a twitch.'

'A *big* twitch,' added Baldwin.

Fletcher concluded. 'We spoke to the accountancy experts in Fraud and they're keen to examine the books and the construction contract.'

Blunt paused not wanting to make a fool of himself again.

'Is that it, DS Fletcher?'

'Pretty much, sir, but like the knife from Forensics found by DI Rose, we're waiting on the auditing of the books and identifying the Hero's heroine.'

'What?' snapped Blunt who hated clever-dick answers which made him look a fool.

'His mistress, sir.'

Smiles appeared although not from Blunt. 'Good work, everyone,' he said sounding insincere. 'So are there any questions or comments about our two persons of interest?'

Not a dicky bird. The silence was embarrassing but only for the SIO.

'Right, well before we move on to the body in the bush, I have another angle on who might have killed the soccer coach.' He paused for dramatic effect. Like his earlier attempt at humour, he performed the old lead balloon trick.

Blunt was poised to pounce with his news, when a voice from the squad stopped him dead. It was Jo Best. 'There might be a third person of interest, sir. Have we looked into the victim's widow?'

He was thrown again. 'What about her?'

'As Mrs Fischer was super calm when told of her husband's murder, have we checked the victim's finances, super, and life insurance to see who benefits from his death?'

Sensible question and possibly capable of solving the murder and yet, not on the agenda, the agenda set by the SIO. Jo Best exposed him.

What a bitch thought Blunt. With a homicide, no stone must be left unturned, and setting out who did what was down to the SIO. Bloody Jo Best had asked an elementary question and, in so doing, pulled down the SIO's pants—metaphorically speaking, of course.

His body language went freelance again. 'Thank you, Senior Constable; I'll deal with it later.' He announced his news. 'My enquiries on the Fischer homicide uncovered information about why the construction project collapsed. I've been knocking on doors with little co-operation from various sources, but using my contacts, I've been given a few interesting leads.' This was bullshit. Of homicide leads had he none. He paused to milk the reveal. 'The word is organised crime might be involved.'

That sounded impressive and, if true, *was* impressive. If only the Homicide detectives knew what really happened to DI Blunt.

'Things will get interesting when I contact my snout who knows the Melbourne underworld.'

This again sounded impressive. If Blunt had a contact who knew about organised crime, and could help the police discover how the underworld had their claws in the construction industry at Heidelberg Rovers, if they did, Blunt could expose a lot more than a murder.

'It's early doors,' he said, and let's continue to pressure Pathology, Forensics and Fraud for results. Oh, and Senior Constable Best, you can chase up the financial situation of the victim and his will.'

'Sir,' said Jo wondering if this was a reward or a punishment.

'I'll do likewise with my source. So, questions?' The tradition of silence under the current SIO continued. 'Right, let's eliminate or accommodate our two main persons of interest, and we can rendezvous at 1400 hours.'

Nobody moved. He stared at his fellow detectives wondering why they refused to move. DS Fletcher put him out of his misery. 'The second murder, sir, the body in the bush.'

Blunt swore. 'Shit,' was a polite reaction to his cock-up. He was so keen to tell the world about his, as yet imaginary foray into the underworld, he forgot to seek reports of the other suspicious death. DI Rose stepped into the embarrassing silence.

'Thank you, DI Blunt. Now perhaps Acting Detective Senior Sergeant Hughes can fill us in on her picnic in the countryside.'

Immediately members chuckled and made cheeky comments. Blunt could never create such a relaxed response. Billy took the floor.

'Thank you, ma'am. I went to Gippsland with DS Melody and Senior Constable Best.' A photo of Max Bowman before his last trip to Licola appeared. 'The deceased was a fit and healthy male, 61, super experienced in bushcraft and outdoor living who stupidly pitched his tent beneath an old tree with a dying branch directly above him. Then the dog-loving bushman threw his dog out of the tent before the branch fell, killing him instantly.'

'That's the template for a suspicious death, Sarge,' said Baldwin.

'Local uniform thought it suspicious, detectives from Sale agreed, as did the three of us. A friend of the deceased, when he heard of the "accident", went to his local nick to say there was no way it could have been anything other than deliberate. The victim would never camp under any tree, and the dog would always be in the tent with his master.'

'What happened to the dog?' asked DI Rose with two rescue dogs at home.

'The widow collected him but not before a clever suggestion from Senior Constable Best, which saw a retired Heyfield vet collect a blood sample for possible future use.'

'Well done, Senior,' said Rose, and Blunt sniffed his anger.

Billy continued. 'I've asked Dr Strange to do the PM, and Forensics to tackle the tent, camping gear and vehicle. Suicide's impossible and an accidental death fanciful, making this a homicide in a remote location. Locals were unable to help with suspects, so we'll start with family and friends of the deceased.'

'And enemies,' added Melody.

'Indeed, and with reports from Pathology and Forensics.' Billy looked at DI Rose.

'Thanks Billy,' said the boss who addressed the group. 'You know how stroppy I get with an unsolved homicide. Now we have two so don't get in my way. DI Blunt, anything further?' He shook his head. 'Right, the SIO for the Licola homicide is Detective Acting Senior Sergeant Hughes, and for Heidelberg, DI Blunt. Let's plan well before we go tearing off. Both SIOs meet with your team then bring me your plan of action. Once they're approved we can get busy. I do not want officers duplicating work or wasting time making separate trips to Forensics and Pathology.' She pointed at her detectives to emphasize the point. 'Fail to plan and you plan to fail. Now get to it and both SIOs in my office in 15.

They entered her office with their plans. She studied them. 'Good; no duplication. And use your fingers instead of your size 12s although

Pathology and Forensics need face to face contact.' She continued reading. 'Why are you running three, Billy while Callum is on his own?'

Billy went to answer only to be gazumped by Blunt. 'Dealing with the underworld and organised crime, ma'am, it's safer and more likely to be successful if I'm working alone.'

DI Rose glared. 'Jo Best has an outstanding record for solving homicides, Inspector. With her on your team, statistics say your chances of a result are greatly increased. Do you rate her? Trust her?'

'Of course, ma'am,' he lied, 'but we're dealing with ruthless bastards. To them, women are fair game. Senior Constable Best is inexperienced with these hardened crims, and you could be putting her in harm's way involving her in what I'm doing.'

Rose sniffed. 'Billy?'

'DI Blunt has a point, ma'am.'

'So who are you dealing with, Callum?'

He hesitated. 'No specifics yet, ma'am; I need more snooping time.'

'Well give me something. For all we know you could be playing golf or taking long lunches in Chinatown.'

Blunt knew the best lies were ones which contained an element of truth. 'I got nothing from a couple of sources but struck gold with a retired crime reporter. He put me on to an old retired lag who knows organised crims involved in the construction industry. These are the heavy hitters and if I can get an insider talking, we could crack the soccer coach homicide and expose organised crime both in one hit. But I stress, it's still early doors.'

He sounded convincing although both women felt they couldn't trust him as far as they could throw him, and with his penchant for Yum Cha, even picking him up was a no-no.

Rose grew angry. 'Callum, I need to know who you're dealing with, when and where you'll be. If your source is a lunatic, I need details. You get whacked in a back lane, and we don't know where you are or who did it.'

'Understood ma'am, and as soon as I have a concrete lead'—he winced at using that word—'I'll inform you immediately and we can use the Soggies if necessary. Right now, it's softly softly. A heavy-handed approach could spook them and we'll get nothing.'

Rose didn't like the situation. 'Okay, Jo Best sticks with Billy.'

'Thank you, ma'am,' said Blunt, pleased he'd won.

'But take DS Melody instead.' Blunt fumed. 'He's more experienced than Best and far less appealing to killers.'

Billy smiled and Blunt didn't. 'Thanks ma'am, and we can take the finances of the widow,' he said thinking he'd won after all.

'Which widow?' asked Billy. Blunt looked confused. 'There are two.'

'I'll take the wife of the soccer guy,' he said. 'You can have the camper's Mrs.' DI Rose and Billy Hughes reckoned Blunt was trying to control the whole situation but agreed to his request. 'I'll tell DS Melody,' said Blunt and left.

He pulled Melody aside. 'Change of plans, Sergeant. You're with me. We'll work on my organised crime gig but you check out the finances of the soccer coach. Look at his will, super, insurance, et cetera. Then liaise with Fraud to check the club's books and the builder's contract.'

'When am I doing that, sir?' asked Melody.

'Now. Call me when you're done and we'll meet to plan the organised crime raid.'

And with that order, Blunt departed in haste. He didn't want new instructions from DI Rose but he did want to crack this soccer club murder, and hopefully expose an organised crime gang.

DI Rose and Billy approached Melody. Jo joined them. Rose explained the new team set-ups. 'And listen, Rick, DI Blunt is dealing with heavy hitters.' She looked around. 'Where is he?'

'Ah, he's gone, ma'am leaving me to work with Fraud.'

Rose took a deep breath. Her blood pressure started climbing. 'Okay,' she said. 'But keep an eye on the DI.'

Chapter 14

Billy Hughes drove Jo to Pathology. 'So any update on the DI?' asked the newly promoted detective.

'Not since I last saw you, Sarge.'

'And what do the quacks say?'

Jo hesitated. 'I haven't had a serious chat yet. I will when Pierre's up and about, and ask him how a DS managed to get promoted.'

'Acting Detective *Senior* Sergeant,' replied Billy with faux indignation. They fell silent until Jo mentioned the elephant in the car.

'Aren't you going to ask if he still wants to marry me?'

That was hard, even cruel, unnecessary and unexpected. Even Jo surprised herself. *Why did I say that?*

'I think that remains in the *Mind Your Own Business* file, Senior.'

Jo wanted to apologise but said nothing. She'd been thinking about Pierre, his new will, and their marriage prospects for days. Her thoughts spilt out without thinking. She struggled with stress.

They entered Pathology to be greeted by the lady herself. 'Welcome officers, and your timing is impeccable. I've finished a quick once over of your boy from the bush.'

'Don't frighten us, Doctor and claim it's a suicide,' said Billy.

'Not likely. It's highly suspicious and good luck in proving how they did it.'

'They?' asked Hughes.

'Well the amount of damage to the body and the estimated weight of the branch suggests at least two and possibly more culprits. What did Forensics find?'

'No word as yet,' replied Billy.

Jo was keen. 'Anything unusual, Doctor?'

'Detective Senior Constable Best, how simply marvellous to see you back in my emporium and working away at being the deranged detective you are.' Jo gave a restrained smile and for a second wondered if the pathologist might have fallen off the wagon.

'It's good to be here, Doctor but I can't believe you haven't found us a clue, the one to set us on the path to catch the homicidal maniac.'

Strange looked at Billy while pointing at Jo. 'She has a way with words, Sergeant. I predict a big future for this girl.'

'We all do, Gabrielle,' replied Billy getting impatient, 'but first your pearl of wisdom if you please.'

The pathologist grinned. She grabbed a photo. 'Pearls plural if you don't mind. First, there's a connection between your two stiffs.'

'What?' exclaimed Billy and Jo as one.

'You might remember I spotted a small cut hidden inside the eyebrow of the soccer chap. Hard to see how it could be anything other than deliberate. Well there's another one.' She picked up another photo. 'There's a similar cut but on the tongue of the second body.'

'Same knife?' asked Billy.

'No,' said Strange.

Jo studied the second photo. 'Is that a bite mark? As the tree branch fell on him, has he bitten his tongue?'

Again Strange looked at Billy while talking about Jo. 'She's good. Did I tell you she has a bright future?' Then she switched to Jo. 'But not bright enough.' Strange picked up a magnifying glass and handed it to the young officer. 'Look above the bite mark and to the left.'

Jo used the glass. 'Yes, I can see it.' She handed the glass to Hughes.

Strange explained. 'Like the cut *inside* the eyebrow, this too is disguised by being placed close to the bite mark.'

'And administered post mortem?' asked Jo.

Strange shrugged. 'Unless he was unconscious before someone screamed "Timber!"'

Hughes had questions. 'So each body has a sort of hidden but not fatal cut caused by different weapons. And from that, Doctor, you believe the homicides are linked?'

More false indignation came from the medico. 'Hey, what is this? Words in my mouth, a leading question or both?' asked Strange. 'Me pathologist, you detective; I offer data, you use or abuse. Capeesh?'

'Thanks,' said Billy, suitably rebuked.

'I'll have a detailed PM on your careless camper by tomorrow. Now, anything else I can help you with?'

Jo jumped in. 'I believe you mentioned pearls plural, Doctor. You've only shown us one.'

'Oh God, I'd forget my arse if it wasn't hermetically sealed.' She looked for her notes. 'Your riverside victim had interesting blood in his veins, and unnatural chemicals in his nose. He overdosed on Valium and breathed in a sort of homemade chloroform.'

Shock hit the detectives. 'He was drugged?' asked Jo.

'I reckon the Valium made him wonky, and the homemade chloroform knocked him out.'

'Homemade chloroform?' asked Billy. 'I've never heard of it.'

'Bleach and acetone; crude but it can work. No chemistry degree required. I can't find any frontal head wounds to show he'd been struck but as the tree landed on target, any wounds won't be found.'

'Was he abused having been drugged? Was it a bizarre sex attack?'

'No sign,' said Strange. 'He was lying on his back when the branch fell on him so examining his front was tricky to say the least. But turning the poor wretch over revealed a pristine posterior, so if that was the assault area, I'd forget sex and concentrate on murder.'

Stephen Payne drove his boss to Forensics. 'Which officer do you deal with, Stephen?'

'Several, ma'am but Alastair Dean is the one I know although I think he prefers dealing with Jo Best.'

'Am I supposed to read between the lines, Senior Constable?'

'Ah, no ma'am; it's a statement of fact.' He wasn't sure she believed him and so slipped on his obsequious jacket.

DI Rose was not a regular at Forensics these days. Decades ago as a Detective Senior Constable yes, but as the fairly recent new boss at Homicide, she assigned such visits to her fellow officers. Alastair Dean knew who she was, saw her and approached.

'Good morning, Detective Inspector.' He introduced himself and nodded to Payne.

'We're hoping you have good news, Alastair to go with our two unsolved homicides. What about the knife?'

'Blood stains were found and DNA results show they're a match for the victim.'

'That was quick.'

'We aim to please, ma'am.'

'Excellent.'

'There is only one set of fingerprints on the knife so if you have suspects and can send us prints, we can tell if you have a match.'

'We have suspects so your work may narrow the field.'

'Happy to help you close a case.'

'Great but what have you got on the Gippsland homicide?'

'Nothing I'm afraid. We sent two officers to Heyfield to examine the vehicle, tent and camping material. The local police suggested we look at the crime scene, but the passage of time and bad weather may provide little if anything, ma'am.'

'Thank you. And you'll send your report?'

'Of course, and anything we get from the bush as soon as it comes to hand.'

'Thanks again.' She shook hands with the scientist and turned to leave accompanied by the silent Senior. They stopped at the door when called by Alastair.

The detectives returned as the scientist looked for a report on his computer. 'We were sent some canine blood from the Gippsland homicide.'

Rose remembered Jo Best having blood taken from the dead camper's dog. 'Did Senior Constable Best bring that in?'

Alastair hesitated. Froze would be too strong a description but he definitely lost his previous friendly flow. 'I think it came by courier.'

'And?'

'It went to a specialist, and we're awaiting their report.'

'Thank you,' said Rose and she and Payne left as Alastair's body temperature plummeted.

'Where to first, boss?' asked Charley Baldwin as he drove DS Fletcher on a quest to find President Hero's girlfriend.

'I'll give you one guess, Detective.'

'Gotcha,' said Charlie and headed for the President's sister-in-law, she with the secrets and a willingness to blab. 'So how do you think DI Blunt is going as the SIO?'

'You'll never make a DS, Charley, if you peddle in gossip.' Baldwin swallowed. 'But I'll shout you lunch if the prick gets through this latest case without stuffing up big time.'

Baldwin smiled as they headed to the President's sister-in-law's abode in Templestowe. They wanted her to be home alone. She was.

'Detectives,' she said opening the door. 'I'm sorry but my sister is not here. She's at home. I spoke to her only five minutes ago.'

'Thank you Mrs ...' replied Fletcher.

'My name is Hanna.' She left it there and the police took her lead.

'May we speak to you, Hanna about the incident at the soccer club?'

'Why, because you think my brother-in-law is the killer?' That stopped the cops. They looked at one another. Hanna stepped back inviting them in. 'Please wipe your feet.'

On their previous visit, they interviewed Mrs Hero at the front door. Now, once inside, they understood the shoe-wiping request. The house was beyond spotless. Meet Hanna the dust hunter.

'You have a lovely house, Hanna,' said Charley Baldwin and Fletcher supported him.

The house-proud woman welcomed the compliment she heard many times. 'Thank you but you've not come here to inspect my carpets.'

'Indeed,' said Fletcher. 'Why do you think we suspect Mr Hero might be involved in the death of the soccer coach?'

'I don't think, I know. He is a manipulative, money-grubbing womaniser. He defrauds the soccer club he professes to love and serve, and Dieter Fischer knew all about his dirty tricks, and was killed to stop him exposing the president.'

Again the detectives were stunned. 'Okay, anything else?' It was not so much what this elf-like woman said but the way she said it. No pauses, and with an air of arrogance and confidence. She finished.

'I see,' said DS Fletcher thinking all his Christmases had come at once. 'And may I ask how you know all this, Hanna?'

'My sister tells me everything, and even the stupid man himself boasts of his exploits, thinking his wife and sister-in-law are idiots. We're women, we know nothing. You must know, officers, there are plenty of criminals who get caught thanks to their stupidity.'

The detectives exchanged glances, and Charley Baldwin continued the interview. 'We're grateful for your help, Hanna, but in any investigation, and particularly a homicide, the police need evidence. Forensic evidence, documentation, recordings both audio and video, witness statements and more all help the police make a case. Your comments, as helpful as they are, need to be supported by evidence. Have I made myself clear?'

She looked at them. 'You sound like my brother-in-law. I think it's called mansplaining.'

Both detectives half smiled and Fletcher acknowledged their faux pas. 'You're absolutely right, Hanna and we apologise. But is there any physical evidence you can show us?'

'How about the name and address of the president's mistress?'

She walked to a desk and removed a photograph. The police looked at one another. This visit proved interesting and was brimming with potential. She handed DS Fletcher the picture. 'Her name and address are on the back.'

He turned it over. 'Thank you, Hanna. May we take this?'

She nodded. 'There are plenty more where that came from. It's part of a war chest for when my sister starts divorce proceedings.'

The detectives absorbed the information. 'Do you have anything else?'

'Just a tip. The mistress is only after his money. Once you tell her he's a suspect in a murder case, she'll drop him faster than she drops her knickers. My brother-in-law lies for a living but once you put pressure on him, he'll crack. If he didn't kill Mr Fischer, he's guilty of fraud, embezzlement and cruelty to his wife. My sister and I will be grateful for any effective policing. The Hero getting justice would serve his wife and her sister very nicely, if you get my womansplaining.'

The males smiled, thanked her and went to the door. Hanna added an afterthought. 'Oh and here's another name for you.' The police waited. 'I don't only gossip about suspect males. You should look at Dieter Fischer's widow. She's a real piece of work.'

And speaking of Elizabeth "Liz" Fischer, DS Rick Melody had been assigned to investigate the woman's late husband's finances. It was a legitimate enquiry but one DI Blunt used to ensure his partner was "out of town" while he, Blunt, launched his raid on a part of Melbourne's underworld.

Melody arrived at the Fischer home. The widow let him in. Seated inside, the Detective Sergeant did the usual condolences routine then tactfully explained how the police needed to investigate Mr Fischer's background.

'Can you think of anyone who might have wanted your husband killed; any enemies he may have had?'

'I've been over all this with the other detectives. Don't you lot communicate with one another?'

Melody apologised and tried to switch subjects. ''It would help us, Mrs Fischer, to know a little about your husband's affairs.'

'Such as?'

'His finances. Did people owe him money, did *he* owe money?'

'You mean can you see my late husband's bank records, his super details, share portfolio and insurance policies?'

Melody felt embarrassed but pleased. Straight shooting helped. 'Well, yes, that would be most helpful.'

'Do you need a court order or search warrant first?'

Melody nodded. 'We can obtain the authority if you so desire.'

'I'll be back,' she said and headed out of the room. Melody waited. He heard a sound and turned as an elderly woman entered.

'Who are you?' she asked leaning on her walking frame.

'Hello. I'm a police officer.'

'Is this about my son-in-law?'

'It is and I'm sorry for your loss.'

'He was never here. He lived at that football club. It's hard to miss someone who's never here.'

Melody wanted to continue the conversation but the younger widow entered with a folder. 'Mum, come here.'

The older woman looked at her daughter and then the detective. 'Don't get old, officer, and whatever you do, don't get mollycoddled.'

Mrs Fischer handed Melody the folder then ushered her mother from the room. When Liz returned, Melody had finished.

'Satisfied, officer?' she asked.

'Thank you. Do you have a copy of your husband's will?'

'No, it's sitting in our solicitor's safe.' Melody nodded wanting the solicitor's details. 'I'll save you the trouble,' she said. 'I get the lot.'

DI Blunt worried. He lived dangerously. He researched Miguel Spaniell. His criminal CV was impressive with his record squeaky clean for the last umpteen years. He'd been found in the vicinity of two homicides, was twice interviewed by police but never arrested let alone charged. Miguel's hands were spotless, meaning others did his dirty work. They were well paid and incapable of rolling over.

Blunt entered the Vino Encantador Wine Bar in Brunswick. It was late morning and the luncheon crowd had yet to appear. Those there toyed with their lattes only moving their eyes. No head turning required, no song and dance reaction to an unknown besuited bloke who had *Pig* or *Copper's nark* tattooed on his forehead. Mind you he did sport a quality piece of tailoring. He and the former head of Homicide, DI Steele, were both modern-day dandies.

Blunt perched on a bar stool. 'Coffee, black,' he said acting his heart out auditioning for the Paul Newman role in *Cool Hand Luke*. The coffee arrived and the dialogue didn't. The others in the café remembered their vow of chastity; no, their vow of silence.

Blunt approached the *How Do I Get Out of This Situation?* stage with sweat pushing to break through his skin when the main man himself wandered in from the rear. Hitler had an escape door and stairs at the rear of his bunker, and Mickey Spillane did likewise. He greeted a couple of the regulars. The Brunswick Brotherhood was strong and tough, and tending towards butch.

Spaniell's spending was kept on a tight rein except for the stock market and his attire. Dressed for a TV interview, he clocked the visitor without being noticed, and made an assessment. *Trouble* he thought. He moved to his perpetually reserved table, and his cappuccino with extra chocolate floated down from heaven. He picked up *The Age* and scanned the financial pages. There was a time when he couldn't spell Forex or rather thought when he first heard the word the speaker meant XXXX the beer.

With his wealth came an enthusiasm for the risk of investing. The bearded barista brought a glass of water to the boss and then subtly returned behind the bar. In no hurry, he sidled towards Blunt and looked at him. The detective fumbled for his wallet. He had no other moves to play. 'Mr Spaniell would like a word,' said the barista, and Callum dropped his wallet. Smiles appeared within the café. Blunt recovered and moved to the only reserved table.

'Good morning,' said Blunt with a barely perceptible nod from the wannabe Mafioso, and Blunt pulled out a chair and sat. The barista appeared. 'I can recommend the Cortado.'

Blunt had never heard of it. 'Fine,' he said and the barista floated away.

Spaniell checked his phone. 'FTSE's on the move. What do you know about Fortescue Metals?'

Blunt swore under his breath then recovered. 'Not my bag, Mr Spaniell.'

'Oh?' queried Mick, 'then what *is* your bag, officer?' The last word glowed in the dark in the daylight at 1049 hours in Brunswick.

'I guess this is where I say "fair cop, guv",' said Blunt and hoped like hell his pathetic quip would not see him banished to Siberia.

'I'm not sure if it's my sixth sense or you gents being dressed by the wardrobe mistress from *The Sweeney,* but I can definitely pick you rozzers. I had a cop in here last year who looked like Dennis Waterman complete with bell bottoms.'

Blunt had no idea about the FTSE or UK cop shows of the 1970s. He'd heard of bell bottoms. Without fanfare he showed his ID. 'DI Callum Blunt, Homicide, Mr Spaniell.'

'Homicide? How is my old mate, DI Steele?'

Shit, thought Blunt. *What does old mate mean?* 'He's no longer at Homicide, Mister Spaniell; moved onward and upward to the AFP.'

Spaniell knew all this but asked questions and initiated conversations to discover all he could about this new cop on the block. 'Feds, hey? So, DI Blunt, great name by the way, tell me, do you have DI Steele's ambition?'

'No-one has DI Steele's ambition.' Good answer, Callum.

'I see you've copied his penchant for bespoke tailoring.'

Blunt enjoyed the subtle compliment, especially coming from a dandy like Mickey Spillane.

'I'm investigating a murder on a building site and understand you're a person with a solid knowledge of the construction industry.' His coffee arrived.

'Would you like more milk?' asked Spaniell. Blunt shook his head and the barista left.

'As I was saying ...'

Spaniell interrupted. He still had his face in his paper. His voice was level and restrained. 'So who gave you my name?'

Callum hesitated. 'Ah, now I think you know that would be an infringement of Rule 29a, sir.'

Without trying, Callum kept giving the right answers. Spaniell loved respect, craved it, and Blunt's language and decision not to give up his source won silent plaudits from the gangster.

'Good answer. So if I can help you, DI Blunt, how and when can you help me—legally of course?'

Blunt's confidence grew. 'I'm happy to discuss same once I see your cards, sir.' Mickey Spillane put down his paper and waited for details. 'We have a homicide at a building site in Heidelberg, and wondered if you had any of your labour force on the job.'

'Barry Clunes,' said Spaniell; 'silly man paid his premium to the wrong agent.' Blunt waited. 'Whoever did the killing, it won't be Barry.'

'I don't suppose you've heard who might be involved?'

'God, you don't want much? Why not give me an honorary degree—Bachelor of Jurisprudence or some such?'

Blunt acknowledged the man's wit. 'We cops are nothing without a good snout.' He wished he hadn't used the word *snout*.

'That's a bit rich coming from a pig.' Blunt was good at pathetic grins. 'I might have a tip which brings us back to my unanswered question.' He paused and Blunt said nothing. 'So if I can help you, DI Blunt, how and when can you help me—legally of course?'

The detective spoke in a softer voice. 'Sometimes having an inside man, a friendly voice on the other end of the line, can be … handy.'

'Handy?' asked Mickey with a rich serving of scorn.

Blunt thought. *Have I ever uttered such pathetic bullshit?*

The gangster looked at his visitor. 'I'll ask around,' he said. Blunt wasn't sure of his next move but reckoned quitting while he was ahead seemed wise.

'Thanks, Mr Spaniell.' The detective gulped his coffee, put his business card on the table, and stood to leave when Spaniell spoke.

'Nice shoes,' he said. They looked at Blunt's footwear. 'And socks.'

Shit! The bastard knows about my concrete brogues.

Chapter 15

Cain Reid took the call. 'Cain, it's Norm from next door to your folks.'

'What's happened?' Cain knew this was bad or disastrous news.

'It's Nipper. I looked out my kitchen window and saw him lying in the back yard.'

'Is he all right?'

'He's still breathing. I called an ambulance and they're here and are gunna take him to the Northern in Epping.'

'Is it his heart?'

'Dunno, he couldn't speak. He made a sort of gurgling sound.'

'Okay, thanks, Norm. I'll go and see him now. The Northern in Epping you said?'

'Yeah and let me know how he is.'

'Will do and thanks.' Cain hung up and called. 'Rosa.'

'What?' she answered from the bathroom.

'Nipper's collapsed at home. The ambulance's taking him to the Northern. I'm off.'

'Okay,' she called. No mention of good luck, best wishes, and most definitely nothing about giving her father-in-law her love.

At the hospital, Cain followed directions and met the doctor in charge. 'Hello, Mr Reid, I'm looking after your father.'

'How is he?'

'He's had a stroke. He's in little, if any pain, and we won't know the full extent of his condition for a while. We're doing tests to get an accurate reading of his problems.'

'Can I see him?'

'Sure, once we've made him stable. But you should be prepared for his appearance and condition. He can't speak and is paralysed down his left side, and his face looks a little strange.' She was being kind.

'Will he recover?'

The medico paused. 'The impact of stroke varies, and the damage caused determines the recovery required. Whatever recovery your father makes will take time.' The doctor thought that if Nipper survived, he could be bedridden for a long time, and spreading bad news over time usually helped soften the blow for the family.

Cain felt awful. His mother was in respite, and her dementia kept getting worse. Being cared for by his father, who now lay in hospital having been ravaged by a stroke, was beyond impossible.

'Take a seat, and we'll come and get you when your father is settled.'

Cain saw the signs banning mobile phones so went to the car park.

'He's had a stroke.' Rosa said nothing. 'It's pretty bad. He can't speak and won't be coming home any time soon.'

Rosa couldn't bring herself to say sorry. 'Have you seen him?'

'Not yet. I'll stay till they let me.'

'I'll tell the kids,' she said. 'Can they visit him?' To Rosa, Nipper didn't have a name other than "him".

'I'll let you know.' They paused. Cain was distraught and Rosa silent. 'If Norm from next door hadn't seen him, Nipper could've died alone beside his tomato plants.'

Cain wasn't trying to score points and Rosa withheld fire. She wanted to say, "He's still not coming to live here," but held her tongue.

'See ya,' said Cain and went back to the ward. He had plenty of time to ponder the situation. Both his parents were now incapable of looking after themselves. Wholly-dependent was a good description.

He thought about renovating the rooms downstairs beside his garage. Both his parents could be housed there. Okay, first problem solved. But who would care for them? Rosa was more or less retired and spent time babysitting their two grandkids but she wouldn't lift a finger to help Nipper. *I can't give up work* thought Cain. The only option involved selling his parents' home and using the money to pay for them to live in care—high care for his father, for both. Could they be in the same nursing home? Would they know one another if they were? When he thought about his old man, Cain wanted to cry. He did.

Chelsea Lilliput came home from work with shopping. Jason was on the phone talking to a musical mate about recording one of his songs.

Chelsea ignored him, which she would have done anyway, and unpacked groceries. Jason ended his call and tried talking to his wife.

'How was your day?' She ignored him and kept working. He decided to bite the bullet. 'What's wrong?'

'Nothing,' she replied and finished putting away their supply of tinned food and pasta. Fresh was a stranger in their house.

'Hang on a minute, will ya?' She did and stared at him. 'This is not your usual strop. Something's wrong so why won't you talk to me?'

'Because there's nothing wrong and even if there was, you'd be about as helpful as a tumour.'

Jason was getting nowhere so lobbed the grenade. It would create one hell of a mess but it might get Chelsea to come clean.

'Your boss called today.'

She came alive. 'Keith rang you?' Jason nodded. Now she was wary. 'What about?'

'The possibility of you being sacked.'

'Bullshit,' she said without any conviction. 'I'm his best worker and he knows it.'

'He said that.'

Chelsea was desperate to know the news. 'So why did he call?'

'He reckons you've been behaving strangely, having a go at customers and even telling him where to go.'

'They deserved it. Some customers are idiots, and Keith never sticks up for his staff. The customer is *not* always right, and he knows it.'

'So if it's not work, and you're not suffering from a mystery disease, what is it?'

'I'm not crook and even if I was, you'd be the last person I'd tell.'

'Thanks for nothing.' Jason decided to try being apologetic. 'Look I'm sorry I didn't put the photos back the right way.' She stopped. 'You usually only get depressed a few days before his birthday so I didn't think that was the reason.'

'It's not so drop it.' She wanted to leave.

'Does your cousin know?'

Chelsea lost it using her hands to threaten him. 'You leave Valerie out of it. You say anything to her and I'll use your best guitar for firewood. Got it?'

Jason understood the words, and her tone left him in no doubt.

He waved a white flag. 'All right, all right, but if you lose your job, don't come crawling to me for money.'

She looked at him, shook her head and walked out muttering, 'You and money; what a joke.'

Jason hesitated than called after her. 'Keith thought it might be the change of life.'

It was easy to upset Chelsea, and his last remark kick-started her anger. She stormed back into the room. 'He said what?'

Jason pleaded. 'He doesn't want to sack you, Chelsea. If there's a reason for your weird behaviour, just tell him.'

'Well that beats everything; middle-aged males discussing women's stuff. You two have zero knowledge and less experience. Why don't you do stand-up? You could call yourselves *Useless and Dickhead*. And you'd make more money than you do from your crap songs, which wouldn't be hard.' She stormed out with her last remark hurting Jason the most. It was true, he was no Glen Campbell.

Chapter 16

Detectives gathered with DI Rose running the show. 'We have several suspects for Heidelberg but none for the bush. Any general comments before we start?'

Nobody spoke until Jo had one of her rushes of blood. She was good at speaking without considering the consequences. 'Is there any connection between the two cases, ma'am?'

Murmurs rippled around the room.

'You think they're connected, Senior?'

'Not sure, ma'am, but Dr Strange found an unusual mark on both bodies. It's a long shot but other far more experienced officers we know have advocated the test-every-possibility approach.'

DI Rose knew the young detective was talking about her grandfather, the long retired DCI Robbo Robertson.

'What are these similarities?' asked DI Blunt.

Rose looked at Jo. 'Senior?'

'Both bodies have a small cut made by what Doctor Strange says was a knife or sharp object. The coach had a nick within his eyebrow and the camper had a nick on his tongue beside what looks like a bite mark. Easily missed I guess but picked up by the brilliant pathologist.'

'I agree,' added Billy Hughes.

'Were the cuts made with the same knife?' asked DS Fletcher.

'No,' said Jo. 'And Dr Strange said either or both could have come from the coach's fight, or the impact of the tree branch on the camper causing him to bite his tongue.'

'But she doesn't think so?' asked Rose.

'No, ma'am.'

'Okay, we'll keep it in mind. Let's start with the Heidelberg homicide. Who's got Pathology?'

Hughes indicated and started. 'Jo mentioned the small cut on each victim. Dr Strange reckoned the weight of the branch and the damage to the victim meant two, possibly three killers were involved. If true it gives us more persons of interest to investigate. And good old Dr Strange kept to her routine of finding something dramatic. She reckons there are traces of Valium in Max Bowman's blood.'

Her comment sparked an interest. Rose led the questioning. 'What, the experienced camper couldn't sleep so popped a mild tranquilizer?'

'It might be mild, ma'am, but there was a fair bit of it. And according to Dr Strange, the victim also had traces of a homemade chloroform in his nostrils.' That caused a bigger response. Billy spoke over it. 'As his family and friends have said, the victim was an experienced camper, so the poor bugger could have been drugged, placed in his tent beneath the tree, and the branch encouraged to fall and kill him.'

'And the dog's all right?' asked DS Melody.

'Thanks Rick,' said the boss. 'Yes, he's back with his family in Melbourne but we'll come to that. Are we agreed this is a calculated homicide which worked a treat?' The room agreed. 'And we have no firm leads as yet?'

'We haven't interviewed the victim's friends, family or workmates, ma'am. We haven't even established a motive,' said SIO Billy.

'Understood; so let's push on. Senior Constable Payne and I went to Forensics. Stephen?'

'We found the knife we believe was used to kill Dieter Fischer in the toolbox of the ute owned by Barry Clunes. He agreed it was his knife. Forensics found traces of blood which matched those of the victim. Only one set of prints on the knife which we're pretty sure will match the builder. Clunes has been arrested and is in custody.'

'Anything from Forensics on the camping equipment, 4WD, and the blood taken from the dog?' asked Hughes.

'Still waiting, Sarge,' said Payne.

'Thanks Stephen,' said Rose. 'So, will somebody tell me why Clunes can't be charged with Fischer's murder? Strong motive, at the scene at the right time, admits he fought the victim who fell and struck his head, and Clunes owns the knife used in the killing with cause of death being the stab wound to the chest. The knife has the victim's blood and most likely Clunes' prints. Why is this not an open and shut case?'

'Is he stupid?' asked DS Fletcher.

'Meaning?' asked Rose.

'He's admitted to everything apart from stabbing the guy. He's refused a solicitor, and not disposed of the murder weapon. Does that make him stupid or is he pulling a sort of double bluff?'

'Or has he been set up?' asked Billy.

Charley Baldwin explained his theory. 'If the guy is as broke and depressed as he claims—lost his wife, kids and business—is this some weird game of suicide by police? Does he want to be banged up even though he didn't kill Fischer?'

'He could be acting cool in interviews because he's innocent,' offered DS Melody.

'May I suggest, ma'am,' said Billy Hughes, 'as we have at least one other strong suspect, that alone is reason to hold off charging Clunes.'

Rose took all this in. 'Okay, we hold off but if his prints are the only ones on the knife and these other suspects fall over, I'll want a bloody good reason not to charge Clunes.'

Jo liked this approach from her boss where she encouraged everyone to contribute. Rose trusted her colleagues, and they spoke their mind not fearing any reprimand or backlash.

Jo thought. *DI Blunt is not like that.*

'So,' said Rose, 'what about these other persons of interest?'

Fletcher reported. 'The president, Alex Hero, has guilt written all over him although not necessarily for the murder. He's given a false alibi, is likely on the take over the construction of the new grandstand, and he does the books for the club.'

'So what's happened about these financial claims?' asked Billy.

'Fraud will look at the club's books and the contract where Clunes was awarded the job. We'll interview Hero's girlfriend. He said he was at home which his wife's sister denies. If he falls back on the mistress, pardon the expression, we reckon she'll give him up. So with fraud charges and a false alibi, the president may fold. Oh, and as Hero hated Fischer and Clunes, he may have killed the coach leaving Clunes to carry the can.'

'Anyone else,' asked Rose.

'The victim's widow, ma'am,' said DS Melody. 'I tried the polite routine. She willingly handed over hubby's financial details. The man ain't on Struggle Street. Share portfolio, big super fund, no mortgage and solid cash accounts. The cracker is his life insurance with a big cover. I asked about his will and she freely said, "I get the lot".'

The room went quiet. As SIO on this case, Blunt knew he needed to make decisions and show leadership. He threw in some questions. 'What about the marriage? Apart from the money, does the wife have a motive to knock off her husband?'

'Too early, sir,' said Melody. 'We need to interview the widow, neighbours, friends, family, and people at the soccer club.'

Hughes looked at DI Rose. 'Not sure we can keep Clunes without charging him, ma'am. There might be a strong case but when you have others who are still in the frame, holding fire might be better.'

Rose took a deep breath but refused to comment on Clunes. 'Maybe. If he maintains his position, we'll release him. Okay, who else? Callum, what news from the underworld?'

He thought she was mocking him. 'I've found a good lead. The word is an organised crime figure is dabbling in the building game. If Clunes refused to pay extortion, he could have been framed for the murder of Fischer.'

'Why kill Fischer?' asked Rose.

'Because he discovered the fraud run by Hero or organised crime or both, and needed to be silenced.' Everyone waited for more. Few trusted Blunt and reckoned his solo efforts were to bolster his career. They were. 'It's early days but I've made contact with a legit labour hire guy who has links with organised crime.'

'He's legit with links to crims? That doesn't make sense,' said Rose.

Blunt wriggled. 'Legit but only as a front.' Blunt convinced no-one.

Billy asked a question. 'Have you tried the Master Builders Institute or the Construction Workers Union?'

Blunt glared at her. He couldn't believe she knew about his two massive cock-ups. She didn't but Blunt didn't know that. 'I've spoken to both and got nothing.'

More silence. 'Right,' said Rose. 'We need Forensics for the camping equipment and 4WD; the president's mistress, the Fischer marriage, the camper's friends, family and associates, and Fraud going over the club's books and the building contract. Anything else?'

'Bluey's blood,' said Jo, 'the dog belonging to the camper.'

Billy jumped in. 'We're waiting on a forensic report. If the camper was drugged, then why not the dog? How did the killers control the dog as the camper was killed?'

'Could it have been the curious incident of the dog in the night-time?' asked DS Melody.

Everyone stopped. 'What are you on about?' asked Billy. Jo knew.

Melody explained. 'Sherlock Homes reckoned because a dog didn't bark, it knew the person who stole the racehorse, the criminal. If Bluey knew the killer or killers of his master, the dog wouldn't have been aggressive, and wouldn't have tried to protect the victim. If the killers were strangers, Bluey would have gone mad.'

Members buzzed. The new detective reads books.

'Thank you for the literary clue, DS Melody,' said DI Rose, and pointed at Jo. 'And thank you, Senior for having the blood taken in the first place.'

Jo felt warm inside, Melody ditto, while Blunt growled.

Chapter 17

Jo wanted to chase up Forensics for news on Bluey's blood. In recent weeks, she avoided the place because of a run in with her least favourite scientist, Alastair Dean. Yes, he behaved badly, even illegally towards her but she led him on. Fluttering her eyelashes to get ahead in the queue was fine but when the recipient took it to mean she fancied him when she clearly did not, things got nasty. He acted like the rejected lover although Jo and Alastair were never lovers.

'Sarge,' she said to Billy, 'I need to check on those results for the dog's blood.'

'Fine but remember the DI's request—walk with your fingers.'

'If you don't mind, I'd like to do a face to face.'

Hughes looked at Jo. 'Not more boyfriend trouble?' Jo didn't answer. Billy waved her away. 'Go on, get lost. And when you next see Pierre, give him my best.'

Jo left feeling better about one meeting and lousy about the other. She arrived at Forensics and looked around. She couldn't see the once lovesick Alastair. She chatted with a woman she didn't know. Jo explained her request and the scientist was about to look for the results when a voice sounded behind her.

'I've got those results.' Jo turned to see Alastair. 'Detective Senior Constable Best, how nice to see you,' he said. He seemed genuine, with nothing sarcastic about his speech or demeanour.

'Alastair,' said Jo, heart racing and smile on dimmer. 'Long time, no see. Are you well?'

'I'm fine. Yourself?'

'Yes, thank you.'

'I see you've been in the news yet again solving homicides and nearly getting yourself killed.'

'I was lucky but not so my colleague, DI Richelieu.'

His face fell. 'Yes I was sorry to hear that. How is he?'

'He's recovering slowly.'

'I'm pleased. Now to the canine blood. It went to an animal lab and they've sent through the result. It's all clear other than for traces of what they think is chamomile tea.'

Jo thought he was joking, mocking her. 'Seriously? Dogs drink tea?'

'I think meat or a treat is soaked in chamomile tea, and the dog eats the food with some believing the tea relaxes the dog helping it to sleep but I've no idea if it's true. Does that help?'

'It does, and thanks for your prompt service.'

He handed her a print out of the report. 'Always a pleasure.'

'Lovely. So how is your mother, Alastair?'

He went quiet and paused then spoke with a softer voice. 'Sadly she passed away.'

Jo wanted to slap herself. 'Oh God, I'm so sorry. Forgive me, Alastair, I didn't know.' She placed a consoling hand on his arm for a brief moment.

'How could you?'

She paused then waved the report. 'Well, thanks again, Alastair. Bye.' She departed and was walking to her car when the first scientist she met, the woman, ran after her.

'Hello?' Jo stopped. 'Look, it's none of my business but I heard Alastair telling you his mother had passed away.' Jo wondered what was coming next. 'She hasn't.' Jo felt sick. 'She's gone into care and I know this because Alastair showed us photos of her in her new place only this week.'

Jo struggled to compute the information. 'Thanks.' She didn't know what to say. What seemed like an end to the problem she had with Alastair became something new and possibly nasty.

Driving to the hospital, Jo worried about Pierre's latest condition and Alastair's blatant lie. She realised his bitterness at being rejected by Jo still lingered. All she needed now was to discover Pierre had relapsed and was back in Intensive Care to make her misery complete. She parked, entered the ICU and was spotted by Katrina, the nurse.

'Jo, hi, how are you?' she asked with a smile to match.

Jo felt slightly better because of the nurse's enthusiasm but waited for the news. 'Hi Katrina. How's Pierre?'

'He's moved.'

'What?' asked Jo with alarm.

'Just next door. He's moved from Intensive Care to High Dependency.'

'Is that good?'

'It sure is. In ICU it's usually one nurse per patient but now he has to share. His nurse will look after someone else as well. He still has a long way to go on his recovery but every little step helps.'

Jo's heart rate slowed. She felt terrific. 'Can I see him?'

'Of course. I'll check for you.'

Katrina left and Jo tingled. Good news about Pierre was the best. She wanted him up and about. Okay, returning to work was not going to happen soon, if ever, but he still had years of life to go and maybe, *maybe* they could be spent with a certain Detective Senior Constable.

Grant Buchanan, the doctor she met before, came into Reception. 'Oh no,' he said looking worried, 'I'm sure I paid that fine, officer.'

He smiled and Jo shook his hand. 'Doctor Buchanan,' she said.

'Grant, we're all on first name terms here, Jo.'

'Katrina told me Pierre has been moved.'

'He has and all because he's making progress, slow but he's heading in the right direction.'

Jo's insides grew tight. 'Can I ask about his prognosis?'

'Of course. I gather from what Pierre said, keeps saying, and from reports of your latest escapade, you are pretty much Pierre's family.'

Jo agreed. 'Yes, I am.'

The doctor led Jo to a seat and both sat. 'As you know, he's had a splenectomy. The injury he received from the car attack left us with little choice. People can live without a spleen but it does mean their immune system is weakened, and they're susceptible to diseases like pneumonia and meningitis. Drugs can be a lifelong requirement.'

'I see,' said Jo feeling better hearing a medico lay it on the line.

'But,' said Dr Buchanan and Jo's stomach plummeted, 'he does have a couple of other problems. I can explain them in more detail but perhaps at another time.'

Jo reckoned he wanted to distribute the bad news in a slow drip format rather than in one lump sum. She appreciated his approach.

Katrina arrived. 'All ready, Jo. The Inspector awaits.' Jo thanked Grant and followed Katrina to Pierre's new accommodation. 'Here's your favourite detective, Inspector,' she said and left Jo to greet the man who set her heart racing.

She wondered if her love was pure love or perhaps a mixture of sympathy and love. Beside his bed were fewer monitors, machines and cables. She took in his hair, his attire and mostly his smile. Of all his winning characteristics, Pierre Richelieu used his eyes, teeth, and lips to greet anyone with his welcoming smile.

She moved to his side. His hands were out waiting to greet her. She wanted to touch him, kiss him but worried about hurting him or damaging the equipment which she assumed monitored his breathing and other vital organs.

'Ma fille chérie,' he said with his smile dissolving into tears.

'Pierre,' she whispered and, holding his hands as much to steady herself, she bent and kissed his lips. They were as soft as always but less energetic, no longer excited. She dabbed his eyes wiping his tears. 'You look wonderful,' she said and he fell back on his pillows—plural. Sitting up tired him.

'As you can see, they 'ave moved me to another palatial suite and they continue to treat me like a king.'

'You deserve nothing less, and they said it's because you are making progress, Pierre. It's wonderful news.'

'Alas slow progress, ma chérie, but I will continue to do so with you by my side.'

Jo had her tear ducts under control until then but now felt the waterworks department getting busy. She switched to work chat hoping to lower the emotional temperature.

'Those two homicides I told you about are keeping us busy.'

'Oh oui, tell me everything, s'il vous plait.'

'And Detective Senior Sergeant Hughes sends her best wishes.'

'Ah, Billy, 'ow I miss you and 'err and everybody.'

Jo explained the two homicides in broad detail. He asked questions showing Jo his mind was fit and well. Yes, he became tired but he was miles better than when she saw him last. He even wanted to know the office gossip which Jo found tricky.

Katrina entered and Jo and Pierre stopped. 'Don't mind me,' said the nurse. 'I need to check a couple of things.'

Pierre took over. 'My dear Katrina, this lady is the reason I am doing so well. She is the inspiration for me to recover and leave this wonderful 'ospital.'

'Careful, Inspector, I may have to breathalyse you for flirtatious chat.'

All three laughed with Pierre beaming being able to show off his true love. He could tell Jo how much he loved her by telling his carers how much he loved her.

Jo thought enough was enough. Regular short visits worked best for both of them. She naturally leant in and kissed Pierre on his lips, squeezed his hand and prepared to leave. 'I'll be back as soon as I can, Pierre and when I do, I expect to see you getting better. Au revoir, Inspector.' She blew him a kiss. 'Bye,' she whispered to Katrina and left without looking back.

Another nurse and Dr Buchanan came out of a room and Jo didn't stop. The medicos looked at one another. This part of the hospital was one place where families and friends of patients became emotional.

Jo drove home trying to sort her work life balance. Solving one, possibly two homicides dominated. But solving her feelings needed someone or something higher or wiser or better than her.

The only person she felt keen on sharing her intimate thoughts with was Gabrielle Strange even though she could be brutal with the truth. Michael Chan she admired for his brilliant clear thinking but the last time she opened up to him, he misread the signs and embarrassed them both.

Her mother and sister would never be consulted on anything in Jo's professional and personal life. Not so her grandfather; there's someone she would willingly open up to but more on the professional than the personal. What would Pop think of her marrying a wealthy Frenchman who would have to retire on grounds of ill-health?

Damn, she thought, *I have no-one.*

Then her phone rang. She used it hands free without checking caller ID. 'Jo Best speaking.'

'Not *the* Jo Best, detective extraordinaire and all round nice girl?'

Jo smiled, even laughed. 'Hello Doctor Carr, long time no see or call. How are you and your wonderful family?'

'We're fine and still talking about your latest triumph against the bad guys.'

'Trust me, Jack, I had clever helpers, one incredibly brave friend and a solid serve of luck.'

'My folks are here and the kids will soon be getting ready for bed and I thought, wouldn't it be great if Detective Best could drop in for home-cooked lasagne, and sign autographs for her two youngest fans.'

'Two *oldest* fans,' cried Hugh in the background.

Jo heard him and laughed and without hesitation accepted the offer. Right now she was not the happiest constable in Christendom, and a home cooked meal with some pretty special people sounded like the perfect pick-me-up.'

'That's a terrific offer, Jack. I can be there in twenty minutes.'

'Don't you dare speed, officer.'

'Bye,' she called and struggled to hit the off button.

'She's coming,' said Jack and to Jo it sounded like they cheered.

Callum Blunt sat at his computer in his Cremorne townhouse and scribbled notes. His objective was to solve the soccer coach homicide, and expose any organised crime involved in the construction of the club's new grandstand. One result would be great, two perfect. His only positive lead was the Brunswick-based café owner and labour-hire guru, Miguel Spaniell known as Mickey Spillane. Blunt had met the guy and asked for help. In return, Blunt offered a friendly ear within the police if Spillane ever needed advice. Surely that's not enough.

What next? Blunt's promotion within law enforcement was due to gladhanding people rather than skill or intelligence. His dedicated pursuit of promotion was what got him where he was today. But now, working alone, his lack of imagination proved a handicap.

Bloody Jo Best would have an idea, more than one. Why can't I figure out my next move?

He doodled on his notepad and listed the people who might help him without exposing him. DI Steele would be worth another call. So too Lockjaw and that old lag Lenny the Mower, and possibly Mickey Spillane although he might well be the target.

He's not thick. If he gives me anything, it'll be to steer me away from him.

Who else? Then he twigged. *What about people on the inside at the soccer club? But who? And are they already on the interviewee list compiled by my colleagues? If so, interviewing them will be tricky. If anyone at Homicide find out I'm talking to people they're talking to, I'll cop it big time. I need someone on the inside who is not on the police radar. But who? And where will I find inspiration?*

Jo arrived and the Carr front door was opened by little Harry, who Jo thought was growing taller every day. The lad's father and grandfather hovered in the background sporting grins the size of a pumpkin. Hugs all round then two female voices sounded in another room.

'We're in the kitchen.'

Jo made a face and led the gents to the kitchen with Harry grabbing Jo's hand. Domesticity was in fine form. Grandma Peg was into the plate-up stage and granddaughter Grace, she with the acquired brain injury from a car accident, moved slowly around the table placing paper serviettes in place. She'd done the same with the cutlery which was set as if governed by a theodolite.

'Ladies,' cried Jo and moved to kiss both. It was tricky as Grace on her stick juggled serviettes and Peg her delicious lasagne.

Everyone sat with Jo between the kids. Hugh played the drink waiter role and Jo felt all the worries of her recent death threat, Pierre's health crisis, Alastair Dean's lie, and the two new homicides fade thanks to the fabulous food and company. Laughter kept interrupting, and the stories by the kids, plus their questions, kept Jo on her toes. She couldn't get over the improvement in Grace's speech or the vocabulary being spouted by her younger brother. The grandparents and parent purred.

After the meal they all retired to the lounge where Grace had a surprise for Jo. The young girl produced a scrapbook. She handed it to the detective who saw the title on the front cover. The letters of *Detective Jo's Scrapbook* had been cut from newspapers and magazines. Actually the last word was *Scrapebook* but a small piece of white paper was stuck on the *e* leaving a space showing *Scrap book*.

Grace ran the show. 'I have been making a scrapbook for you, Jo.'

'Grace, that's wonderful.'

Grace had trouble leaning across to reach the edge of the cover and get started. 'First, you open the book.' She struggled to do so.

'May I help?' asked Jo.

'Yes please.'

The cover was opened and there was a picture of Jo in her police uniform. She looked smart. 'Oh my goodness,' said Jo,' that's ancient.'

'No, that's you, Detective,' said Harry in case she was in any doubt.

'So it is,' said Jo. 'I wonder what else I can find.'

She turned the page and saw a photo of Jo taken from a web page of a TV station with their report of one of Jo's earlier cases. There were more photos, and beneath each Grace had written things like *Detective Jo Best solves a case* or *Detective Jo Best rescues a missing girl* or *Detective Jo Best catches a criminal.*

Jo felt a lump in her throat. This scrapbook was a labour of love. 'Grace, you've done a brilliant job. You're a very clever young girl.' The look on the girl's face was priceless. She'd been waiting ages to show the lady who inspired her, the tribute she lovingly created. To have her praise was the best. Her family members were thrilled.

Unbeknown to Jo, young Harry was busting to do *his* tribute and had, until now, been gazumped by his big sister. His father had promised him a turn and Harry was under strict instructions to wait.

'Dad?' he asked with a sing-song voice.

Jack nodded. 'Okay mate, you can ask Detective Jo now.'

The scrapbook was returned to its creator as Harry moved to the centre of the lounge room.

'Detective Jo, I have been practising for when I grow up and become a policeman.'

'Wow. I'm impressed, Harry. What have you been practising?'

'First, I have been practising my saluting.' He stood to attention and saluted Jo. From her sitting position she gave the best salute she could.

'Excellent, Officer Harry.'

'Then, my marching,' he said and hurried to the double doors, turned before marching all of three metres to where he once stood. His swinging arms could not be faulted. Jo clapped.

'Excellent cadet Police Officer Carr.'

Harry grinned. 'One more, Harry,' said his father, 'and then it's time for bed.'

The lad thought about his next routine then moved to his grandfather who handed him a small empty milk carton with a straw poking out of the top. Harry approached Jo. She was intrigued and couldn't imagine what the young boy had been practising.

'Excuse me, lady,' he said.

'Madam,' said Hugh.

Harry remembered. 'Excuse me, madam. Will you please blow in this machine?'

Jo hesitated then threw back her head and shrieked with laughter. The others except Harry joined her and finally the boy got excited. Hugh collected him and whispered in his ear.

'Thank you, madam, you passed,' said Harry mimicking what his Pop had whispered.

Jo held out her hand, Harry hesitated then moved forward and shook it. She gently pulled him closer and kissed his head. Hugo took Harry, and Peg helped Grace who now walked using only one stick.

'Say goodnight you two,' said Hugh, and the kids did and departed.

Jo looked across at Jack. 'That's the happiest hour I've had in a long time, Jack. Your kids are a credit to you and your folks.'

'Especially my folks. I'd be lost without them. So, how are you, Jo, really I mean?'

'Much better since I walked down your drive.'

'That business in your flat with those two crazy women must have been a nightmare.'

'It was.'

Jack hesitated. 'God, I'm sorry, I shouldn't have brought it up.'

'It's fine; it was just another day at the office.'

Jack shook his head. 'Liar,' he said in a soft voice.

Jo forced a smile and wanted to change the subject. 'Grace is making so much progress. Her mind is as sharp as ever, more so.'

'True and it's a real blessing. Her speech is improving every day and if we can get her motor skills firing, she'll be as good as new; well, almost.'

'And Harry with his breathalyser routine was hilarious.'

'He kept asking what he could do and Dad suggested the roadside stop. Way too young for a child to be testing for alcohol but he loved the idea.'

'We all did.'

Peg poked her head around the kitchen door. 'Coffee?'

'Please,' said Jo and Jack.

There was a pause when both didn't know what to say. Then Jo remembered. 'I met a friend of yours the other day, Doctor Grant Buchanan.'

'Jock Buchanan—lovely guy and a brilliant specialist.'

'I guess he's told you about my colleague in Intensive Care.'

'He has; terrible situation. How's he going?'

'Well he's alive and after what happened, it's a miracle. I had a chat with your friend today and I think he's softening me up for bad news.'

'Well you're in good hands, the very best.'

Hugh entered. 'My ears are burning. Are you talking about me again?' He sat next to Jo and she slipped an arm into his.

'You would have been a brilliant medico, Hugh,' she said and he went all coy and mimicked.

'Shucks, I bet you say that to all the boys.'

Peg came in with a tray of coffee, cups and cake. Jack jumped up and helped his mother, and all four sat and sipped with the three residents studying their guest.

'It's lovely to see you, Jo, at any time,' said Peg, 'but after what we've seen and heard of your cases on the telly, it's as if you've been to Hell and back.'

'If you ever want a bodyguard, Jo, I'm available,' said Hugh whose offer received appropriate scoffing from his family.

'Thank you, kind sir,' said Jo, 'but I don't think I could afford you.'

That's a lie, she thought. *If I marry Pierre and/or if he dies, I can afford a hundred bodyguards.*

'With your colleague out of action, what happens about staff replacements?' asked Jack.

'A new DS started last week and a long-serving DS was promoted.'

'But not you?' asked Hugh.

Jo smiled. 'Hardly. I'm a beginner when it comes to promotion. I think Senior Constable is my lot forever.'

'Even when you're the smartest detective on the squad?' asked Peg.

Jo scrunched her face. 'You're too kind, Grannie, but most cases are solved by lots of detectives each contributing their bit. Anyway,' said Jo pointing at the woman, 'you're biased.'

'We're all biased,' said Hugh and Jo gave him a smile to melt his piece of sponge.

The supper finished and Jo made her excuses. 'I've had a fabulous night. The kids inspired me and your kindness gives me a real lift.'

'Any time, Detective,' said Hugh giving her a hug. The hug from Peg lasted a fair while.

'Look after yourself, young lady,' said the grandmother. 'Cut back on those car chases and shootouts.'

'I'll try, I promise.'

'I'll see you out,' said Jack, and they wandered up the drive.

'You're a lucky man, Jack Carr. You have a family to be proud of with more than enough love to go round.'

He laughed. 'Thanks, Jo but you only see us once in a while. We can have our off days too.'

'I'll have another chat with Doctor Buchanan about Pierre.'

'Give him and your Inspector my best,' said Jack.

'I will, both of them.'

They reached her car. She had a memory flash of Jack kissing a blonde woman in this very spot. He had a memory flash of his in-laws witnessing Pierre kissing Jo and taking delight in describing the scene to the GP.

She faced him. 'Thanks again, Jack. I really enjoy your company.'

'Likewise,' he said. They looked at one another and then, as if on cue, embraced. They had never hugged like this. They both enjoyed the sensation of the other's body and smell—pleasant as they were.

They released their embrace and Jo hopped in her car as quick as she could. He bent to see her face. 'Take care,' he said and she looked at him, paused then started her engine. He closed the door and she drove away looking in her mirror to see him holding up a hand.

It had been a relaxing and lovely break from her life of hard work, miserable memories of almost being shot, and then watching her colleague, friend and lover fighting to stay alive.

Heading for home, the tears trickled down her face.

Chapter 18

Fletcher and Baldwin drove to a Kew address. Quiet street, old-money properties, and gardens watered by systems using NASA technology.

'Nice work if you can get it,' said Baldwin.

'I'll lead,' said Fletcher, 'but jump in with any apposite remark.'

Baldwin wasn't sure what apposite meant and didn't ask because the front door opened. There stood a woman, either side of 40, with enough hair to make Samson jealous, and more bling than an up-himself rapper. Her white and gold-trimmed jacket with white slacks were never on special at Kmart. She eyed them through the safety door.

'No hawkers,' she said. 'Are you illiterate as well as desperate?'

Two IDs appeared and Fletcher spoke. 'Police, madam; are you Ms Cassandra Huntington?'

'Why?' was all she said although with a marked drop in attitude.

'We're Homicide detectives, madam, and believe you may be able to assist in a case we're investigating.'

'Do I have to?'

'No, madam but ...'

'And why me? I know nothing about any homicide.'

'Do you know a Mr Alex Hero, president of the Heidelberg Rovers Football club?'

'He's my dentist.'

That threw them. 'Oh, your dentist?' Baldwin saved Fletcher.

'If you're concerned about our claims, madam, we could have a patrol car with uniformed officers come to verify our IDs if that would make you feel safer, and with a female officer too if you prefer.'

Fletcher was impressed with his Senior Constable as the lady of the house unlocked her security door and walked inside. They had to open the door. The fewer police on her street, let alone inside her home, the better. 'If you must, come in,' she called, 'and wipe your feet.'

Baldwin winked at Fletcher, and they entered the sitting room with its expensive furniture and furnishings, most of which were imported from Europe. She sat without inviting her visitors to do the same. She crossed her legs, flaunting her gold heels the cost of which impacted the gold price.

'May we sit, madam?' asked Fletcher. She gave a mini nod. They sat and prepared to take notes. 'You say you know Mr Hope professionally as your dentist.'

She hated the police and her flared nostrils indicated her displeasure. 'He's not my actual dentist. He owns the practice where I have my teeth done.'

Judging by her choppers, her last visit included one with the lot.

Fletcher cracked on. 'As you may have heard, there was a death at the soccer club, and Mr Hero has told us he was with you on the night the coach was killed. Can you please confirm that?'

'Is Alex a suspect?'

'If you could answer the question, madam.'

'When did this ... thing happen?'

'Last Tuesday between 8 pm and midnight.'

The detectives were sure they could hear her mind calculating the consequences and costs of the possible answers she might offer. She shook her head. 'No, I was home alone.'

'Mr Hero was not here at all on Tuesday evening?'

'Are you deaf? I just told you.'

'Thank you, madam. Did Mr Hero ever discuss soccer club matters with you?'

'Never. Why would he?'

Fletcher hesitated and Baldwin took over. 'Can you think of any reason why Mr Hero might tell us he was with you on the night in question?'

'Because he suffers from delusions of man-duer. His wife is a mouse impersonating a dried prune, and by claiming me as one of his patients, he gets to bask in my class and beauty. Alex Hero is nothing to me, and if he tries to drag me into his sordid little world, I'll sue him for every cent he's got. And you can tell him that too. Now, I have a hair appointment so you have to leave.' She walked to the door. The detectives made faces and followed her. She stood back to give them easy access to their world.

'Thank you, madam,' said Fletcher.

'And don't come back,' she snapped closing the doors.

As they walked to their vehicle, Baldwin had a question. 'What would she pay for a short back and sides?'

Poor old Alex Hero; it wasn't his day. He'd been losing sleep ever since the new grandstand project fell over, and to have the coach murdered within spitting distance of his office put the wind right up the Prez. Life with his mistress was rocky, and having him as a suspect for Fischer's murder was the absolute pits. But then his life became worse.

Worse? How can my life possibly become worse?

Three cops in suits arrived with a warrant to inspect the books. What!? *I do the books. I know where the bodies are hidden. Help!*

As he paced the corridor wondering not if, but when the fraud chaps would grill him, in came those two homicide detectives—again.

'Good morning Mr Hero,' said Fletcher. 'Remember us?'

'What now? There are three police officers here already.'

'Oh?' asked Fletcher, confused.

'As if the situation isn't bad enough, they have a warrant to examine the club's accounts. They reckon they could be here for hours.'

'Well we won't take long, sir. We wanted to check the alibi you gave us for the night of the murder.'

Hero lost it. 'I've already told you. Don't you people take notes?'

'We do, sir, and you told us you were at home with your wife.'

'Thank you. Now is that all?'

'Only she now says it isn't true.'

The president stopped and took a deep breath. 'Okay, I can explain. She's starting to forget things. I'm going to get her checked for signs of early dementia.' He was a lovely chap was Alex.

'She said she was with her sister and her sister has confirmed that.'

More pressure for Hero. 'Okay, I might have been home alone.'

'Giving wrong information to the police is a serious matter, sir. Lying to the police in a murder enquiry is potentially dangerous for your bank balance and possibly your freedom. I advise you to answer truthfully this time.'

The president felt the knot in his stomach grow ever tighter. 'Okay, understood and I'll tell you the truth only I would ask this doesn't go any further.' The police said nothing. 'I was with a friend on the night of the murder.'

'Name?' asked Fletcher.

Hero flushed. 'Is this necessary?' he snorted. 'My friend has nothing to do with the club or ...'

Fletcher announced. 'Alex Hero I'm arresting you on suspicion of ...'

Hero was all hands, protesting. 'All right, all right, her name is Cassandra Huntington, she's a patient at one of my dental clinics, and is going through a nasty divorce. I've been giving her support.'

Is that what they call it? thought Baldwin.

Fletcher continued. 'And how is this lady involved in your alibi?'

'She's not involved in any murder and nor am I because at the time of the murder I was with Ms Huntington in her home until midnight.'

The detectives looked at Hero. He was sure he'd been removed from the list of suspects for Fischer's murder. Fletcher delivered the bad news Mr President was not expecting.

'We've interviewed Ms Huntington, Mr Hero, and she claims she was home alone on the night of the murder.'

Hero looked like he'd been shot. 'No,' he gasped, 'I was with her.'

Baldwin twisted the knife, and read his notes. 'Ms Huntington said, "Hero is nothing to me and if he tries to drag me into his sordid little world I'll sue him for every cent he's got. And you can tell him too".'

The detectives stared at Hero who lost his power of speech. His alibi was shot, he'd been dumped and threatened with legal action. Shock set in. *The bitch,* he wanted to say. *And I knocked a grand off her new implants.* He meant teeth. She paid full whack for her other implants. Before Hero responded, a detective came out of his office.

'Mr Hero, we need an explanation for these amounts.'

Talk about it never rains.

'Does DI Blunt know you've bunked off school?' asked Jo as DS Rick Melody drove her to interview Max Bowman's widow, Kylie. She'd been to ID her husband's battered body with plenty of warning beforehand. The staff worked hard to make Max presentable. They had the widow stand on the less horrific side. Melody was present when Kylie and Max's brother, Shorty Bowman attended.

'DI Blunt's busy fighting the Melbourne Mafia,' replied Melody. 'He gave me the five minute job of setting Fraud onto the soccer club's books, so DI Rose re-assigned me to continue working on the bashing in the bush.'

'What did the widow say when identifying her squashed spouse?'

'Not much, and now the top brass want me to see first-hand how the wonder detective struts her stuff.' Jo looked to see he was smiling. 'Your reputation precedes you, Detective Senior Constable Best.'

Jo studied him. He was hard to read. *Was that a friendly quip or a putdown from a male senior officer?* 'Sarge, you know we have no leads, and no persons of interest?' He nodded. 'How will we play this?'

'I lead and you swoop in to score the try at the death.'

Jo laughed. 'You're not from around here are you?'

He looked at her. 'Sorry?'

'You reckon we're the Mexicans, south of the border. Victorians dob a sausage but only a banana bender or New South Welshman would score a try.'

He understood his mistake, laughed and eventually they parked outside the Bowman residence in Pakenham. Kylie was waiting. She worked nights at one of Pakenham's nursing homes, and let them in. Bluey was there. He missed his master but at home always welcomed visitors and barked a greeting. Jo and Bluey hit it off. Melody expressed their condolences then began questioning the widow.

'As you know, Kylie, we're pretty sure Max met with foul play.' She nodded. 'With his expert camping skills and love for his dog, there is no way he would have camped where he did and left Bluey on his own.'

Kylie beckoned Bluey who sat next to her. She nodded. Jo wasn't sure if the widow kept quiet to stop from crying. Melody continued.

'Did Max have any enemies, money troubles or work problems?'

She spoke for the first time. 'No.' Short answers were in vogue.

'How was his health? No problems with his heart, no sign of cancer or something else serious?'

Again she shook her head then decided to talk. 'There's no way he would kill himself. He was not that sort of a man. He used to reckon people with depression were weak. Even if he was sick, he would always go to work. He would never ever leave Bluey.' The dog's ears twitched at the mention of his name and by someone he knew.

'What about family and friends? Is there anyone we could talk to who might know something?'

More head shaking from Kylie. 'His best mate, *only* mate is Finn Ruby, and his only family is his brother, Shorty, but they were as shocked as me.'

'Shorty?' queried Melody. 'Was he the tall guy at the morgue?'

'His name's Graeme but because he's six seven, everyone calls him Shorty.'

'Sounds logical.'

'Max was only five ten.'

'A Collingwood six-footer,' said Jo with Kylie nodding, and Melody clueless.

'Can we have details for Shorty and, what did you say Max's friend's name is?'

'Finn Ruby.'

Jo took notes as Kylie found the details for Shorty and Finn.

The DS seemed to be running out of questions. He looked at Jo; she looked at Kylie. 'May we have a look around his study, bedroom and garage? We're up against it, Kylie. His vehicle and equipment are being examined by Forensics but anything from here would be great.'

Kylie led them down the hall. 'Our bedroom's down here. I don't think Max would know what a study was. The garage and his shed are out the back.'

'I'll start in here, Sarge, if you want to try the yard.'

Melody felt uneasy about being told, albeit politely, what to do by a junior officer but away he went. Kylie stayed with Jo who, pulled on gloves and started a gentle search, looking at photos then looking under the bed. She stood and pointed to one side.

There was a romantic novel on one bedside table, and Jo pointed to the opposite side. 'That's Max's side, right?' Kylie nodded and looked uncomfortable. 'I don't know too many men who read Mills and Boon.'

Kylie tried again to smile. 'Tea or coffee?' she asked.

'Thanks, I'd love a cuppa; milk no sugar please,' and Kylie left then popped back in again.

'And your mate?'

'Oh don't worry about him. He'll be in the shed looking at the women on the Pirelli calendar.'

Kylie nodded and disappeared. Jo moved to Kylie's bedside table opening the top drawer. Mundane minutiae stared back at her. The contents of the second drawer were more interesting, especially a wedding photo. Then it was over to the victim's side of the bed. Nothing of interest in the top drawer but in the second she withdrew a receipt from a gun shop for the purchase of ammunition, a booklet from a funeral service, and a map with handwritten directions. She took photos of the receipt, the map, and the funeral booklet noting a handwritten phone number on the back.

Kylie arrived with a mug of tea and a packet of cheap biscuits. 'Sorry,' she said, 'it's the maid's day off.'

Jo laughed and took the tea. 'Thanks, oh my favourites,' she said dunking a shortbread.

'Any luck in the garage or shed?' asked Jo as she and Melody headed back towards Melbourne.

'I got nothing; you?'

'Could be. Max recently bought shotgun cartridges, went to a funeral, and has a map with handwritten directions.'

'To where?'

'Not sure. I took photos.'

'We'll need to talk to his brother and his mate. Who first?'

'We might catch Shorty at his brother's place.'

Melody looked at her. He'd heard Jo Best was good but this was the first time he'd seen her smart work in action. 'Meaning?'

'I think the brother-in-law is comforting the widow in her grief.'

'And you know that because?'

'Well the bed hadn't been made properly, and Max's side was disturbed right down to the foot of the bed.'

'Long legs you mean?'

'And under the bed were a pair of men's slip-ons worn I'm guessing by Gulliver on his travels to Lilliput.'

'You've lost me.'

'And there was a faint dust outline on the wall in the corridor where a photo once hung, again I'm guessing, for many years.'

Melody sniffed. If both detectives were being assessed on their inspection skills, she was an A+ student and he barely scraped a pass. 'Even if you're right, the photo could have been anything.'

'True,' said Jo, 'but there's a wedding photo of the happy couple in the bottom drawer of Kylie's bedside table, upside down and complete with dust on the top of the frame.'

'Wow,' whistled Fletcher, 'it's true what they say about Bestie.'

Jo smiled and they discussed the possibility of the widow and brother having the motive and opportunity to knock off poor old Max.

'Kylie and Shorty would know the method of killing was hopelessly contrived, hopefully putting them in the clear,' said Jo.

'Because we'd never see them as being so stupid?'

'Double bluff,' added Jo. 'Why don't we try the mate at his garage in Ringwood?' Melody nodded. 'You can exit at Eastlink, Sarge.'

'Will the widow be home?' asked Baldwin as he and DS Fletcher headed for the nearby suburb of Doncaster.

'Could be. She works in the local library and is on bereavement leave.'

'So tell me again why we're still interviewing her?'

'I think it's called "for the purposes of elimination". We know her old man was loaded and she's the sole beneficiary. She has an alibi for the night but standing to inherit a small fortune, did she have someone else knock him off?'

Baldwin wasn't keen. 'And if she did, you reckon she'll break down and confess?' Fletcher looked at the Senior Constable. Baldwin argued. 'She's one cool female, Sarge. If she's involved, she won't come easy.'

'Patience, Sunshine and all will be revealed.'

The door was opened by the Fischer's teenage grandson, 14, a student and breeder of acne.

'Gran's not home,' said Timmy. 'She's gone to feed Winston. You can come in and wait. She won't be long.'

The police were aware of interviewing a minor without an appropriate adult so sat and discussed Timmy's education and favourite football team. It turned out to be Manchester United thanks to his now deceased grandfather. Time ticked by and the detectives made eye signals wondering how much longer they should wait.

'Gran's not usually this long. She goes to Penelope's house, the one in Melbourne, to feed Winston when Penny's at her beach house.'

Both men wanted to ask about Penny but knew that way madness lies. Then a car arrived, and Mrs Fischer came in at a lively pace. The detectives took note. She flicked the passive aggressive switch.

'Did we have an appointment?' she said, her temper on a slow burn.

'No, Mrs Fischer,' said Fletcher, 'but we were in the area and had a couple of questions.'

'And interviewing a child without an appropriate adult present must surely be illegal.'

'It is,' replied Fletcher. 'Timmy asked us in to wait and we only discussed his studies and favourite football team, and despite it being Manure United, we decided to hang around.'

The pathetic quip fell flat and Timmy wanted to help. 'And Winston,' he said turning his grandmother's anger into a rage.

'You what?' she snapped at her grandson who flinched. The police looked on with interest as Mrs Fischer gave Master Fischer the rounds of the lounge room. 'I told you never to discuss Penny with anyone.'

'I'm sorry,' whispered her bullied boy. The detectives were hooked. The widow played it badly. Had she been calm and brushed aside her grandson's comments, the issue—whatever it was—may well have been forgotten. But now her tantrum piqued the cops' interest.

'Go to your room,' said Grandma, and Timmy departed without a sideways look at the detectives. His grandmother had no qualms in staring at both men. 'I don't appreciate you calling at my home when I'm not here, and certainly not interviewing my grandson who is a child.' Those last few words were loaded with anger. Fletcher used the woman's anger to his advantage. He knew people who lose their rag often lose their logic, and thus say and/or do silly things.

'Look, Mrs Fischer, Timmy simply explained your absence, how you were doing a friend a favour by feeding her cat. No harm done.' That seemed to work and Liz dropped a notch or two on the upset scale. Then Fletcher pounced. 'You should be congratulated for continuing to help a friend while she's away at her beach house when you are grieving.'

He left it there but she didn't. Her blood pressure soared and she was ready to scream, "How dare you?". Fletcher milked her sudden loss of temper then pushed harder.

'Did Penelope know your husband?'

'No. She only met him once and had nothing to do with him.'

'That's for the police to decide, Mrs Fischer,' replied Fletcher. 'Who is Penny and how does she know your husband?'

The widow's mood and body language threatened to catch fire. She couldn't hide her annoyance. 'She's a friend I met at our Book Club. We share interests in reading and nature. She has a house in Sorrento and I sometimes visit her. When she's away, I feed her cat and change its litter tray. She has no connection to my husband. So can you please ask your questions and stop wasting time on someone who has absolutely nothing to do with my husband's murder?'

The detectives wanted more information on Andrew's finances and what his widow knew of the finances at the soccer club. Did he discover corruption or mismanagement and tell his wife? Is that why he was murdered?

'I have no knowledge of the soccer club's finances. Andrew never spoke about his work. After a match, I could tell from his mood if the team won or lost. Now, is that all?'

Charley Baldwin asked a cheeky question. 'What was his mood after a draw?'

Again she glared and her mood became white hot when they asked for Penny's name and address. She gave them the details through gritted teeth and the detectives left, each with their own flea in an ear.

Chapter 19

Cain came back into the hospital and struggled. The doctor took him to see Nipper and the condition of his father was shocking. Nipper was seriously ill. Cain's confusion pushed him to ask more questions.

'Can my father hear us?' he asked the doctor. She moved away from Nipper. Cain joined her. 'Please Doctor, when do you think my father will recover, and do you think my wife and I are able to look after him?'

The female medico copped these types of questions often. 'As you can see, he's had a major stroke, and may not ever fully recover.' Cain swallowed. 'He may regain some movements, but he'll need a great deal of therapy to get back to any form of normality. As for you and your wife caring for him, that depends on many factors. Some families take in an elderly parent or parents while others feel the best care is found in a nursing home. When your father leaves, it'll most likely be in a wheelchair and your home, if not already, will need updating to cater for someone with severe disabilities.'

'I'm a handyman; I can do that.'

She wanted to be brutally honest. 'Special facilities in the bathroom, ramps, no steps, et cetera, and unless you and your wife are physically able to become his carers, you could damage your health and possibly your relationship. I've seen families suffer after taking on the care of an elderly dependant parent. Is your wife keen to help?'

Nipper said, 'Sure,' quickly, too quickly. 'Can I speak to him now?'

'Of course, but be prepared as he may not answer you or do so in a strange and hard to understand way. Okay?'

Cain nodded and followed the doctor.

Nipper wasn't going anywhere. The sheets with hospital corners kept him "incarcerated". Meet Nipper the permanently retired crim.

'G'day Dad, it's me, Cain.' Nipper's eyes became his words.

The doctor explained. 'His speech will need time to recover but he can hear and understand you.' She looked at Cain who again had tears in his eyes. 'I'll leave you alone, Mr Reid. Come and see me later.'

Cain knew he had to be strong. His mother was in respite. She was due home next week. What home? The house was there but her carer, the only relative to look after her, lay in a hospital bed unable to move.

Cain chose not to mention his mother. He talked about Nipper's grandkids and the latest footy results. No mention of Rosa. He squeezed his father's hand, promised to return tomorrow, leant in and kissed his old man then left. He didn't look for the doctor. He knew the answers. He wanted out of this hospital.

Forget going home, he headed straight for the nearest hardware store. His mind was made up. He had tools and timber aplenty at home but no paint. He remedied that situation.

When home, he ignored Rosa. She saw him put items in the garage. She left him alone, and didn't ask about her father-in-law, not wanting to hear bad, possibly terrible news. Her hatred for Nipper lay dormant in the back of her mind.

Half an hour later, she heard banging sounds and went downstairs to what was once the games room for their kids. She entered and swirls of dust attacked her. Waving a hand in front of her face, she yelled.

'Cain!' He stopped hammering. 'What the hell are you doing?'

'What does it look like and, Nipper's fine; thank you for asking.'

There was anger and hatred aplenty amongst the renovations.

'I hope you're not doing what I think you're doing.'

Cain gave her both barrels. 'He's had a massive stroke, Rosa. He's helpless, can't feed or wash himself. His speech is a mix of slurring and dribbles. I assume he wears a nappy.'

'I'm sorry,' she said with about 5% sincerity. 'But he can't live here.' Cain picked up his hammer. 'Even if you put in facilities, he'll need 24 hour care. Who's gunna look after him when you're at work?'

'I'll get a nurse.'

'And what happens if she's late or off sick or quits because he's a vegetable and needs professional care? In a nursing home that's what he'll get. You can visit every day if you like. It's not the best solution, Cain, it's the *only* solution.'

'He's not lost his marbles. He'll know he's living with strangers, and been abandoned by his family.'

'Sell your parents' house and put them both in the same nursing home. They have places for couples.'

Cain flared looking ferocious. 'That would be worse than him being on his own. Mum doesn't know him. She'll think a strange bloke is in her room. She'll start screaming and depress him even more.'

Rosa was losing the argument. 'Turning this into a parents' retreat is crazy. You're sacrificing your life and stopping your father from getting the best care.'

Cain was determined. 'This is something I want to do, *have* to do. I will not let him die surrounded by strangers. He's never forgotten what happened to Tommy, and every day he suffers for what happened.'

'*He* suffers?' She yelled. '*He* suffers?'

As her volume rose, his level climbed to match it. 'How many more times? It was an accident, Rosa. He didn't mean to do it, and if he could take it back he would do so in an instant.'

She pointed at her husband. 'I do not want him in this house.'

'Fine, this is the annexe. He'll live here, you'll live upstairs and neither of you will ever meet.'

The hatred and despair she'd allowed to fester for decades made it easy for Rosa to object. He tried to reason.

'When your parents were crook, I built a ramp to help them stay in their home until they couldn't. I took your father to games. I went to visit him when you put him in a home. I did my bit.'

'Yes, but my father didn't kill my son.'

'*Your* son?' Cain exploded. 'He's *our* son!' He grabbed the hammer and, without thinking, flung it. Rosa screamed, ducked, and the hammer smashed against the wall. She fled in fear. He froze in shock.

Jesus, what have I done? I might have killed her.

Finn Ruby had been mates with Max Bowman since they were kids. Finn ran a panel beating business and the cops pulled up in his forecourt. They wandered inside.

'Finn Ruby?' asked Melody.

'Yeah,' said the boss. The detectives settled in the company office which was last cleaned when St Kilda won the premiership. Before the subject of Max's death could be broached, Finn let rip.

'This was dead set a murder. If criminals are supposed to be stupid, whoever killed Max gets the prize for Idiot of the Century. Have you arrested who done it yet?'

'Not yet, Mr Ruby,' said Melody looking at his watch, 'it's only just gone lunchtime.'

Finn pretended to miss the sarcasm and continued his rant. 'What idiot would try and make it look like an accident or suicide? Max was never depressed and started camping when he was a kid.'

'His wife told us that,' said Melody.

'That slag,' snapped Finn, his anger out on show.

Jo jumped in. 'We reckon she's friendly with Shorty.'

She surprised Finn and Melody. 'Friendly? Is that what you call it? They're at it like bloody rabbits.'

Melody sensibly pulled back and let Jo run with this topic.

'How do you know?'

'Max told me. He has, had a mate who lives near their house. Whenever Max went camping, that big streak of shit would rock up and stay the night. What? To play Monopoly?'

'So Max knew about their affair?'

'Of course he knew.'

'Well why didn't Max tell his brother to get lost or why didn't Kylie divorce him?'

Finn didn't answer. He sniffed. The detectives looked at him but he didn't make eye contact.

'Finn?' asked Melody.

'Because Max said if she divorced him he'd kill her.'

The detectives took a breather. 'Would he do that?' asked Melody.

Finn nodded. 'He's always had a wild side. When we were young, we were mad on motors. He was magic with engines. He could hot up any car; make it sound like a jet. He was basically a nice guy but we drank too much, chased birds, and drove way too fast, and if anyone crossed him, he could lose his temper big time. If Kylie went for a divorce, he would see it as a real humiliation.' Finn remembered their youth. 'Oh yes, killing his wife would never faze Max Bowman.'

Jo and Melody left the panel beater and headed for the nursery in Croydon owned by the dead man's brother, and apparently the current lover of Max's widow.

'Should be pretty easy to find him,' said Jo. 'He'll be the giant amongst the pansies.'

Melody laughed. He took his time assessing his junior partner. He heard she was the smartest detective in the squad, and witnessed an example of that in the Bowman house. The missing photo—why was it taken down in the first place?—and the unmade bed featuring a certain pair of long legs, were clever observations.

'We have two topics for Shorty,' said Melody. 'His response to the allegation he is shagging his sister-in-law, and his alibi for the 24 hours before his brother was murdered.'

'So you reckon it's a Cain and Abel scenario, Sarge?' asked Jo.

Melody's parents were atheists and he'd never even heard of, let alone read, the Book of Genesis. He sniffed to cover his ignorance.

'Let's stick to those two topics,' he said, not wanting to admit he didn't have a clue what she meant.

They drove in silence for a while until Melody broached a delicate subject. 'So how come you're back on the job so soon after DI Richelieu's attack?'

She looked at him wondering if he was asking out of genuine interest, trying to get under her skin, or draw her into a confession.

'Someone told me when you fall off the horse, Sarge, the best remedy is to jump back on as soon as possible.'

He nodded. 'Good for you.' Neither spoke for a while. 'So what's the latest with the DI?'

Jo wondered if the relatively new DS knew about her relationship with Pierre. 'He's a fighter and all his friends and colleagues are betting he'll be out of ICU any day now.' He was but Jo kept quiet about Pierre's progress knowing it could be one step forward and two steps back. Her chest ached as she desperately hoped he continued to make progress.

Melody changed the subject and Jo thought he might be half-decent. She'd met a few unusual officers, Steele and Blunt being two examples, and fortunately the good guys outweighed the pricks.

They pulled up outside a large nursery. Melody surprised Jo by asking her to lead and to go hard. They wandered towards the office. The only staff member, towering over the plants, served a customer. He looked back at the detectives. 'Be with you in a minute,' said Shorty.

'No hurry,' said DS Melody.

When he approached the detectives, he knew they weren't interested in native plants for their 5 acre plot beyond Lilydale.

'You're cops,' he said, confident he was right.

They showed their ID and introduced themselves. Shorty was expecting a visit, and thought they would express their condolences, and ask a few questions about his brother's enemies and financial situation. He wasn't expecting their first question, and coming from the female officer gave him a serious fright.

'How long have you been sleeping with your sister-in-law?' asked Jo with a deadpan expression. The shock on Shorty's face was priceless.

'What the ...' he gasped and froze.

'It's a simple question, Mr Bowman,' said Melody who couldn't stop himself from jumping in.

Jo reckoned it was a rhetorical question so moved on. 'Where were you last Tuesday night from 6 pm and for the next 24 hours?'

Shorty was in strife. His love life was obviously front page news, and now he was a possible suspect in his brother's murder. He decided to make a grab for the moral high ground and, being a giant, he went pretty close but missed and crashed back to earth.

'I don't have to answer your questions,' he fumed. 'What right have you got to come barging in here accusing me of being involved in my brother's terrible death?'

'You don't want us to answer that, do you Mr Bowman?' asked Melody who again couldn't allow his colleague to run the show.

Shorty tried to sound threatening. 'I'm saying nothing without my solicitor.'

Jo teased him. 'Go on, I bet you haven't even got one. You heard that line on the *Underbelly* series.'

It was a smart retort made even more powerful because it was true.

Melody followed up with one of his own. 'Don't leave town, Mr Bowman. We'll talk again soon.'

The DS turned and walked back to the car with Jo following. Shorty needed the loo.

'Can you drop me near St V's, Sarge?' asked Jo as they left the freeway heading up Victoria Parade for the CBD. She didn't offer an explanation.

'Sure,' said Melody and didn't ask why but then added, 'if the DI asks, what do I say?'

'She won't ask,' said Jo. Melody needed time to translate that. 'And over here will be fine.' He pulled over and she got out. 'Thanks, Sarge. See you soon.'

She darted across Victoria Parade, her mind buzzing with conflicting thoughts. *I know I love him. Does his precarious health influence my feelings? Do I feel sorry for Pierre? Am I here because he changed his will? Why do I cry when I think of him and his current predicament?*

Climbing the stairs to the ICU she bumped into Grant Buchanan descending.

'Good afternoon, Jo. How are you?'

'Hello Doctor.'

'Grant,' he said smiling.

'Grant. How's the patient?'

'See for yourself. Come and find me before you go. Bye.'

The encounter put her nervous nerves on edge.

Surely if Pierre was at death's door he would have said.

She entered the ward and nearly died. Nurse Katrina was arm in arm with Detective Inspector Richelieu in what was a poor interpretation of a walk. Smiles went off like crackers.

'Ma fille chérie,' exclaimed Pierre and nearly fell. Katrina held on tightly and Jo flew to Pierre's other side to help. He tried to turn his head pursing his lips. Jo was intent on keeping him upright and didn't see the offer to osculate. The nurse saw the romantic byplay and shrieked with laughter. Jo looked up to see what was funny, then kissed the patient in a short, sharp smacker. They stood still.

'What are you doing?' Jo demanded of the Frenchman.

'I am in training for the marathon, mon chérie.'

More laughter and assistance finally saw Pierre back in his bed. His regulation hospital attire did nothing for his dress sense or privacy. With the patient tucked in and sitting up, Katrina took her leave. Pierre held out a hand and Jo took it. Their eyes met and she moved in and kissed him, properly this time.

'It is wonderful to see you, Joanna. As usual you look, 'ow you say, slightly more attractive than sensational.'

She smiled and felt her stomach wanting to speak. 'If you are allowed out of bed, surely you have earned your promotion from ICU.'

Pierre boasted. 'But of course and soon, I 'ope and pray, I will move to a general ward.'

'But Pierre, that's brilliant.' Her tears welled.

'I am inspired to recover by the girl of my dreams.'

Oh God, I'm going to cry again. Jo's tears were interrupted by Katrina. 'Tea or coffee, Jo?' she asked. Jo placed her order and pulled a chair close to the bed. Pierre was ebullient.

'Tell me about your detection triumphs, s'il vous plait, so I can rejoice with you.'

'Dull and boring I'm afraid; progress but at a super slow pace.'

'Still there are two 'omicides?'

'Oui, and DI Rose has allotted teams to each murder committed about 240 kilometres apart, but I am thinking outside the box to see if they are in any way connected.'

'Ah, the brilliant Joanna Best mind, always creative. But enough talking shop because I 'ave something to ask my favourite detective.'

Jo's mouth went dry but before Pierre continued, Katrina arrived with refreshments.

'Katrina,' said Jo, 'I can't believe the progress Pierre has made; no doubt due to you and your wonderful medical team.'

The nurse smiled. 'We aim to please.'

'They are all magnifique,' gushed Pierre.

Katrina checked on Pierre's readings. 'Now don't you go getting ahead of yourself, Monsieur. Slow and steady progress is what you need.' She turned to Jo. 'I'll see you later.'

The visitor settled and studied the patient. He'd made remarkable progress in the relatively short time he'd been in hospital, and even more so in the last few days.

'Detective, pass me that envelope s'il vous plait.' Jo did and Pierre opened it and produced a document. 'Mademoiselle, this is a legal document establishing for me an enduring power of attorney. My lawyer in Paris 'as recommended a Melbourne lawyer who 'as produced this document.'

Jo's face couldn't disguise her fear. 'Pierre,' she said but he interrupted.

'As a lawyer, Mademoiselle, you will know all about this document.'

Jo nodded. 'I do.'

'Then I wish for you, Joanna Claire Best, to become my enduring power of attorney. Please, will you do this honour for me, your friend and admirer, the man who cannot 'elp but adore you?'

'Of course,' said Jo without thinking, 'but you are getting better, Pierre, and you're a young man.' He laughed and it hurt him to do so. 'You should be planning your new life when you leave hospital.'

'Ah,' said Pierre with eyebrows raised. 'My new life, you say. What will it be, s'il vous plait?' He looked into her eyes. 'What do you think I could do if I am no longer a gendarme?'

Jo struggled. 'Pierre, you ask difficult questions. Your life has been changed, forever, and you will need to think about your choices but not today. You have plenty of time to decide.'

'It may be difficult to choose what I do but easy to choose with whom I do it.' Their eyes were working overtime. Not knowing what he might say next caused her heartrate to accelerate. Not knowing how she would respond made it even faster.

'Pierre, we haven't talked about your attack, those responsible for it, and what you did in changing your will. We need to talk about those things. But not before you recover, and regain your strength and health. It's all I care about now, and all I will care about until you reach the best condition you can.' She paused. 'Have I made myself clear, Inspector?'

'Always,' he smiled.

'So, please Pierre, can we agree on one thing? You get a full medical discharge from this institution, and then we'll sit down and discuss everything about the past, the present and our future. Agreed?'

He smiled. 'ow could I not? And I like so much the part about *our* future. 'owever, Mademoiselle, there is one important condition.'

Jo sighed. 'Oh please, Pierre. We made a deal.'

'The condition being on every visit you make to see me, I am allowed to kiss you at least twice.'

Jo slumped. She was expecting a tricky condition putting her under real pressure when in fact his request was one she would agree to without thinking. He held out both hands. She moved to him, placed her hands either side of his head and kissed him tenderly. Neither chose to stop. Jo stood back when she heard footsteps.

'Are you still here?' asked Grant Buchanan. 'Who is solving the homicides of Melbourne?'

'Of Victoria, Doctor,' she replied. 'And yes, I must be going.'

The doctor addressed Pierre. 'I keep hearing good things about you, Inspector. What is driving you to get better and leave? Is it something or some*one*?'

Pierre put on a hurt persona. 'If you must know, it is the lack of French cuisine, Monsieur Médecin.'

All three laughed. Katrina appeared and Jo gave Pierre a wave and blew him a kiss.

'Mademoiselle,' he called, holding up the envelope and its contents. Jo came back.

'Ah,' said the doctor. 'Your colleague has asked me to be one of the signatories, Detective. He was very insistent.'

Jo looked at Dr Buchanan, Katrina and then Pierre. They were all smiling. She took the envelope, blew Pierre another kiss and left. She was halfway down the stairs when the doctor called.

'Jo, may I have a word?' He joined her. 'I think you should know a couple of things. Pierre has made great strides in his recovery, and we all hold high hopes he'll be able to leave and live a long albeit less active life.' Jo's stomach was on a double shift and wanted to head south. 'Having a car tyre roll over your body can trigger different reactions. The impact was between his groin and heart, and with his spleen removed, if that was the end of his problems, we'd be looking to move him to a general ward. And that may well happen. But I think you should be aware his situation may flare up when least you expect it.' He looked at her and her shock. 'Sorry to be so cold.'

'No, no,' said Jo. 'Your friend Jack Carr once told me about hanging black crepe.'

Grant smiled. 'And how is the GP par excellence? Give him my regards and tell him he owes me lunch.' The doctor squeezed Jo's arm. 'Good luck,' he smiled and darted back up the stairs.

She headed to Homicide and hoped to have run out of tears before she arrived.

Chapter 20

Jo arrived at Homicide as the meeting started and her arrival stopped proceedings. DI Blunt waited for the latecomer to cop a reprimand. None came. 'Good news, Senior?' asked the boss.

'Yes ma'am,' said Jo. Most knew she referred to DI Richelieu.

'And?'

'DI Richelieu has been moved from ICU to Advanced Care and was, with help, walking today.'

It was almost a cheer as a collective gasp of approval was heard; several applauded. Jo sat and DI Rose continued.

'Thank you, Senior, and long may it continue.' She steered the squad back to the cases. 'So nothing further on Mr Clunes,' who had been released without charge. 'What about Mr Hero?'

'He's in big trouble, ma'am,' said DS Fletcher. 'His alibi is shot with his bullied wife taking a stand against him, we think, for the first time, and his mistress dropping him right in it.'

'Meaning?' asked Rose.

'He could have been at the football club on the night, seen or heard the fight between Clunes and the coach, then, when Clunes left, Hero could have slipped in and stabbed the victim.'

'With Clunes' knife?' asked Billy Hughes.

Fletcher agreed. 'Yes, there's a problem explaining how it ended up back in the builder's ute but Hero could have put it there later that night or the next day. Clunes was slack with security and Hero knew his new address.'

Rose hated loose ends. 'Because the wife and mistress won't support his alibi doesn't mean they're telling the truth. Is the mistress lying to get back at him? Does she simply not want to be involved?'

Fletcher and Baldwin nodded. 'Could be, ma'am,' said Fletcher.

Rose surveyed the room. 'So is there anyone else for Fischer's murder? What about the widow?'

Charley Baldwin reported. 'The victim has substantial assets and his wife is the sole beneficiary. She's got a girlfriend and may have been planning to leave Mr Fischer and shack up with her.'

A buzz began. 'And how do we know that?' asked DI Rose.

Charley was less enthusiastic. 'The 14 year-old grandson let it slip.'

Rose flushed. 'What? He said that in front of his grandmother?'

Fletcher and Baldwin grimaced. 'No, ma'am, she hadn't arrived.'

Rose lost it. 'Oh no,' she groaned in disbelief. 'Tell me you didn't interview a minor by himself?' She shouted. 'Tell me!'

Fletcher hurried to explain. 'It wasn't an interview, ma'am. The kid invited us in saying his gran was due any time. We talked about his schooling and football. He came up with the grandmother's friend.'

Rose shook her head. 'And any half-decent barrister will make you look like conniving incompetents.' The silence lingered. 'What else?'

'The wife has a strong alibi for the night in question,' said Fletcher.

Rose was unhappy. Unsolved homicides were a real pain, plus a negative mark on her career prospects. But charging a suspect only to have him or her released because of lack of evidence or worse, discovering someone else had done it, was a sharp smack in the chops.

'Right, more work to do on the Fischer murder. Get the truth on the alibis and check out the wife's girlfriend.' Heads nodded. 'Now let's have news on our murder by tree.'

DS Melody began. 'It's a gum, ma'am, and I believe, *Eucalyptus radiata*.'

A big Ooooh filled the room. 'Smartarse,' was the most polite reaction.

Billy Hughes took over. 'The only suspects to date are the victim's wife and brother.'

'Her brother?' asked Rose.

'No his.' Billy indicated DS Melody. 'Rick.'

'The wife is sleeping with her brother-in-law, Graeme, known as Shorty because he's six seven or eight.'

'What's that in English?' asked the DI.

'About 204 centimetres, ma'am.'

'Go on.'

'Preliminary financial checks show the brother-in-law owns a nursery which is badly in debt. The victim was a self-employed tradie with healthy super, and sickness and death cover. With Max out of the way, the lovebirds collect the cash and ride off into the sunset.'

'Good motive. Evidence?' asked Rose.

'Circumstantial only, ma'am, but we reckon there's more to come.' He looked at Jo.

'The victim's best mate said Max was a violent man, and had threatened to kill his wife if she ever chose to divorce him.'

'What,' said Rose, 'the lovers were afraid of the victim so killed him out of fear?'

DI Blunt wanted in on the action. 'Why would the two people who knew the victim would never camp under a tree, kill him under a tree?'

Jo answered. 'Perhaps it's a sort of double bluff. His family knew his camping habits, so they killed him in an obviously contrived and stupid way to deflect attention from them.'

'What's happened with Forensics?' asked Rose.

Billy responded. 'Still waiting on the 4WD, tent and camping gear but reports suggest there was homemade drugging of the victim and now his dog.'

Everyone, including DI Rose, gasped. 'The dog was drugged?'

'Melbourne vet found traces of chamomile tea in the dog,' said Jo.

Rose thought it incredible. 'Tea?' she scoffed.

'It's supposedly a form of sedative. Meat is soaked in the tea.'

'Which suggests what?' asked Rose.

No immediate reply. DS Fletcher had a go. 'Could be amateur assassins or clever dicks trying a con.'

Rose nodded. 'Alibis?'

Melody replied. 'The wife was working in a nursing home in Pakenham but the brother refused to answer any more questions without his solicitor.'

'Right, bring him in, and chase up Forensics on the vehicle and equipment.' She clapped her hands. 'These are not crimes of the century. Put pressure on people; arrest and charge, if you please.'

The squad broke up and Rose approached Jo. 'Grab Billy and bring her to my office.' She did and the women wanted to hear about Pierre.

Jo explained. 'I couldn't believe it, ma'am. He was out of bed and walking with a nurse.'

Rose's eyes widened. 'He was walking?'

'He was leaning on her.'

'I bet he was,' said Billy and regretted saying that.

'I spoke to the doctor who gave me a mixed report.'

'Mixed?' asked Rose.

'Terrific progress to get where he has but they're worried the damage he suffered could cause problems down the line.'

There was silence. Rose and Billy had questions but chose not to ask them—for now. 'Thanks, Jo,' said the DI. 'See you tomorrow.'

Heading home, Jo checked her phone. She'd missed a call from Michael Chan. Waiting for her train she called him.

'Detective Senior Constable Best, a very good afternoon to you.'

'Hang on,' she said. 'You don't have Caller ID.' Silence. 'You have! Doctor Chan, you've let your Luddite membership lapse. Welcome to the real world.'

'Ha ha.'

'Michael, I'm sorry I missed your call.'

'So you should be. What happened to our dinner date?'

'Nothing, it's a matter of finding a time.'

'How about now?'

'Now?'

'I'm whipping up Pepper-Steak Stir-Fry.' Jo's mouth began to leak. He sniffed. 'The aromas in my kitchen are sen-sa-tion-al.'

'I thought we agreed to eat out.'

'We did but then I know you want to pick my brains on your tricky homicide, and a restaurant is not the ideal place.'

'Are you psychic?'

'And Alan has been asking when you're going to call.'

'Tell him I'll be there in an hour.'

'Great,' said Michael and grinned. His grin when alone was always bigger than his grin when with company. Alan wanted to try his master's starter.

At home, Jo rang Gabrielle Strange. She answered with her Gothic voice and appalling so-called joke. 'Strange speaking.'

'Good evening, am I speaking with the pathetic pathologist?' A cackle exploded. 'I'm tempted to say, "What's up, Doc",' said Jo.

'What's up, Dick,' said Strange still laughing.

'Can I drop in tonight, about 9? I need a sprinkling of sage advice.'

'The only sage here, girlie, is in my condiment drawer. See you then.'

Click. Jo smiled at the attitude, philosophy and language of the pathologist. *If I had to take someone to a desert island*, thought Jo, *Gabrielle Strange would definitely be on the list.*

As she walked along the side of Michael Chan's warehouse cum studio, she remembered how they first met and how he readily agreed to help her sort a problem. Jo's mother, Shirley, had been defrauded, a victim of catfishing, and in trying to help her Mum, Jo discovered Michael Chan was the best IT expert in town; probably the country. Since then the two had worked on several cases and, despite many hair-raising moments and near misses, they always greeted the judge.

His tech equipment told him she was on the property, and he opened the door as she arrived. Both remembered a recent meeting in this place. Embarrassment reigned. Both were determined to avoid such a misunderstanding again.

She leant in and kissed his cheek. He purred as they strolled towards the kitchen/dining component of his cavernous warehouse. Jo couldn't figure out why, wherever they sat, it was never cold. Michael's engineering skills matched his IT expertise. Alan the cat showed off his perfect manners. Jo bobbed down and the cat purred and rubbed against her thigh. His master fancied such a move.

The food was delicious. *Is Michael Chan the perfect husband?* Jo remembered how she once told Michael he would make a wonderful wife. Today, such a remark was definitely not a good idea. Jo asked him about his work, most of which was so technical he might have been talking Russian. He steered her round to the cases.

She described both homicides always stating only facts and never opinions. *Let him take the details and draw the conclusions.*

'The others don't agree but I have a nagging suspicion the cases are connected,' said Jo.

'What, with hundreds of kilometres between crime scenes, widely different methods of killing, and no known connection between the victims? I like your optimism, Detective. You always were one for outrageous theories.'

Jo's face shouted disappointment. They were such good friends, both could say exactly what they thought without fear of causing offence. Oh, except for straying into the field of romance.

'Thanks for nothing, Michael. May I have more of your superb coffee?'

'Of course,' he said, pouring. 'And you're probably right.'

'What?' she gasped. He gave his half grin. 'You bastard, you've known all along.'

He ummed. 'Perhaps not known but I did have an inkling.'

'So tell me where, how, what's the key?'

'You're missing your third monkey.'

She felt her heartbeat quicken. This man had a mind to worship but he could be bloody annoying when teasing out his reply. 'Third monkey?' asked Jo.

'Oh come on,' encouraged Michael, 'see no evil, hear no evil, and speak no evil.'

Jo still hadn't cracked it until the lightbulb glowed. 'The cuts on the eyebrow and tongue,' she cried.

'You need a third corpse with a cut on its ear.'

'Michael, you're brilliant. The same person or people killed both men because of something they said or saw.'

He wasn't sure. 'Possibly but what about this third homicide? Is there anything on the books? It could be a missing person or a so-called accidental death?'

'I don't think so. I would've heard.'

'If a body turns up with a small cut on its ear, you'll have the set.'

Jo sat on the settee. Alan hopped up on her lap and enjoyed his ears being stroked.

'Your theory reeks of possibilities, Michael, but what if no third body turns up?'

'What if it has already?'

'Sorry?'

'Maybe body number three has already arrived.'

Jo loved the way Michael's thinking kept pushing the boundaries.

'You mean dead but not murdered?'

'Possibly, or not believed to be murdered.' They fell silent. 'What have you done to discover any connection between your two bodies?'

'Both widows were asked if they knew the name of the other victim and both said no.'

'And searching the victim's houses, places of work, vehicles and such produced nothing?'

'Not that I've heard.' Jo took out her phone. 'I found items in the camper's bedside table.' She flicked through her photos. 'There was a map with whacky directions, a receipt for ammunition and a funeral booklet.'

'And?'

'Nothing made sense.' She looked harder. 'There's a phone number scribbled on the funeral booklet.'

'And?' said Michael again.

Jo looked at him. 'I rang it several times and it went to a recorded voicemail.' He simply stared at her. She twigged. 'You couldn't?' she asked remembering what this man could do with digital software.

'I couldn't what?' he asked taking her phone. He went to his control panel which consisted of hardware major corporations would love to own. She put Alan on the settee and followed Michael.

Lights came on and machines whirred. He typed the mobile phone number into a piece of software. He watched the screen, one of many he used, and typed again. More data appeared and finally, Michael pushed back his chair inviting Jo to look at the result.

She gasped when she read the name of the person listed as the owner of the mobile phone number she found in Max Bowman's bedside table.

Dieter Fischer.

She was almost home having forgotten her date with Gabrielle Strange. So excited was she at having a definite link between the two homicides, Gabrielle had slipped her memory. The suburbs involved, Northcote (Michael), Fitzroy North (Gabrielle), and Clifton Hill (Jo), were adjoining so doubling back was not an issue.

Gabrielle opened her door. 'I thought you'd stood me up.' She set off down her polished wooden floor hallway and propped in the kitchen. Jo followed then felt terrible—no chocolates.

'Oh Gabrielle,' she said, 'please forgive me.' Such was Jo's sincerity, the good medico genuinely thought a dreadful event had taken place.

'What?' she asked, alarmed.

'I forgot the drugs.'

Gabrielle roared as much with relief and poured Jo's coffee. 'Unforgiveable, Detective,' she said producing a box of expensive dark beauties. They tucked in and Jo buzzed about her new discovery. She told Gabrielle her news of the link between the two homicide victims.

'I've told you before, girlie, you'll make yourself powerful enemies—showing up experienced cops makes 'em mad.'

'Not all of them, surely?'

'Some men especially,' said Strange. 'But even my elementary sleuthing skills tell me you didn't come here to gloat about your breakthrough. You want to talk about the Frog.'

Jo slumped. She did want advice about Pierre. She described his solid progress, about what Dr Buchanan told her, and then explained the Enduring Power of Attorney request from Pierre.

'Interesting,' said Gabrielle.

'I'm sorry, Gabrielle, but I don't want a commentary. I want advice.'

The doctor pondered her reply. She loved the young woman and could think of nothing better than to guide her in this difficult time.

'I don't think Pierre is perverse.' Jo was shocked. 'I don't think he's trying to trap you.' Now Jo was confused. 'He doesn't want to trick you into marriage. Apart from being hopelessly in love with you, he trusts you. He believes if anything happens to him, you are the one person he wants to make decisions on his behalf.'

Jo thought about the answer. 'You mean if he dies?'

'Dies or becomes so ill, he's out of it. He wants you to control his affairs.'

'It's a financial and personal power of attorney; it's not for medical matters.' Gabrielle shrugged. Jo felt tears well up. 'How can I say no?'

Strange looked at the detective. 'You can't,' she said. 'So help him.'

DI Rose and Billy Hughes both received the same text.

Ma'am and Sarge
There may be a link between the
homicides. Bowman had Fischer's
phone number in a drawer of his
bedside table. More in the morning.
Jo

DI Rose heard her phone ping and looked at the message. She wasn't surprised at the news or who sent it. She wondered how Jo Best found the link, and if her discovery would help solve either or both homicides.

Billy Hughes was in the bath when her phone pinged. She called to her husband. He was often the office boy for his wife's late night messages and pushed his wheelchair to her phone. 'Is it important?' she called.

'It's from Jo Best,' replied hubby and read the text.

'That girl,' said Billy and slipped beneath the bubbles.

Mind you, both female detectives would be confused in the morning when they received details of an arrest involving domestic violence. The uniformed constables at the scene were told what the attacker said to his victims.

Those words threw a spanner in the works of the Fischer and Bowman investigations.

Chapter 21

It was dark and the house had no outdoor lighting on a timer. Inside, the kitchen light threw its beams to the driveway. The intruder crept along ducking behind the car in the carport in case someone happened to look out the window. The darkness helped the intruder. He heard a woman talking to children; time for bed. The intruder paused, listened and waited. His heartrate accelerated. When the voices inside fell quiet, he crept to the darkened back yard.

There was a flyscreen door, never locked. The intruder slowly opened it causing the hinges to groan. He let this opened door rest against his body and slowly tried the main door handle. Once fully turned, he paused ready to enter, pushed hard and hit a brick wall. This wasn't Fort Knox but the locked door didn't budge.

He froze and listened. No sound came from within, and then the light in the kitchen went out. There was no-one in the back of the house. For the intruder, it was now or never. He wanted the element of surprise but if a forced entry was required, then crash and bash it was. He wished he had one of those sausage-shaped metal objects the cops use to break down a door, the so-called enforcer or big red key.

The lock was about halfway up the height of the door. Turning the handle to make sure the latch bolt was withdrawn; the intruder leaned back then threw his left shoulder against the door, level with the lock.

His shoulder wanted to scream as the pain exploded but the cheap plywood door didn't fancy a fight and waved the white flag. The noise of the splintering door was loud. The intruder crash-landed on the kitchen floor.

The light came on, a woman appeared and screamed. She was a good screamer. Scrambling to his feet and suffering great pain, the intruder pointed at the woman and yelled. 'Come here, bitch.'

She'd already grabbed a frying pan, often used though not often cleaned, and swung it at the man. He saw it and instinctively raised his left arm—the one attached to the throbbing shoulder—and copped a crack on his elbow. His right arm and shoulder were pain free but dear God, his left side needed the largest Panadol ever created.

Despite his agony reaching 7.3 on the Richter scale, the intruder reckoned he could defeat the woman, that is until a man appeared and pushed the odds dramatically in favour of the residents. The two men traded ineffective blows with no points awarded. The woman called the cops. The men swore, spat and struggled. The intruder grabbed the male resident in a headlock and warned him.

'I'll do you mate, just like I done that bastard at the soccer club.'

More threats, more amateur wrestling, before the woman and the previously used frying pan joined in for a second time, now tickling the intruder's right elbow. Whack! The excruciating pain had the intruder on the floor and beaten.

He lost the will to fight, and the uniformed constables arrived and made the arrest. As the cuffed and miserable attacker was dragged to his feet, the cops asked for his name.

He swore. The woman gave him up. 'He's Barry Clunes, my ex, and the man who murdered the soccer coach in Heidelberg.'

The cops looked at one another. What they thought was a domestic looked like being a step up in the arrest stakes. Neither had nabbed anyone for murder before.

'I heard him confess,' said the winner, 'we both did.'

She nodded. 'I'll do you mate, just like I done that bastard at the soccer club, is what he said,' and Barry landed in the back of a divvy van.

DI Blunt felt shithouse. His plan to bust organised crime and solve a homicide on his lonesome stalled. His contacts in the criminal fraternity gave him nothing. Desperation set in. He played his last card, went to the scene of the crime, and parked near the incomplete grandstand of the Heidelberg Rovers Soccer Club. What a mess; planning meetings, grants, tenders, contracts and all that work and for what? An eyesore as here stood failure, a useless end product.

A high cyclone wire fence protected the shell. Attached to the fence was a sign—Betta Security. Blunt wondered about the death of spelling as he looked on his phone for information. Betta Security's office was in Preston not far from Heidelberg. He had nothing else so drove there.

The Betta Security building had good security but no architectural merit. It was a box. Blunt entered Reception and decided to pull back a little on his usual bombastic approach. Maybe making a fool of himself at the Master Builders, and being given free footwear thanks to the Construction Workers Union tipped him towards being less of a prick.

'G'day,' said a bloke sitting alone in the office. 'Can I help you?'

Blunt showed his ID and even used a pronoun other than I. 'We're investigating that homicide at the Heidelberg Rovers Football Club.'

'Oh yeah,' said Bram Coker, the manager.

'Have you guys seen anything suspicious around the building site?'

Bram shook his head. 'We swing by a few times a night but we've never had any break-in or reports of stuff being nicked.'

'Would you know if something illegal was going on?'

'Like what?'

'Corruption, extortion, even murder.'

Bram's business was doing okay. Telling the cops about pilfering wasn't worth it. Murder and corruption were tricky subjects. Best to keep your head down and mouth shut. Callum would get nothing here.

He thanked the bloke—another seismic shift for Blunt—and headed for the door.

'Hang on,' said Bram. 'You might wanna have a word with one of the subbies, Mufti I think he called himself. He reckoned the job would never get finished because of the backhanders and shady deals.'

Blunt's heart pumped harder. 'Mufti? What, as in civilian clothes?' Blunt didn't know of the alternative definition, Islamic scholar.

Bram didn't know either definition. He shrugged. 'Adrian'll know.' He tapped his phone. 'Adrian and Mufti had a smoke together when Mufti worked overtime.' The phone was answered. 'It's Bram. Listen, how did you contact Mufti the subbie at Heidelberg?' Blunt's excitement grew. 'The cops are trying to solve that murder.' Adrian kept asking questions. 'Yes, there's a cop here now.'

Blunt slipped back into old habits. 'Tell him I want Mufti's number now.'

'Did you hear that?' Adrian had bad news. 'You haven't got it?'

Blunt's rollercoaster of emotions plunged back to Earth. 'Does he know anything?'

Bram listened then ended the call and explained. 'Adrian reckons he's a former digger who worked in counter-intelligence, and uses a code name to stop enemy agents from finding him.'

Blunt felt a thrill akin to sexual pleasure. His scheme took flight and became way, way better.

'Yes but how can I find him?'

'Adrian says he drinks in the Cherry Tree Hotel in ...'

'Cremorne,' said Blunt trying not to hop about like a lottery winner. *It's my local!*

He thanked Bram and set off for home. Life kept getting better.

Blunt lived a Jack Dyer drop punt from the pub. He dressed casual and wandered into the Cherry Tree Hotel. It was reasonably well patronised. He ordered a craft beer and tried to look relaxed. He had no idea what Mufti looked like and wondered if he relaxed in uniform. Weird. After a couple of minutes, the bartender approached and made small talk.

'Busy day?'

'So so,' said the detective wanting to ask one simple question.

'I haven't seen you in here before.'

'No, I'm on the road a bit.' The bartender nodded. 'Listen, you wouldn't know a guy who drinks in here called Mufti?'

The bartender looked surprised. 'What's your name?'

Callum felt trapped. *Why does he want my name?* Then he knew any smart-alec answer would backfire. 'Callum,' he said.

The bartender pointed at Blunt. 'Callum,' he said before pointing at a drinker a metre and a half away, 'meet Mufti.'

They greeted one another. 'Can I buy you a drink?' asked Blunt.

'Does Bill Gates have a dollar?' answered Mufti.

Callum saw an empty table. 'Over there,' he nodded. Mufti drained his glass and headed for the spot.

Blunt joined him with the drinks. 'I need your help. I'm a cop investigating a homicide at the Heidelberg Rovers Soccer Club.'

Mufti knew all about that place and the murder. He was 43, looked ten years older having bought his moustache from a walrus. 'Plenty of stories from that disaster,' he said, and Callum unconsciously licked his lips.

'I'm interested in your name. Were you once in uniform?'

'What? As opposed to once in royal David's city?'

Callum was lost. 'Sorry?'

'Special Ops, ADF, no can speak, if you get my drift.' Blunt nodded. 'So what do you want to know? The killer's name and inside leg measurement? Or how about details of corruption and backhanders which brought the house of cards a crashing down?'

Callum thought his trembling leg might be seen beneath the table. 'Are you serious? You know who killed the coach and who's corrupt?'

'I'm one of the subbies owed thousands, and unless a court case gets sprinkled with pixie dust, I'll be lucky to see a cent in the dollar.'

'I'm sorry,' said Blunt trying to sound sincere. 'But what I need is solid evidence. You once being in Special Ops would know all about that. Do you have anything concrete?'

Again Blunt winced, having mentioned that word, and thinking about his custom-made footwear.

Mufti took his time, produced his phone and tapped a few times. He placed the phone in front of Callum and hit Play. 'Does this help?'

Chapter 22

Jo arrived early. She knew DI Rose and Billy Hughes would want chapter and verse on the text she sent them last night. Charley Baldwin, who had never been late for anything, saw Jo arrive.

'Hello, here's trouble,' he joked then had a horrible feeling Jo was early because something terrible had happened to DI Richelieu.

'Good morning, Charley,' she said smiling and Baldwin relaxed. 'Is the DI in yet?'

'What have you done this time?' he asked. 'You've cracked one of the cases, you sneaky little minx.'

'No I haven't and ...' Jo stopped as DI Rose and Billy Hughes arrived. Squad members settled and waited.

'Good morning,' said Rose. 'Two important items uncovered in the last few hours. Detective Senior Constable Best has found a link between our two victims.' Members craved the news making Jo feel great. She wasn't sure why the DI hadn't contacted her for more details but felt less great when the second item was revealed. 'Last night Barry Clunes, our main suspect for the Heidelberg homicide, was arrested by uniformed officers over a domestic violence incident. At the arrest, he confessed to killing Dieter Fischer.'

For once in her life, Jo doubted the genius of Michael Chan.

Detectives had questions and then comments aplenty but Rose called for quiet asking Jo to tell all. She did.

'When I searched Max Bowman's bedroom, I found a funeral booklet for the former racing car driver, Brody Miller. On the back of the booklet someone, presumably Bowman, had written a phone number. I tried the number a few times but always got a recorded message. I put it to one side meaning to follow it up later.' Now Jo worried because explaining how she found the phone owner's name was not according to Hoyle. 'I passed it to the experts who came back with the name Dieter Fischer. And that's about it, ma'am.'

Billy was the first to speak. 'And by experts, do we mean Victoria Police's favourite IT specialist?'

Jo hesitated. 'Ah, there's an outside chance you might be on the right track there, Sarge.' Most officers followed this conversation. Melody and Blunt remained ignorant.

Rose wanted to move on. 'So one victim had the other victim's phone number; what does that mean?'

'Could be nothing,' said DI Blunt. 'They're mates from years ago who met by chance at a funeral and wanted to catch up later.'

He sounded reasonable. 'Anyone else?' asked Rose.

'Why did Clunes confess to uniformed police and not us?' asked DS Fletcher.

Rose explained. 'My understanding is he told the assault victims he would kill them just like he killed Fischer. The victims told the uniforms so the cops didn't actually hear Clunes confess.'

'We need him back in here pronto,' said Charley Baldwin.

'He's en route as we speak,' said Rose. 'But we need to explore this connection Jo found. Talk to the families of the victims. Does anyone remember their deceased family member talking about the other victim? Is there a relevant link and, if so, what is it? What else? DI Blunt; what's your news?'

'Getting there, ma'am. I've obtained amateur footage of a crime boss together with an official of the soccer club which may implicate both men in corruption. The video quality's pretty poor and I'm having it repaired as we speak.'

'Sounds good, Inspector but we're investigating two homicides. If you've rumbled organised crime, pass it to the relevant squad and concentrate on who murdered our victims.' Blunt nodded but fumed inside. 'SIOs in my office in ten; Jo in my office now.'

Jo entered the boss's office and remembered entering this room in her early Homicide days, and getting the best bollocking of all time. She was even sacked in this office. DI Rose was no such boss.

'Sit, Jo and tell all. Is this you and Michael Chan again?'

'Yes ma'am.'

'For God's sake don't let any prosecution fall over when a defence barrister has the case thrown out over illegal gathering of evidence.'

'I could obtain a warrant and do it officially.'

'See to it.'

'Ma'am.'

'So what's your theory?'

'My theory's looking shaky now Clunes confessed to killing Fischer.'

'Okay, what *was* your theory?'

She explained the Michael Chan three monkey idea with the tiny cuts linking the victims. 'The phone number reinforced the possibility but the third monkey, if it exists, is unknown.'

'Okay,' said Rose. 'Talk to Billy and work on the basis the victims knew one another. How did they know one another and ...' Rose didn't know what else to say.

'See if they were killed by the same person?' asked Jo.

'That'll do. I'll give you 24 hours.' Jo frowned. 'Okay, 48. Now go.'

Barry Clunes waited to be interviewed. Rose asked Billy Hughes and DS Melody to explore the claim the builder admitted murdering Dieter Fischer.

'I'm glad to see you're using a solicitor this time,' said Melody. Clunes grunted. He looked like a beaten man. His marriage, kids and livelihood were, for him, long gone. Whatever punishment he would cop from the cops was of little or no consequence.

I may as well be hung for a sheep as a lamb.

Billy gave him the usual warning and the interview began.

'Tell us about last night, Barry?' asked Billy Hughes.

'No comment,' he muttered with neither energy or spite.

Billy quickly assessed his mood. Badgering him, being sarcastic or even pleading would get nowhere. At first she tried the good news approach. Melody was impressed.

'Barry, Fraud detectives are investigating the Heidelberg Rovers accounts, and the contract between you and the club.'

Good move, Billy because Clunes lost his sullen insolence and showed a flicker of interest.

'Preliminary reports show various discrepancies which will need explaining from the President, Mr Hero.'

Clunes grunted. He spoke something other than no comment. 'It couldn't happen to a nicer bastard.'

'Not sure if any findings will assist you financially, Barry, but if we can eliminate you as a suspect in the Fischer homicide, you could have one or two big ticks against your name.'

His sarcasm returned. 'Whoopee.'

'The alleged assault last night doesn't look so good.' Clunes stared at Billy and remained tight lipped. 'Want to tell us about it?'

He was back on script. 'No comment.'

Billy sat back which was the pre-arranged signal for Melody to play the Bad Cop role.

'We have you at the crime scene at the time of the murder, your prints on the knife with the victim's blood, *your* knife, your motive of revenge after being ripped off by the President, your admission of punching the victim, and now, as of last night, your admission to your ex and her boyfriend that you killed Dieter Fischer. We call that a rock-solid case; watertight. Ask your legal adviser. And ask him about the difference in possible sentences between denying the charge and pleading not guilty as opposed to coming clean, pleading guilty and copping a reduced, possibly much reduced sentence.'

Billy was impressed with Melody's speech. She thought the DS should become a prosecutor. Clunes showed little response so the Bad Cop tried the Good Cop approach.

'You obviously love your kids, Barry. By pleading guilty, with all the grief you were going through, you'll get to see them before you become a grandfather.' Melody paused. 'What do you reckon?'

Clunes looked at one detective and then the other. 'No comment.'

The interview ended and Barry Clunes was charged with the murder of Dieter Fischer. Nobody fancied his chances of bail.

'That was quick,' said Michael Chan. 'I'm still drying the dishes.'

'Are you free for the next 24 to 48 hours?' asked Jo Best speaking on her hands-free mobile as she drove to Northcote.

'Do you mean free as in "available" or free as in "at no cost"?'

'I'll take that as a yes. I'm on my way.'

Michael was chuffed. A chance to stretch his brain, to outwit a law-breaker and a chance to work with a gorgeous girl—out of his reach unfortunately—in what was for him a case of *I did but see her passing by, and yet I love her till I die.*

He told Alan he may be away for a day, and the cat didn't budge. 'Sometimes, Alan, you might show a tiny bit of appreciation.'

Jo arrived. Michael gave her the sweeping gesture of welcome and Alan, to demonstrate his finicky nature, hopped on her lap.

She told Michael her news and explained her plan of attack. 'We contact anyone who knew the victims asking if they knew the other victim and from there, we build details of how the victims knew one another.'

'Sounds good.'

Jo knew Michael had something else in mind. 'But?'

'The old teaching motto of *Start from the known and proceed to the unknown* might work here.'

'Damn you, Michael. I hate it when you know what I don't.' He looked peeved. 'Sorry, you know I'm genuinely jealous; please explain.'

'What do we know about that funeral? Why did the dead camper have the funeral booklet with the soccer coach's phone number?'

'No idea. And I told you I only got a recorded message.'

'Well if the owner of that number is dead, he sure won't reply.'

Jo cringed. 'He is dead.' She had no idea. 'Okay, what next?'

'So the known is the funeral. To move to the unknown, we study the event. Who died?'

She grabbed her phone and flicked through the pictures. She read the details. 'Celebrating the life of Brody Keith Miller.' She read his dates and the date of the funeral.

'Sounds like a good starting point,' said Michael, and headed for his console. In only a few seconds he found various articles about the death of the racing car driver who was killed in a car accident in Tasmania. 'Is that him?'

Jo looked at the photo on the funeral booklet and then at Michael's screen. 'That's him,' said Jo. 'So how is the funeral relevant?'

Michael tapped away. 'Let's see, Kiddo.'

'Kiddo? Michael, Richard Hannay would never even *dream* of saying Kiddo in *The 39 Steps*.'

Michael's half smile appeared as he found all sorts of information about Brody Miller. 'Famous rally car driver. Won Bathurst three times. Won the marriage stakes three times.'

'What?'

'He had three wives. His funeral was attended by hundreds of people. His casket was adorned with his crash helmet and steering wheel.' Michael sounded serious. 'Okay, here's something.'

Jo leant in and read the headline; *The Dark Side of Brody Miller*. She skimmed through the article which was an exposé of a young man's addiction to speed and women. 'Interesting,' said Jo, noting the by-line and using her phone.

'How interesting?' asked Michael who turned to see Jo making a face as she waited on her phone.

'Tazmin Gallagher please.'

'I wish you'd get a move on, Detective; you're so slow off the mark.'

Jo held up her hand as a stop sign, and Michael went to make coffee.

'Tazmin Gallagher,' said the journalist.

'Hi, Tazmin, my name's Detective Senior Constable Jo Best from Victoria Police Homicide Squad. I've read your piece on Brody Miller.'

'Which one?'

Jo was thrown. 'I'm sorry?'

'There are three pieces on Miller.'

'Oh, ah, the one headed *The Dark Side of Brody Miller*.'

'So how can I help you, Detective?'

'I'm working on a case and you might be able to give me some background. Can I buy you a coffee?'

Tazmin received many calls, most of which were from time wasters but she reckoned this was different. 'Sure and I want you to know I'm a paid-up member of the back-scratchers' society.'

Jo laughed. 'I'm financial too. Look, I'm out of town but can we say I'll call you when I'm in your foyer in about an hour?'

'See you then,' said Tazmin.

Jo gathered her bits and bobs and patted Alan. Michael held up a pot of freshly brewed coffee. 'Oh Michael, I'm sorry.' She moved to him. 'You've given me a promising lead—as always.' She kissed his cheek. 'I'll show myself out,' she called heading for the door. 'Bye Alan.'

She left and Michael turned to his cat. 'Coffee, old bean?'

Tazmin and Jo met in the foyer of the newspaper's building. 'Let's try our canteen,' said Tazmin leading the way.

'But I'm paying,' said Jo.

They stopped by an empty table away from other diners. Tazmin spoke softly. 'If I'm ever in need of a tip from a Homicide officer, shouting her a coffee seems a good place to start. Cappuccino?'

'Perfect,' said Jo, 'and thanks.'

Both women checked out the other's clothes, hair, jewellery and footwear. They might have been sisters; similar age, healthy natural hair, plain, if that's the word, but classy clothes, and fashionable but practical footwear.

Tazmin arrived with coffee. 'I'm Taz,' she said, 'short for Tazmin.'

'Jo, short for Joanna,' replied Jo.

'You're the famous Jo Best, the shy and hard to photograph detective who always gets her man.' The detective groaned inwardly. 'If my colleagues hear I'm consorting with the elusive super cop, they'll be ropeable.'

'Enough of the soft soap, Taz. Let me tell you what I'm after and then we can negotiate the quid pro quo. Deal?'

'Deal,' said Taz.

Jo was good at not giving away state secrets and definitely not to a reporter. Taz twigged to that straight away. 'We may have a connection between our two homicides and the funeral of Brody Miller. Do the names Dieter Fischer and Max Bowman mean anything?'

Taz shook her head. 'Only as recent murder victims; sorry.'

'So without identifying your sources, where did you get your info on Brody's bad behaviour?'

'A bit of luck and the Me Too movement. Brody was no movie producer or high-flying financier, but he made money and found fame driving fast cars. A lot of women fell for his charms. Decades later, people, women, reckoned the truth should be told about his seduction techniques with questions of drugs and under-age sex. One middle-aged woman, who read my feminist pieces, contacted me and told me about her relationship with Brody Miller. She gave me names and next thing I had women and their friends, siblings and parents all describing Brody as a poor man's Jeffrey Epstein.'

'Did your articles lose their sting when Casanova popped his clogs.'

'Bastard,' said Taz. 'I reckon he did an Epstein and topped himself.'

Jo was surprised. 'I hadn't heard that.'

'What, a highly skilled and experienced professional driver fails to take a bend when not wearing a seatbelt? Before he died, I contacted him about the articles. Before he hung up, he told me to die.'

Jo pondered. 'You think your exposé tipped him over the edge?'

Taz pondered and grimaced. 'I try not to think about it.'

Jo's mind was working overtime. 'Any chance of a favour?'

'Depends.'

'Could you contact a few of your women and ask if they know the names of my two victims?'

Taz pondered. 'You might do better if you do the asking; cut out the middle woman.'

'You'd do that?' asked Jo trying to contain her excitement.

'For a price,' said Taz. She paused, waiting for Jo to react. She didn't. 'You give me first dibs if and when you crack the homicides.'

'Sounds fair but I thought you were the feminist writer.'

Jo's eyes laughed and Taz twigged. But the journo wanted more.

'Plus I get a one on one interview with the super detective.'

Jo shook her head. 'Too much, Taz.' Neither spoke. Jo explained. 'Look, if I agree to the story with the glamour pic, I'll cop scorn from colleagues, my critics will go harder than ever to bring me down, and every well-meaning no-hoper will send me useless tips on why Sam Neill and not the dingo did it.'

'Fair enough,' said Taz smiling and working her phone. 'How many names do you want?'

Jo was thrown. 'Three would be great.'

'Let's say four. What's your number?' Jo handed her phone to Taz who typed in names and numbers. 'Now I've given my word these ladies will remain anonymous, so you're going to have to find a way to explain how you have their details without involving moi. Oui?'

'Oui,' said Jo, wondering if she was now on the slippery slope to becoming a corrupt cop.

Taz handed back Jo's phone. 'Good luck,' she said, 'and don't forget I get first crack when you nab your killers.' They finished their drink.

Jo stood. 'I'll dig out my back scratcher, and thanks for the coffee.'

She returned to Homicide, and knocked on the boss's door.

'Jo, come in. Tell me your good news.'

'It would take too long, ma'am, but I've found women who might, repeat might know either or both of the victims 20 or more years ago.'

'Which means what?'

'Not sure, but if any of them do know something, it might be another way into cracking the cases.'

'Case,' said Rose. 'We've charged Barry Clunes with the Fischer murder. Massive motive, he was at the crime scene, victim's blood on his knife, and now his admission he did the deed. And for your theory, he was nowhere near Gippsland when the tree fell on Bowman.'

Jo had nothing to say. Disappointment festered.

'How's Pierre?'

'Ah there's strong improvement there, ma'am, with hopefully more to come. I'll pop in tonight after I've finished these interviews.'

'Do you tell him about your work?'

Jo wondered if she should confess. 'Only the essentials because too much may remind him of what's he's missing.'

'And will never work on again.'

Jo nodded. *Is she asking me to tell Pierre that?* Jo stood. 'I'll get going, ma'am.'

Rose called. 'Give Pierre my best.'

Chapter 23

Blunt could not believe what he saw on Mufti's phone. It was a short video, shot at night with limited lighting and poor audio, but the Inspector was sure he recognised the two men—Alex Hero the club president and, wait for it, Miguel Spaniell, the labour hire boss with the scent of *Underworld Villain* his favourite cologne. He'd only seen photos of Hero but Spaniell he knew. Then Mufti confirmed the IDs.

He willingly sent the video to Callum's phone as the two sat in the Cherry Tree Hotel. 'Take it,' said the sub-contractor owed thousands. 'If you can nail that labour hire bastard or fraudster Hero, you'll have done me a favour. I was so angry I even asked a mate to check on the price of hitmen.'

'I didn't hear that last bit,' said Blunt. 'Let me get you another drink. Oh and do you know a good technician who could improve the quality of your clip?'

'Yeah, I do.' Mufti gave Callum the details of a top quality A/V engineer and after a genuine speech of gratitude—hard to believe, but true—Blunt gave Mufti his card and told him if ever he needed a favour from a top cop—Blunt's words—to call his number.

Ten minutes later, Blunt was home and replaying the footage on his phone. This was gold. Two birds with one stone. Okay, probably not the homicide but to nail a fraudster and an underworld heavy, and on his own, was no mean feat.

He rang the audio engineer who had bad news. 'Sorry mate, I'm absolutely flat chat at present.'

'Name your price,' said Callum trying not to sound desperate.

'It's something like "not all the tea in China", and speaking of which, there is an ABC who is pretty good at fixing A/V.'

Callum didn't know what an ABC was and didn't ask. All he wanted was the footage made good. He wrote the name and number of the new technician, thanked the audio guy, and rang the second number.

'Michael Chan,' said Jo Best's best friend.

Callum failed to pay attention in Homicide meetings unless the subject involved him, and so failed to realise to whom he was speaking. Michael listened with interest.

'My name's DI Callum Blunt and I've been given your name as an expert in improving A/V footage. I'm working on a major homicide, fraud and organised crime case, and need this material fixed super quick. It's only a minute long. Name your fee.'

'Well I'd need to see the footage first. Can you email it to me?'

'Whoa, no way. This is super secretive, and I'll need you to sign the Official Secrets Act before I even show it to you. Can you do it now?'

'Does Australia have an Official Secrets Act?'

Callum grew tense. 'Figure of speech, man. Come on, I'm begging.'

Michael wondered what Jo Best would think of this call. *Is it genuine?* 'Okay, bring it over.'

Callum was so happy he wanted to cry. He grabbed Michael's details and took off.

Twenty-five minutes and several speed limit violations later, Michael saw a man approach his front door. He opened it. 'I'm Michael,' he said extending his hand. Blunt shook it.

'Callum.'

'And this is Alan.'

Blunt saw the cat but no other human. 'Sorry?'

'The feline.'

Blunt thought it was a joke. He showed his phone to Michael and started the clip. Michael watched it.

'So, can you make it sing?'

'Warble perhaps,' said Michael who was starting to irritate the cop. 'Walk this way.'

They finished up at Michael's console. 'Bloody hell,' said Blunt. 'What is this, NASA Down Under?'

Michael held out a hand. 'Your phone.' Blunt was immediately defensive. 'Officer, I can't repair what is not in my machine.'

'I don't want a copy kept, sent or anything else.'

Michael excelled at irony. 'Do you have the Official Secrets Act form?'

Blunt reluctantly gave Michael the phone. He transferred the footage to one of his machines and started work. Blunt watched in amazement. The audio became clearer; not perfect but so much better.

'That's as good as I can make it. Now for the visuals.'

Michael's phone rang and he answered much to Blunt's frustration. It was not on speaker.

'Michael Chan.'

'You know who this is, you've got Caller ID,' said Jo.

'Oh hello, Honey. It's great to hear from you. How are you?'

Jo groaned. *Oh no, Michael is back being a lovesick Romeo.* 'I'm fine, darling. How are you?' she said with a large serve of sarcasm.

'I'm fine, Babe. What's happening?'

Jo twigged. 'Oh shit, sorry Michael. You're busy. Look, I can't find the missing link and need your input. Please, can I come over?' The last word was laced with desperation.

'Okay Gorgeous, but tread carefully. I'll see you soon.'

He ended the call and worked on the visual. He made it brighter which helped although not dramatically. 'You might need a specialist to get this any sharper. Don't you cops have technicians?'

'Tits on a bull, mate. What if you make it black and white?'

Michael tried more approaches with a marginal improvement. He asked for Blunt's phone and the cop again went defensive. 'Do you want the new and improved toothpaste or not?'

Blunt had his expectations too high but knew he now had a better product. As to whether the content would support a charge was fifty-fifty. Michael transferred the file, and Blunt struggled to say thanks.

Michael's alarm sounded causing Blunt to panic. 'It's okay,' said the guru, 'it's a friend. Actually she's a cop; you might know her.'

Blunt's face auditioned for a cartoon. 'She?'

'Detective Senior Constable Jo Best. Does the name ring a bell?'

'Vaguely but this footage is top secret. Is there a back door?'

'Sure,' said Michael leading Blunt to the exit for desperados.

At the door, Blunt threatened. 'Erase all trace of the footage or else.'

'Will do, officer,' said Michael saluting with his index finger. Blunt dropped two fifties and fled. Michael hurried through his warehouse and opened the door to another Homicide detective.

'You alone?' she asked.

'Now I am,' he said, gesturing.

Michael let her settle before he dropped his big news. Jo was dumbfounded. 'DI Callum Blunt?' Michael nodded. 'He with the expensive haircut and imported shoes?' More nodding. 'Well, come on, tell me everything.'

This time Michael's head went east to west. 'Sorry, Official Secrets Act and all that.'

'You rat. How did he get onto you?'

'I thought *you* recommended me.'

'Me! Michael, that … officer hates my guts.' She didn't handle this news well. 'I hope you haven't switched sides.' She gasped. 'You have! You're two-timing me!'

Michael's half-grin appeared. 'Not exactly; but the pay's better.'

She gulped. 'He paid you?'

'Two fifties as he fled via the back door.'

'He's just gone? Why? Did you tell him I was coming?'

'I did and he said he knew you vaguely and fled.'

'Vaguely?' It was Jo's turn to shake her head. She went for a wander much to Alan's chagrin.

Sit down, woman. I fancy sitting on your lap. Those were Alan's thoughts not Michael's although it could have been either.

Michael brought matters to a head. 'Are we going to bother about an insecure detective who is not good at what he does, or should we get on and discuss what you came to discuss?'

She stopped her walkabout and sat, much to Alan's delight. 'May I ask what DI Blunt wanted you for?'

'To improve a 60 second video clip taken on a phone at night where two blokes were talking about money and said, in my 'umble opinion, ma'am, nothing of an incriminating nature.'

Jo recovered. 'Thanks. I'm sorry. Now, do you have any tips on lying or misrepresentation?'

'Pardon?' he asked genuinely confused.

'The journo who wrote that article you found has given me a few of her sources, and I need to contact them without involving the journo.'

Alarm shone from Michael's eyes. 'A journalist revealed her sources? That's impossible. And why?' Jo made a face. He twigged.

'Ah, the old mutual back scratching. So what did it cost you?' She made another face. He was shocked. 'You haven't sold your soul to the Devil?' She refused to answer. 'You *have!*'

'I deny everything, Doctor Chan, but my question remains.'

'No idea.'

'Oh come on, Michael, I have to get these women to talk to me.'

He thought about it. 'Honesty with a carrot,' he said.

'What's that in English?'

'You tell them the truth about who you are but you offer them a chance to crack a case which might burn their enemy.'

Jo thought it possible. 'But how did I get their number? The journo gave me their details on the one condition she isn't the source.'

'Then you're gunna have to lie, lady.'

He was right. 'Okay, can you make a short clip of TV coverage of the mourners at Brody Miller's funeral? All the news channels covered it.'

'Sure,' he said and started work. Jo looked at the first name and number and made the call.

'Hello,' said a middle-aged woman.

'Is that Kimberley Burton?'

'Kimberley Chappel. Who's calling?'

'Sorry Kimberley, I can't read my own writing. I'm a police officer, Detective Senior Constable Jo Best, and I'm hoping you can help me.'

'How?' asked the now worried woman.

'We're working on an unsolved homicide, and need information about people who are persons of interest?'

'I've got no idea what you're talking about.'

Jo began her fibbing routine. 'We've been looking at TV news clips covering the funeral of the racing car driver Brody Miller.' Jo paused but Kimberley said nothing. 'We have face recognition software and from footage your face came up.' *How many lies can I invent?*

Kimberley growled. 'That cop told me my record would be gone.'

'Sorry?' said Jo looking at a fascinated Michael.

'All those years ago I got busted for having a ridiculously small amount of weed, and that lying cop said the details would be erased.'

'Look I'm sorry, Kimberley, I must have the wrong number.'

'No, wait.' There was a long pause. 'I was at that funeral.'

Jo was thrown. 'Oh, okay. But look, our enquiries have nothing to do with you. We want to talk to anyone who might be able to identify some mourners.'

Another pause seemed to never end. 'All right,' she said. Jo was rapt. 'So who else is on your list?' Jo needed to think super quick.

'Only you, Kimberley.' More fibs and Pinocchio's nose grew longer.

'There were a few of us women there.'

'I'm sorry. Who are us women?'

'We're survivors of Brody's bastardry and keep in contact online.' Kimberley gave Jo names and numbers. Jo tried not to purr. Alan did.

'Thanks a million, Kimberley. Now when can I come and see you?'

'Pretty much anytime. My social calendar is stuck on 1999.'

Jo took the address and agreed to meet Kimberley in an hour.

'You're good,' said Michael when the happy detective ended the call.

'You can talk,' she said. 'I remember a certain Australian Born Chinese ringing a Swiss Bank and posing as a South African.'

Michael used his Joburg accent. 'Eish, we're having a braai tomorrow.'

'Right, can you please put the news clips on my laptop and then we can get cracking.'

'We?' asked Michael in genuine surprise.

'Oh come on Watson, the game's afoot, old chap.'

Michael hurried to finish the simple IT task and get ready to leave.

'Watson?' he said. 'Last time you called me Captain Hastings.'

Kimberley and her two Jack Russell dogs lived in Murrumbeena. She worried when a male appeared with the female cop but as he looked harmless and wore a permanent half smile, she soon settled.

After explanations from Jo, Michael opened the laptop and ran the funeral footage. Despite her detailed knowledge of the deceased driver, Kimberley knew bugger all about the deceased Messrs Fischer and Bowman, the whole point of the visit.

She pointed to several women naming them; all members of the Brody Hate Club. 'There's Madison. You need to talk to her.'

Jo looked. 'Why?'

'She's knows everyone and keeps us all together. I'll give her a call.'

Jo and Michael looked at one another. This was going well, almost too well, and Jo loved the fact there were now two degrees of separation between her and the journalist.

Kimberley obviously convinced the woman on the phone and covered the mouthpiece. 'Maddy's in Oakleigh. Can you go there now?'

'Sure, we can be there in fifteen.' The appointment was confirmed.

Jo was thrilled, thanked Kimberley and drove to the next suburb.

Michael did his usual squashing of expectations routine trying to keep Jo's high hopes in check, and soon they sat in Madison's lounge room.

'We appreciate you helping us, Madison.'

'Maddie, and no problems. So you reckon Brody was murdered?'

Jo did a double take. 'Murdered? We're not sure about that.'

'Kim's been saying it for ages. I thought that's why you wanted to speak to us. Do you reckon the killer was at his funeral?'

Michael's squash-expectations-routine started whistling.

Jo opted for the vague reply. 'We're certainly looking at every possibility. Now Michael has news footage of the funeral and we wondered if you could identify anyone.'

'No problem,' said Maddie. Michael opened the laptop and Maddie watched. 'Oh my God, it's them!' she spat. Michael hit Stop.

Jo moved in closer. 'Who?'

Maddie pointed. 'There's Brody's two mates, the bastards who joined him in their rape routine. What are their names?' She couldn't remember. 'Nah, we only knew a nickname.' Jo flattened her feet on the floor to stop her knees from knocking.

'When you say "we", who ...?'

'They probably killed Brody or would know who did. They knocked around with him for years and the three raped more women than you've written parking tickets.'

The mood grew dark as murder and rape joined the agenda.

'Can we back up a little, Maddie?' asked Jo, now quietly worried. *Am I dealing with a fantasist?* 'Are you saying those two men were mates with Brody Miller?'

'Thick as thieves they were.'

'And you think they may have murdered Brody?'

'I heard he shafted them. He made big bucks, found fame then dropped them as losers. He only let them hang around until he was sure they'd never dob him in. They hated him for being a star and having women throwing themselves at him, so they ran him off the road in Tassie. That's where he died, right?'

I am dealing with a fantasist.

Jo's high hopes crashed and she glanced at Michael whose inscrutable face spoke volumes. "I tried to warn you," said his eyes.

'So how do you know those men?' asked Jo.

Maddie continued looking at the vision but answered. 'Once seen, never forgotten even after all these years.' Then she froze. 'Je-sus. That's her!' she yelled. 'Stop the film. Go back, go back!' Michael obeyed. 'There,' she pointed, 'there she is.' Jo and Michael stared at the screen. Maddie touched it. 'God, talk about a blast from the past.'

'Who?' asked Jo.

'Chelsea Smith as was; not sure of her married name. Bloody hell, some things you never forget. Fancy her being at his funeral.'

Jo was itching to know the back story but wary because Maddie may have delivered two useless and misleading pieces of information.

'Was she a friend of yours?'

'Besties we were, although I don't think we called each other that back then.' She remembered. 'It was first-best friends.' She paused. 'Never again though once those bastards gang-raped her.'

Jo no longer had the fantasist vibe. 'Did she tell you she was raped?'

'She didn't have to, I was there, in the car with her and those pricks. I helped wipe the blood off her in the toilets at Blairgowrie, combed the sand out of her hair, and washed her face as ...' She remembered. 'Useless it was as she couldn't stop bawling. Then I backed up her pack of lies about us being late because we got trapped by the tide.'

Maddie changed. She went back in time, some 30 years. The memories of that appalling night roared into life. Her face twisted and tears filled her eyes. Jo was afraid to coax her. Something terrible must surely have happened decades ago.

Jo whispered. 'I'm sorry, Maddie. Can I get you something?'

Maddie spoke through her distress. 'I thought I'd buried that night. It's funny how seeing Chelsea brought it all back.'

'And you and Chelsea have lost touch?'

Maddie nodded. 'She blamed me. She reckoned I told her parents about the rape. But I didn't say a thing. Her parents must have worked it out. She was a mess. They wanted her to have an abortion. She dropped out of school and moved away. Someone said she went to an aunt's house in the bush.' Maddie looked at the laptop. 'But fancy her going to Brody Miller's funeral. She must have wanted to spit on his coffin. Piss on it more like. Wow. Chelsea Smith and all three of her rapists together again. How about that?'

The visitors watched Maddie re-live a shocking memory.

Jo murmured to Michael. 'More footage please.' He nodded.

'Hang on,' said Maddie. 'I heard she moved to Drouin a few years ago and I think she married a musician. But, if she copies me, by now it could be a new bloke and a new location.'

Jo spoke. 'You've been a big help, Maddie. Do you know if the police investigated the rape?'

'Don't think so. They would have asked me if they had, surely.'

Jo nodded. 'Yes.' She paused. 'Have you seen Brody's two mates around anywhere?'

Maddie shook her head. 'Nah, until seeing them just now, they could be dead for all I know. Maybe some of the other women in our group might know them.'

Jo said nothing about their demise. Obviously Maddie didn't follow the news. Because of his fame, the one name they all knew was Brody Miller

'And looking at the footage, you're sure those two men are the ones who raped Chelsea?'

'Two faces I'll never forget. Those two took me into the sand dunes, and only my protests before we reached their rape spot saved me. And the only thing that still haunts me is they joined Brody and did to Chelsea what they planned to do to me. How lucky was I?'

'Don't blame yourself,' said Jo with a sliver of anger. 'Women apologising or blaming themselves for being raped or accidentally causing a friend to be attacked is a big no-no.' She spoke with emphasis. 'Never blame yourself.'

Maddie turned morose. 'I sometimes wonder what happened to her. Did her parents kick her out? Did she have a kid? Did she turn to booze or drugs? Looking at her in those shots she doesn't look fantastic.' Maddie indicated herself. 'Of course I can say that, I'm Miss World.' She laughed a hollow laugh.

'Is there anything else you can tell us about Chelsea or those men who raped her?'

Maddie thought about it. 'I'd like to see them all six feet under. Now there's only two left.'

Not quite.

'Do you reckon Chelsea felt the same way?'

What a stupid question. 'Would you?' asked Maddie looking at Jo.

Jo nodded and spoke softly. 'I guess I would.'

'I haven't seen her for ages. I dunno what she'd say to me if we met. But I'd like her to know I never said a word about the rape until now.'

Jo reckoned the interview was over. She gave Maddie her card and told her to ring if she remembered anything else, no matter how insignificant. Michael spoke for the second time following his 'Hello' when they arrived. This time it was 'Goodbye'.

They sat in Jo's car. 'What do you reckon?' asked the detective.

'It's called a can of worms,' he said.

'I think I'll give those other women on the list a miss today. Can you please get more footage and photos from the funeral with particular attention to our two victims and their rape victim, Chelsea?'

'Will that be all, Officer?'

She looked at him. He wasn't having a go at her but she did sound like his boss.

She was genuine. 'I'm sorry, Michael.' She put her hand on his. 'I swear to never take your expert talents for granted ever again.'

'So help me God,' he added.

She smiled and playfully whacked him. As she started the car and prepared to set off, Maddie appeared and tried running, well, moving at a quicker pace than normal, down her driveway, waving and calling.

'Wait, wait!' she yelled, approaching the car.

Jo stopped and lowered her window. 'Problem?'

'I rang Helen, she should be on your list, (she was), and she reckons Chelsea's surname is Lilliput, and she's a check-out chick at a Drouin supermarket. She doesn't know which one.'

'That's brilliant,' said Jo. 'How do you spell Lilliput?'

Maddie looked pained. 'God, I can't spell; L something.'

'Don't worry, the oracle here knows everything.'

Maddie looked in and saw Michael's famous half-smile. He *could* spell anything – a n y t h i n g.

Chapter 24

As Maddie waved her visitors goodbye, the latest person of interest, Chelsea Lilliput, was scanning groceries in a Drouin supermarket. Staff training required employees to be polite and friendly. Chelsea failed her training. No greeting, and if a customer said "Hi", Chelsea grunted. She became robotic in her movement of items. Most customers ignored her but one retired old codger objected.

'Do you have to treat the items so roughly?' he asked with a touch of anger in his voice.

Chelsea stopped and looked at him. Hooked onlookers watched. Chelsea reached for the next item and lifted it as if it was something valuable and fragile. The item travelled on a magic carpet over the barcode section then on its heavenly journey to the customer's bag.

He was being mocked, and the surrounding onlookers grew in number and curiosity.

'Now you're being stupid,' he said. 'I want the manager.'

'Fuck you,' said Chelsea, dumped the item on the counter, and stormed off to the staff room. Tongues wagged. The adjacent checkout operator grabbed her phone and called the manager. He arrived, apologised profusely and put another operator in place. He set off to find the bandit.

Chelsea was clearing her locker when the manager stormed in. 'That's it, you're sacked. Get out and never come back.' Chelsea gave him the finger. 'You're lucky I haven't called the cops.'

She turned on him. 'Do and I'll tell them about you having a perv right here in this change room.'

The manager was once caught in a tricky situation. He entered the empty change room trying to find the source of a bad smell—a dead mouse as it happened. Chelsea came in and was changing into her uniform. The manager should have announced his presence but didn't.

He hid then knocked over a mop and was sprung. Chelsea gave him hell and now used her trump card.

The police were not called but Chelsea's behaviour was enough to have her sacked. She was.

Arriving home early, she woke her husband from his afternoon siesta. 'What are you doin' here?' asked Jason.

'I knocked off early. I'll get y'tea then I'm off.'

'You got sacked.'

'I'll be away for a while.'

'How long?'

'Dunno,' she said preparing a meal. Whatever else Chelsea could do, cooking wasn't her forte.

Jason smelt of anger. 'What other job will you get?'

'Dunno; I'll go to Centrelink.'

'We can't pay the bloody electric. You'll have to get another job.'

She fired at him. 'Why don't *you* get a job? You're not a cripple. Your useless gigs make peanuts. Get off your arse, Jason, give the pot away, and do something useful for once in your life.'

'There's an agent in Sydney looking at my new songs next month.'

She stopped chopping vegetables, screamed in frustration, turned and hurled the kitchen knife at her partner. It missed him by a foot or so but once en route, Jason lost the blood in his cheeks as the knife whizzed past and clattered against the il cheapo wood panelling.

'Fuck your fucking songs!' she screamed, and stormed out of the kitchen. He needed time to figure out what had happened.

Did she just try and kill me? Why is she angry? What's wrong with my new songs and, most importantly, what'll I have for tea?

He picked up the knife, replaced it on the kitchen bench—he'd only lived here for six years so didn't know its proper place—and looked around for Chelsea. He heard footsteps and then the front door slam.

He hurried to the front bedroom and looked through the window. He saw his partner throw an overnight bag into their car, hop in and start the engine.

'Hey!' he yelled and raced out the front door. He ran towards the car which reversed at a dangerous speed. The treeless property meant anyone walking past could have seen the speeding vehicle. It bounced onto the road. By the time Jason reached the front gate, Chelsea had engaged first gear and accelerated, leaving her partner fuming and confused. He needed a joint.

Cain's building project in the former games' room of his house was not on schedule. Apart from the silent treatment from his wife, going to work, and visiting both his mother in respite care, and his father in hospital following his stroke, the home renovations died.

The administrator at his mother's nursing home saw him and called. 'Oh Mr Reid, may I have a word please?' Cain entered her office. 'Have a seat.' He sensed bad news and was right. 'Your mother's respite finishes this Sunday. Is it possible she can be collected before lunch? It would really help us.'

'Okay ... but is it possible she could stay for another week?'

'Unfortunately no; our respite room is heavily booked.'

'But my father's had a massive stroke and is helpless in hospital.'

'I'm sorry but if we extend your mother's stay, it means other people who have booked and paid will have to be turned away.'

Cain's misery wrapped itself around him like a lovesick fog. It was going nowhere. The administrator took pity.

'I can give you the name of other respite places but you may find they're just as full as we are. Have you thought about putting your mother in a nursing home as a fulltime patient?'

He spoke as a beaten man. 'I am hoping to have both my parents come and live with me.'

The administrator made a face. 'Oh, are you sure? Your mother is showing more signs of dementia and if your father's had a major stroke, having them both at home sounds like mission impossible.'

Cain didn't mean to cry but he did. Not buckets but the same tears which had been shed a lot in the last week as the health of his beloved parents went from terrible to tragic. The administrator offered him a box of tissues—she had a diploma in supplying paper handkerchiefs.

Cain pulled out a hanky, did a trumpet like nose blow, stood and said he would be back on Sunday morning to collect his mother.

Alas fleeing the nursing home brought no relief as he headed to the hospital where his dribbling old man lay there refusing to die. Did a life of crime help hardened crims fight to the bitter end?

The doctors had encouraging news which meant Nipper was still alive—if you can call that living.

'When he recovers enough to leave,' said the administrator, he'll need high care in a nursing home and probably for the rest of his life.'

That information was cruel but less so than Cain's visit to his old man's bed. At least now Nipper could raise his one working arm and Cain squeezed the hand that moved. The baloney Cain was about to speak would make a copywriter drool.

'You're looking great, Dad. I've been to see Mum who sends her love.' Mum thought Cain was a nurse. If Cain ever read Shakespeare he would agree with the Bard. *When sorrows come, they come not single spies, but in battalions.* The son gave up on the home renovations, and began looking for nursing homes with high care facilities.

DS Rick Melody knocked on DI Rose's door. 'What news?' she asked.

'We poked around, ma'am and found Bowman's lanky brother, Graeme a.k.a. Shorty, is in serious financial trouble. He's borrowed against his nursery having failed to raise any dough on his house.'

'Does he own the house and business?'

'Yes but with hefty mortgages on both. He came unstuck when his wife divorced him and took half their assets. He decided to buy her out, borrowed big time and the house of cards is starting to wobble.'

'I hope that's not the whole story.'

'Seniors Baldwin and Payne had a chat to the widow's work colleagues and neighbours, and Jo Best's info about the widow and brother being an item is spot on. The dead man's finances are sound and his work insurance for a sole trader is healthy, and would bail out the brother leaving the lovebirds free to move in together.'

Rose was satisfied. 'Okay, let's have them in for a chat but separate and simultaneous arrests. Don't let the other know what's happening.'

'Will do, ma'am,' said Melody and left. Two of Max Bowman's relatives were about to come under serious pressure.

Jo drove Michael back to his warehouse. They discussed their outing. Michael, who had been totally silent throughout the interviews, now felt free to have his say. Jo wanted his opinion.

'The Chelsea woman could be interesting,' said Jo.

'Agreed; and could you use the rape to win her confidence?'

'Landmine territory,' said Jo. 'Makes eggshell walking a cinch.'

'Why didn't she report the rape to the police at the time?'

Jo was blunt. 'Only a man could ask that question.'

He fired back. 'Men get raped too, Detective.'

'Touché. Sadly, Michael, tragically, many rapes go unreported and for many reasons. And why would this woman want to talk about something which obviously caused her immense physical and mental suffering, and probably still does.'

They fell silent and pondered the events as described by Maddie. Close to Michael's place, Jo thanked him.

'As usual, Doctor Chan, I am in your debt, and it's great to be working with you again.'

'What can I say? Everyone knows with Team Best it's once in, never out.'

She laughed. 'Idiot. Oh and if you can find more of the funeral footage, I'll owe you a second dinner.'

She pulled up and he hopped out. 'What happened to the first one?' He revealed his immaculate teeth and closed the door. Jo drove to a friend's office, a solicitor she first met at Melbourne University's Law School years ago when they were students. They met for a drink every Christmas.

Jo's appointment was the last for the day. Lauren, the lawyer, opened the door. They hugged, smiled and joked. Settled, Jo produced the document given to her by Detective Inspector Pierre Richelieu. It was to appoint Joanna Claire Best as his enduring power of attorney. The women spoke briefly about the document.

Jo knew everything was in order. Lauren made sure, and with all the legal requirements complete, Jo asked a favour. 'I'd like a copy please, darling, but will you park the original in your safe?'

'Done,' said Lauren, 'now tell me all about this man. Is he the French detective involved in that terrible hit and run accident? And what are you doing with his power of attorney?'

Jo hated explaining the story. She did and Lauren felt sick.

Chapter 25

Few people enjoy being arrested. And when the charge is murder and the cops arrive unannounced, blood pressures take off. The detectives coordinated their approach and the plan worked to perfection.

Shorty was doing a stock-take on his Australian natives, and Kylie was ironing her uniform for her shift at the nursing home. Shorty's arrest was easy with a cop at either end of his nursery, and two to nab the subject. First reactions are important to police. Will the arrested throw up his (or her) hands, state it's a fair cop, Gov, and come quietly? Will he be shocked or glad the whole thing is over? Will he express outrage and vehemently protest his innocence? A conscience can create heavy pressure when murder's involved. Shorty came quietly. He asked if he could lock up his failing business, and hang up the CLOSED sign. DS Fletcher and Senior Constable Charley Baldwin followed him wherever he went.

In her Pakenham home, Kylie answered the door thinking it was a bit late for religious fanatics or telco callers from on a working holiday from Dublin. DS Melody and Billy Hughes arrested her on the doorstep and her reaction spoke volumes. 'I wondered when you'd come. It was that female detective, Joan Best, wasn't it?'

The detectives smiled at their colleague's new name, waited while Kylie locked the house with Bluey being led next door for dog sitting.

News of the arrests reached DI Rose, and interview teams and tactics were arranged. Rose felt better knowing the Fischer homicide was under control, and now the prospects of the Bowman homicide being wrapped up were looking good. However, her mild euphoria balloon was pricked when Jo Best called and her boss replied.

'What news, Senior and remember, only good news about DI Richelieu is permissible?'

'I'm on my way to see Pierre, ma'am, but I wanted you to know I've found evidence of a strong link between our two victims. They definitely knew each other going back many years.'

'Shit,' said Rose to herself, wondering if the best laid schemes o' Vice an' men / Gang aft agley. 'Tell me.'

'Both attended a funeral last month, and were seen conversing at length. I have a witness who knew the deceased and our two victims were known to one another, and all three are alleged rapists.'

Rose slumped in her chair. Stephen Payne tapped on her door waiting for the DI to look at him. She did. 'Both arrest parties have arrived, ma'am.'

She put her hand over the mouthpiece. 'Make sure neither sees the other,' she snapped.

'All in hand, ma'am,' said Payne and disappeared.

'I need a full report a.s.a.p., Jo. How soon can you be here?'

'I'm on my way, ma'am. I just need to drop off something to DI Richelieu, and then I'll be with you, half an hour tops.'

'Don't be late.' She ended the call and sighed. What appeared to be two homicides in the bag now looked messy.

Jo worried. *I thought she would be pleased.*

Rose met her detectives prior to the interviews. She said nothing about Jo's last call, and the detectives noticed her lack of enthusiasm. A final check on tactics began. Billy Hughes and DS Melody would interview Kylie, and DS Fletcher and Charley Baldwin would tackle Shorty.

Billy was curious. 'Something wrong, ma'am?'

'There will be if we can't crack either or both of our guests.'

She didn't sound convincing but chose not to announce Jo Best's news. It might amount to nothing, and with two likely suspects about to be grilled, things might yet turn out to be fine.

The suspects remained ignorant of each other being arrested or simultaneously interviewed. Shorty had a solicitor although how the hell he was going to pay him was anyone's guess. Kylie was depressed and declined legal representation. Both wanted to make a phone call to the other but were afraid to do so being worried about their situation.

Shorty spent time with his solicitor. The giant gardener adamantly protested his innocence and therefore wanted to go the "No comment" route. His wily solicitor reminded his client that if he, the solicitor, was blindsided during the interview, Shorty might come a cropper. The suspect thought about it but stuck to his guns.

'I never killed my brother,' he said, and the solicitor told the police they were ready to begin.

Kylie was already under way. Billy gave her a final chance to have a solicitor with Kylie refusing, wanting the thing over and done with. Billy began.

'Why do you think we suspect you of killing your husband, Kylie?'

'No idea.'

'Kylie, it's pointless us arresting anyone without a reason. Why did we arrest you?'

The suspect thought about it. 'Because Max and me were finished.'

'And?' asked Billy wanting to run with that thought.

Kylie was reluctant to admit it. 'Because Graeme and me are having an affair.'

'Did Max know about you two?'

'Of course he did.'

'What did he say?'

'Nothing.'

'Nothing? What, not a word?'

'He didn't care. He never liked his brother, and he sure didn't care what happened to me.'

'Tell us about Max's financial situation.'

'Why?'

'Are you the only beneficiary in Max's will?'

'You know I am.' They did now.

'Tell us about Graeme's financial situation?'

'You know that too.'

'Are you sure we know?'

'No, but why else would you arrest me? You think I murdered Max to get his money to give to Graeme.'

'And did you?'

'What?'

'Murder Max?'

Kylie turned sarcastic. 'Oh sure. I drove all the way to East Gippsland, knocked him out then picked up and dropped a bloody big branch precisely on him to make it look like an accident.'

'Did you get Graeme to do that?'

She stalled and seemed uncertain. Was she ready to change her story? She summoned up strength and defied the police. 'Prove it,' she said not realising she'd made her first mistake.

Billy looked at DS Melody and tipped him the wink.

'What do we have to prove, Kylie?' he asked.

The suspect became even more confused, and didn't want to mention the charge she faced. 'I'm saying nothing more.' She didn't and was returned to her cell.

Shorty faced DS Fletcher and Senior Constable Charley Baldwin. The suspect came armed with his solicitor, while the police came armed with a large dossier of circumstantial evidence.

Fletcher used the same tactic as his colleagues next door. 'Why do you think you're suspected of killing your brother, Graeme?'

'Because you've found out about me and Kylie, and you reckon I had to get rid of Max so me and Kylie could start a new life together.'

'That's a bit over the top. Why not just move in together? Max couldn't stop you. Why kill the poor bugger?'

'I didn't.'

'So you have the romance motive; what about the financial benefit? We know you're drowning in debt, Graeme, and that Max has a solid pot of super, and death and injury insurance. If you knock off your nipper, you'll knock off your debts.'

Shorty remembered his plan to say nothing so slipped back into the "No comment" lane.

Fletcher continued. 'I should point out, Graeme, Kylie is being interviewed next door as we speak and ...'

Shorty slammed the table. 'You leave her out of it!' he threatened.

The solicitor placed a hand on his client's arm and gave him a glare. Shorty understood and lost his attitude. Fletcher paused using the silence to increase the pressure. When he spoke, he maintained his calm approach.

'What is "it", Graeme?'

He glared at the detective. 'No comment.'

Fletcher had another ace to play. 'Graeme, let's talk about your financial woes, and your affair with Kylie.'

His anger exploded. 'It's not an affair. We love each other.'

Fletcher kept on keeping on, same pace, same level of voice and no emotion. 'But what we don't know is where you were at the time your brother was killed.' Silence. No response. 'You give us a watertight alibi, Graeme, and you're free to go.' Still no response. 'Is it because you were in East Gippsland to kill your brother?'

Shorty looked at them with contempt and gave the same answer as Kylie. 'Prove it.'

Jo bounced up the stairs to the ICU wanting to tell Pierre her news about the murder break-through, and to give him a copy of the signed and sealed legal document confirming Jo as his enduring power of attorney. Nurse Katrina greeted her.

'Hi, Jo. The patient has disappeared.' She saw Jo's look of horror. 'Pierre's been moved to a general ward.' Jo's look changed in an instant. Katrina pointed. 'You should head upstairs to the fifth floor.'

Jo headed for the lift. 'Thanks, Katrina, that's brilliant.'

'Good luck,' called the nurse and felt good being able to deliver positive news for a change.

Jo entered reception and was directed to Pierre's room. It was well described because he alone occupied the only bed in the private suite.

There he was, sitting up supported by a posse of pillows and reading a tablet.

'Knock, knock,' said Jo smiling with delight at his transformation.

'My darling girl,' he exclaimed and held out his arms. She placed her shoulder bag on the chair, leant in and kissed him. He seemed so much warmer, more excited, and more alive. Their kiss lingered before he guided her back. 'Let me look at you.'

'Pierre, this is wonderful, you are out of the ICU, and you look so much like your old self.' Doubly so because he was wearing silk pyjamas. *Where did they come from?*

'And it is all because I am determined to be fit and well for my beautiful Mademoiselle. You are my inspiration, Joanna; you are my reason for living.' She cried. 'No, no, no, I forbid any tears of sorrow, only tears of joy s'il vous plait.'

She kissed him again then opened her bag. 'I have something for you, Pierre.'

'For me? A present? Magnifique!'

She handed him an envelope with a copy of the legal document. He studied it briefly, saw the signatures then beamed. 'Is this true? You have my enduring power of attorney?'

'Oui, Monsieur.'

'Merveilleux,' he said putting the document aside and beckoning her to him again.

Their kiss was interrupted by a soft door knock, and Dr Grant Buchanan stood in the doorway.

'Pardon, Monsieur et Mademoiselle, or should I say, officers?'

All three laughed as the specialist came in and stood on the other side of Pierre's bed.

'Wonderful news, Doctor,' said Jo still reluctant to call the medico by his first name.

'Indeed,' said Grant, 'but Jo, I need you to tell Pierre he must take life slowly. His body took some seriously heavy punishment, and trying to climb Mt Everest in silk pyjamas is definitely a step too far.'

All three smiled. 'I will place him under close arrest the moment he steps out of line,' said Jo. The men laughed.

'Lucky you,' said the doctor departing and pointing to Pierre, 'slowly, Monsieur, lentement.'

Jo sat on his bed. 'You heard the boss, Pierre.'

'Joanna, I am so lucky to 'ave you as my commanding officer.'

Jo picked up her bag. 'I can't stay, Pierre. I have found a connection between our two homicides and must explain all to DI Rose and DS Hughes.' She kissed him quickly and moved to the door. 'I'll be back as soon as I can.'

'And when you do, I 'ave another favour to ask of you.'

He blew her a kiss, she waved and left. *Another favour?*

The squad discussed the two interviews. 'Why won't Shorty give us an alibi?' asked Fletcher. 'If he loves his sister-in-law and had nothing to do with his brother's murder, why not provide an alibi?'

Billy had an opinion. 'They're not under enough pressure. If we push Kylie on his alibi, she might crack.'

DI Rose approved. 'Agreed, and I've heard from Jo Best about a connection between the victims. She's on her way now. Once we know more, we might have another way to crack either or both of these two.'

'Speak of the devil,' said Fletcher as Jo arrived.

'Right,' said Rose. 'Let's hope your connection is relevant, Senior. The floor is yours.'

Jo worried wondering if her information carried weight. She explained her news starting with the existence of middle-aged women who claim to have been sexually abused by the late racing driver, Brody Miller. 'A Melbourne journalist has been writing about the apparent seamy life of the dead driver.'

'Bet it's a female journalist,' said DI Blunt, still smarting from his visit to see that bloke who apparently is Jo Best's bosom buddy.

'One woman told me the racing driver and our two homicide victims allegedly raped a woman 30 years ago, and when I looked at news footage of the driver's funeral, our two victims were there as was the woman they allegedly raped.'

Colleagues admired the research and results produced by Jo although one jealous colleague, Callum Blunt, wanted to boo and carp.

'Can you link the alleged rape to our homicides?' asked Billy.

'Not yet, Sarge,' replied Jo. 'The woman's name is Chelsea Lilliput and from the video footage she's in her 40s. She lives and works in Drouin and that's about all I know and yes, she doesn't look the type who would murder men who were much bigger and stronger than her.'

Charley Baldwin gave his opinion. 'As usual I say kudos to Jo for linking our victims but as Clunes coughed for the Fischer murder, and if we crack Shorty or Kylie for Bowman's death, then this ancient mateship link means nothing.'

Jo liked Charley. She remembered his support on her first day at Homicide but at times she reckoned he had trouble thinking outside the box. *You have to take a punt occasionally, mate.*

Rose decided. 'Billy, you and Jo spend a day on this Chelsea woman. I'll sit in with DS Melody and have another go at Kylie. Fletch and Charley, you crack on with Shorty. The rest of you make sure Clunes is our man. Yes?'

The others agreed and went off to battle. Jo and Billy sat and discussed their plan to investigate Chelsea.

'My memory's good, Senior,' said Billy. 'You've pulled off a few long shots in your short and chequered career but this one seems far-fetched even for you. So what do you reckon?' Jo looked genuinely surprised. 'Come on, it's your baby, Senior.'

Jo reckoned Billy was covering her backside in case this Chelsea woman turned out to be a dud.

'How about we ring her home in Drouin,' suggested Jo.

'What, and tip her off?'

'But if we drive 100 clicks and she's here in Melbourne, what then?'

'What's her number?'

Jo produced it. Billy looked at her. 'I had my friend use White Pages.'

Billy knew all about Michael Chan. She dialled the Drouin number. The speaker was on. Jason answered. He was doubly miffed because not only was he convinced his wife had tried to kill him, but worse, she'd left him to fend for himself. 'Hello?'

'Mr Lilliput?'

''Yeah.'

'My name is Acting Detective Senior Sergeant Hughes from Victoria Police.'

He sounded agitated. 'Have you got her?' The police were thrown. 'Chelsea tried to kill me. Have you got her?'

'Not yet,' said Billy. 'We're not sure where she is.'

'She'll be with her cousin, Valerie; 27 Lisle Avenue, Coburg. Chelsea's lost it. She was sacked from work, threw a knife at me then drove off like a lunatic. You've gotta stop her before she really does kill someone.'

'Okay, sir, we'll have a chat with your wife now.'

'Don't have a chat. Lock her up.'

'Has something upset your wife?'

'Dunno but she's been acting real strange of late.'

'In what way?'

'Sulking, arguing with people, doing things she did years ago.'

'Like what?'

'Personal stuff, you wouldn't understand. Look, stop pissing around and get her locked up.' He paused. 'And what's the number of the Chinese takeaway on Princes Way?' The detectives were shocked.

He slammed down the phone. The detectives looked at one another.

'I used to live in Coburg,' said Billy as she led Jo out of the building.

Fletcher and Baldwin made a plan about going hard at Shorty Bowman; *Take no prisoners* being their motto. They would alternate in a good-cop/bad-cop scenario only there would be no good-cop. They would apply relentless pressure. Both men were fired up and needed willpower to hide their overt body language. The DS won the toss and prepared to attack. Before he could speak, the solicitor interrupted.

'My client wishes to make a statement.'

The pent-up energy of the detectives fizzled. Fletcher nodded. 'Okay,' he said and the solicitor began.

'My client admits he was in the area of Licola at the time his brother was murdered. He admits he went there to confront his brother about his relationship with Kylie, and about his brother's threat to harm her should she seek a divorce. He had no intention to harm his brother. When he arrived in the area, my client saw a car he thought he recognised as well as its driver. My client panicked and drove back to Melbourne not having even seen his brother. As it turned out, my client was mistaken about the car and its driver.

'Had my client discovered his brother's body, he would have immediately reported the so-called incident, collected the dog and brought it safely home. My client told his sister-in-law nothing about his trip until he returned.

'This statement is signed by my client who will answer no further questions.'

And Shorty was true to his word. He went back to his cell while the police decided if his statement was a ruse to avoid being charged with fratricide.

Fletcher contacted Rose and Melody as they chatted to Kylie. The interview stopped as the message was relayed. Kylie worried almost to breaking point. The interview resumed and Rose went for the throat.

'Kylie, Graeme has made a statement.'

'No,' she shouted mimicking her lover by slapping the table. Anger dominated her face. 'He's only saying that to protect me.'

'Saying what?' asked Rose.

'That he planned to drown Max and make it look like an accident.' She froze, horrified. She didn't know what Shorty had said in his statement. Had he confessed? If so, to what? Had she been tricked? Too late, she broke the rule they agreed to if ever they were arrested. Say nowt.

Rose paused waiting for the suspect to lose steam, then spoke in a soft, understanding voice. It was as if she offered an invitation. 'Why don't you tell us what really happened, Kylie?'

She did and her statement supported her lover's although both were in on the plan. Both were charged with conspiracy to murder Maxwell Malcolm Bowman with the possible upgrading to murder subject to further enquiries. With Barry Clunes charged, and now Kylie and Shorty likewise, both homicides were wrapped up. President Hero escaped a murder rap but hit an iceberg labelled fraud and corruption.

DI Blunt was at sixes and sevens. He had evidence of a sort; the president and the gangster meeting at night discussing matters financial. But was it enough? Were their comments likely to excite the Office of Public Prosecutions?

And if Callum told DI Rose—and he knew he could, should and must do that—he'd lose the surprise element. He wanted to make an arrest and then announce his superior sleuthing to the world. However, if he went alone into the lion's den in Brunswick to collar Mickey Spillane, the DI could, should and more than likely would get himself a slap or a slug. Oh my, what to do?

He hit on a plan, which included a solo visit to the Vino Encantador Wine Bar. Good luck with that, Callum.

The fat lady began to gargle.

Chapter 26

'Should we have back-up, Sarge?' asked Jo as they sat parked in Lisle Avenue, Coburg.

'No,' said Hughes. 'I reckon you're the equivalent of at least half a dozen Soggies.' Jo didn't even smile. 'Come on,' said Billy getting out of the car, and Jo followed, not oozing confidence.

The neat brick house, a maisonette, dozed. Rose hit the doorbell. Sounds were heard and through the frosted glass an approaching shape was seen. Val, Chelsea's cousin, opened the door.

'Valerie?' asked Billy.

'Yes. What do you want?'

'We're police officers,' said Billy as she and Jo flashed their ID. 'Could we have a word with Chelsea, please?'

They were terribly polite. Val called. 'Chelsea.'

'What?' came from down the hall.

'There are two cops here to see you.' Silence.

'Tell 'em I paid that speeding ticket.'

Val called back. 'They don't look like traffic cops.'

The detectives could see down the hall and a woman's head appeared. Slowly she headed towards them.

'Hello Chelsea. We're detectives from Victoria Police and we're hoping you can help us with our enquiries.'

Chelsea stood beside her cousin examining two smartly-dressed women. 'You don't look like cops,' said the person of interest.

'We're plain-clothes officers,' said Billy.

Wearing a daggy tracksuit, Val had been checking out her visitors. 'Your clothes don't look plain to me.' Jo enjoyed the compliment.

'What's this all about?' asked Chelsea.

'We're investigating two suspicious deaths and we're hoping you might be able to help us.'

'Why me? I know nothing about any suspicious deaths and anyway, how did you find me?'

'It's important, Chelsea,' said Billy ignoring her questions. 'And we can drive you back here as soon as we're finished.'

The cousins looked at one another. 'Go on,' said Val. 'They've got you confused with someone else. And we can go down the pub for tea.'

Chelsea agreed, collected her bag and followed the police out into the street. 'Car's over the road,' said Billy, and the trio headed towards it. When almost at the vehicle, without warning, Chelsea took off running along the street.

It was comical. The woman trying to escape was middle-aged, going to seed, and hadn't run since her school sports day in the U13 relay sometime in the last millennium. Even then she came second last.

'Chelsea,' groaned Billy. 'Come back.'

Jo took off and with her superb fitness and constant cross-country running, could have nabbed Chelsea in a few strides. Instead the detective ran parallel and pleaded with the older escapee.

'Chelsea, this is silly. Come on.' No, the Drouin damsel kept blundering forward. Jo jogged closer. 'Be careful, you might fall.' And, as if on cue, Chelsea tripped and impersonated a sack of spuds leaping off the back of a truck. She cried out in pain and fright. Jo bent to check her for injuries. Billy arrived.

'Is she okay?'

'No,' snapped Chelsea, '*she* is not okay.'

Her ferocity indicated Chelsea was far from death's door. The detectives helped her to stand, walked her back to the car, and popped her inside on the back seat. Jo joined her with Billy driving.

'Now,' said Billy, 'do we need to go to hospital, Chelsea?'

She had recovered although her pride still ached. 'No.'

'So why did you run?'

'Because I don't want to be arrested and locked up for murder.'

This made the detectives think. Did it ever? In the car they shared glances. 'Whose murder?' asked Billy.

'See,' she said, pointing at them. 'You make up a case or try and trick me. Everyone knows the cops plant evidence, and listen to people who weren't even there. It's bullshit.'

Jo admired the way Billy behaved, how she had always done right from the day Jo joined Homicide.

'Nobody's accusing you of anything, Chelsea. We've got questions which you don't have to answer.' Chelsea settled a little. 'But when someone runs from the police, we become curious.'

Chelsea seemed back on terra firma but not for long. 'If you say I killed him, I'll never confess to something I never done.' Billy sighed and prepared for the arrest but was interrupted. 'When I left home, my useless husband was still alive! He even chased me down the drive.'

They nabbed Chelsea on a specious charge of resisting arrest and took her back to town. Explaining her rights, giving her the opportunity to be legally represented, and having a doctor give her the all clear was going to take time. The detectives were keen to have a serious and formal interview but their enthusiasm took a whack after they booked in their prisoner and went to report to the boss.

'What?' exclaimed Billy with Jo equally shocked.

'Both cases done and dusted,' said DI Rose. She explained the confessions from Kylie and her lanky lover. 'So what news from the woman at the funeral?'

'We brought her in,' said Billy.

'Oh?'

'She did a runner and covered all of 30 metres in about two minutes.' Jo smiled. Rose didn't.

'And?'

'She may be a little unwell in the mind, boss, but we'd like to have a chat anyway; no stone unturned. And if you want to pin the Licola murder on the star-crossed lovers, this woman may have some info.'

Rose looked unimpressed. 'Okay, I did say 24 hours.'

'Actually it was 48, ma'am,' added Jo and copped a glare.

'When will you interview her?'

'Not till tomorrow; she needs the usual tests and lawyer talk.'

Rose dismissed them. 'Well if this is the famous Jo Best being Mr Holmes and proving the police stuffed up yet again, I reckon you're due a failure one day, Senior. It could even be tomorrow. Be gone.'

They left. 'Still confident?' asked Billy.

'No but as my grandfather used to say, "Nothing ventured, ...'

They spoke together. '... nothing gained.'

Billy walked away calling, 'Say g'day to the dashing DI.'

Ah, Pierre, she thought. *What present can I take you?*

Cain signed the paperwork and felt marginally better. After what he felt were a million phone calls, he finally found accommodation for his parents in the same nursing home. It was luck as a married couple died within two days of one another, and the home had no other couple on their list; singles yes but couples, no.

Cain spoke of the high care requirements, and felt fantastic when the manager explained how keeping the couple together but apart for medical reasons was possible. Cain cried; his relief palpable.

He visited his mother who needed reminding of who he was, then told her, not that she understood, how she would soon be moving to a unit with Nipper. He kissed her and she looked surprised.

Then he went to see his father, still in hospital. He could see a slight improvement. The medical staff said there were positive signs his mind was functioning better, and his mobility was taking baby steps in the right direction.

Cain sat next to Nipper and spoke clearly. 'You have a new unit, Dad. You and Mum will be together. It's a lovely place. You'll have this big room with a door out to the beautiful garden. You'll both love it. They're nice people and we can visit you whenever you like.'

Nipper moved his head. It was a signal meaning come closer. Cain put his ear next to his father. 'Yes, Dad?' Nipper tried to speak.

'Sorry, Dad, I didn't understand.' Nipper tried again. Cain thought he understood and repeated what he thought his father said.

'I'm sorry?' Nipper nodded. 'You don't have to be sorry, Dad, ever.'

'No,' gasped Nipper.

'You're *not* sorry?' Nipper shook his head. 'You *are* sorry?' Nipper nodded. 'But I just told you. There's no need to be sorry.'

Nipper beckoned again. Cain put his ear beside his father's mouth, and heard the one word the old man uttered.

'Tommy.'

A dagger plunged into Cain's heart. He hated being reminded of his toddler son's accident caused by Nipper. But to see the never-ending suffering endured by his father for doing what he did all those years ago caused Cain even greater grief. When would the pain of the sins of the grandfather end?

Driving home, he thought yet again of how he could help his father before the old man died.

How can I give Nipper peace in his final days?

Jo bought flowers. Pierre was a man of taste and style, and even the thought would be enough. She headed for the ICU but remembered and instead, took the lift to the general ward where the Frenchman was on the mend. She entered Reception and was spotted by a nurse.

'Excuse me,' said the nurse, 'are you Jo Best the famous detective?'

'Not sure about the famous bit,' said Jo.

'I was wondering if I could get your signature. It's for my boy. He wants to join the police when he grows up.'

How could Jo refuse? 'Sure, have you got something to sign?'

As the nurse searched, another nurse quietly entered Pierre's room.

'It's his birthday and I bought this card. His name is Sean.'

There was an awkward moment when Jo didn't know what to do with the flowers so they were taken by the nurse who handed over a pen and the card. Jo signed and wrote a good luck message.

'I hope it does the trick,' said Jo returning the card.

'Oh that's brilliant,' said the beaming nurse returning the flowers. 'He knows all about your famous cases.'

'I've come to see Monsieur Richelieu. I hope he's been behaving.'

An even bigger smile appeared and the nurse seemed giggly. Jo wondered if Pierre had been distributing his French savoir-faire amongst the staff. 'He's well today.'

Jo returned the nurse's smile and headed to Pierre's room. She bumped into another nurse on her way out. What with the minor collision and handling the flowers, it took Jo a moment to fix her eyes on the patient. Oh dear. Shock was hardly the reaction.

Pierre was up, dressed and enjoying the view from his window. It was nothing to rave about but the patient's stance was a winner.

'Pierre,' gasped Jo. 'Look at you.'

He turned, switched on his Gallic smile with afterburners and opened his arms.

The flowers landed on the bed, and Jo almost leapt into Pierre's arms. She faced the delicate conundrum of wanting to hug her man without doing him some serious mischief. They embraced and kissed with feeling. He managed to stay upright doing so by spreading his legs and planting his size 10s for balance. He spoke, holding her so as to stay upright.

'Bonjour, my darling. You are even more beautiful than when last we met.'

The thing about Pierre's chat-up lines was their sincerity. They were totally believable, and if you fancied him they packed a helluva punch.

'Look at you. I can't believe you are out of bed and dressed.'

He shrugged. 'I need to look my best for my favourite girl.'

She hugged him then moved to the bed to collect the flowers. 'I brought you these, Pierre.' She turned and nearly died. He was no longer standing. In fact he was kneeling. She thought he'd collapsed. 'Pierre,' she exclaimed and threw the flowers back on the bed a second time. The roses groaned.

'No, no, Joanna, I am 'ere deliberately.'

She froze. Her heart started pushing towards her windpipe. The lump in her throat went from golf ball to tennis ball. He looked up at her and smiled.

'My darling girl, please, will you marry me?'

A whole box of tissues would fail to assist the Senior Constable as her tear ducts exploded. Three nurses, well in on the event, hugged and cried outside the door.

'Yes,' gasped Jo, 'oui, oui, oui!'

He lifted his hands towards her. She took them with love and trembling not aware he needed a hand to get up.

They embraced and kissed as three nurses entered unseen by the loving couple. One nurse took the flowers soon to return with them in a vase. Another coughed to attract Pierre's attention. He looked away from his true love for the first time, and the nurse wiggled her left hand indicating a finger. Pierre was so emotional he'd forgotten that certain item.

He removed the small container from his pocket and opened it to reveal an engagement ring. It was modest in size, simple in design and eye-watering in cost. He reached for Jo's hand. She opened her fingers and he slipped the ring with ease onto the ring finger of her left hand. It was a perfect fit. More clapping from the audience—they didn't get to help a patient prepare to propose all that often; more like never, and the couple embraced again. One nurse distracted Jo wanting a close look at the jewellery as the other two helped Pierre to sit.

An orderly arrived with champagne bucket, the bubbly and glasses. Excitement spread like wildfire, and glasses were filled and distributed. 'To Pierre and Jo,' said the senior nurse and the staff members raised their glasses.

'Right, out, you lot, out,' said the senior nurse, and Jo and Pierre were alone.

Pierre sat back in his chair and smiled. Jo knelt on the floor beside him. 'Merci, Madame Richelieu,' he said, 'although of course you may wish to retain your single name, Mademoiselle Best.'

'I rather fancy Madame Richelieu, s'il vous plait.'

'That is for tomorrow, my darling. Now we can make plans at our leisure. It is your day and you choose when and where and 'ow you wish to be wed. I will do whatever you wish, and become the 'appiest man in the world.'

Jo shook her head. 'You are a very interesting man, Inspector.'

He feigned sadness. 'Interesting? You say only interesting?'

'It was the nicest surprise of my life.'

Good,' he said as she held his hand.

'Pierre?'

'Oh dear, she is 'aving second thoughts already.'

'Never, but we are at a delicate stage in these two homicides. If I announce our engagement today, the squad will go a little bit ...'

'Crazy?'

She nodded. 'Oui. Would you mind if we wait a day or two until these cases are wrapped up before we make the big announcement?'

'Of course not but you 'ad better disguise the fact you are wearing a certain ring.' Jo looked again at the sparkler. 'Do you like it?'

'No, Pierre, I do not like it, I adore it as much as the man who gave it to me.'

'Please, my darling, we can change it if you wish.'

'You cannot have it back, Monsieur, you are stuck with me and this ring forever.'

They mused on their life together to date, and of their life together to come. A gentle tap and a nurse entered. 'Sorry to break up the celebration, but the budding bridegroom is also a patient and needs to 'ave 'is medication.' Her lousy attempt at a French accent produced heart-warming laughter.

Jo hopped up, helping the nurse get Pierre mobile. His smile disguised the pain he felt.

'I must away, Inspector,' said Jo.

'Au revoir, detective,' he said and kissed her. Jo squeezed his hands. At the door, she blew him a kiss then left. In Reception, staff members came from everywhere to congratulate the young woman and to wonder at the engagement ring. Jo asked if they would keep the news to themselves until she had the chance to announce it herself. The medical staff agreed but just one with a media contact could let the cat out of the bag. A journalist's nose was finely tuned with spies everywhere. She finally broke free and headed home.

What now? If I tell family or friends, it will be all over the squad and seriously interrupt my investigation of these two homicides. It was crazy as one of the happiest days of her life was put under wraps.

How would she sleep? How could she even eat? For safekeeping, she put the ring on the ring finger of her right hand and turned it around. She knew her parents and sister should be told but figured a 24 hour delay would be fine. She'd need time to prepare the answers to inevitable questions.

The lack of any celebration worried her. Staying in, doing nothing and telling no-one taunted her. She fought back by slipping into her running gear and hitting local roads, lanes, footpaths, parks and bridges. As her right hand rose and fell, every once in a while she would turn her palm inwards and look at the stone in her new engagement ring. It took her mind off the exercise and onto something else—someone else.

I'm engaged!

Chapter 27

Jo's sleep was interrupted, often. She rose at dawn, invigorated, wanting to ring Pierre, to hear his voice and tell him she loved him and couldn't wait to become his wife. She placed her engagement ring on the correct finger and kept looking at it as she prepared for work.

Why am I hiding what I am thrilled about and proud to wear?

She forgot to ask Pierre about insurance and thought leaving the ring in her flat was risky. So again she put the ring on her right hand, turned it and used a flesh-coloured plaster to cover a pretend cut. She admired it and smiled. It was there but not there. Jo felt warm knowing her secret was Pierre's too. And soon it would not be a secret.

She arrived at Homicide waiting for the congratulations and ribbing. *Someone must have blabbed,* she thought. One of the hospital staff would know someone who knew a journalist or a copper, and news tips can mean decent money for the bearer of good (or bad) tidings.

Well, either squad members were brilliant at poker faces or no-one knew. Billy and DI Rose conversed and the boss beckoned her over.

What's up?' asked the DI. 'You look like the cat that got the cream.'

They do know. 'Nothing, ma'am; I'm ready to roll.'

'How's the DI?' asked Billy.

'He's doing well, Sarge.'

'When did you last see him?'

Jo didn't fancy her acting skills. 'Ah, yesterday, after work.'

'And what did he say?'

'Say, Sarge?' asked Jo trying to look calm and disinterested.

'Yes, what are his plans? If he'll open up to anyone, it'll be to you.'

Oh God. Jo hated lying but was in too deep now. 'I think he *has* got plans, Sarge.'

'Yes, yes and you want to say, mind your own business.'

Jo's smile was pathetic. Billy gave her a look of suspicion.

'Right,' said Rose. 'Let's hear what your star witness has to say. If she's a lost soul from the days of fast cars and free love, drop her and prove Kylie and Shorty not only planned the deed but did it.'

The DI left and Billy again gave Jo a quizzing look. 'I hope you haven't got something up your sleeve, Senior, and plan to pull it out making me look a goose.'

Jo wanted to suck air hard. She did have something hidden which would make everyone sit up and take notice. 'A goose, Sarge? You're a long way from being DI Blunt.'

Another doubting look from Billy, and they went to interview Chelsea Lilliput.

Their plan was simple. Treat her as a witness to a nasty crime. Give her space. Encourage her. Make no attempt to trick or intimidate her. If she reveals something which supports the case against those charged, so much the better. If she knows nothing relevant to the homicides, thank her and see she gets home safe and well.

Outside the interview room, Rose put a hand on the door and paused. 'You lead,' she said, and looked at Jo whose pulse quickened.

Chelsea looked better; her cousin from Coburg brought a change of clothes, and a little attention to basic hygiene, hair care and fresh lippy made Chelsea look, even feel happier. A Legal Aid solicitor sat next to her meaning everyone in the room was female.

'Good morning, Chelsea,' said Jo and introductions were made. Chelsea had her rights explained with her solicitor, Genevieve, giving support and explanations where necessary.

'Let's start with what *we* know, Chelsea,' said Jo. 'We're investigating the death of two men who we now believe knew one another. We know this because they were seen talking at a funeral of a third man.' Jo produced a still from the news footage of the Brody Miller funeral. 'Do you recognise anyone in this photo?'

Chelsea sat forward, and studied the print. 'Madison Wright,' she said, 'Maddie,' and sat back.

The detectives were thrown, particularly Jo, who hid the fact she knew the name and the woman.

'Who's she?' asked Jo, sort of lying to the witness.

'She's the person who told you about the people in this photo.'

Jo hoped she wouldn't blow the interview. Chelsea sounded like a damn good witness. 'Can you tell us who else you know in the photo?'

Chelsea took her time and then put a finger on each person as she named them. 'Me, Fischer, Bowman, and in the coffin, is Brody Miller, and all three of those fucking bastards raped me in the sand dunes at Koonya Beach 31 years ago last January.' She looked at the stunned detectives. Even Genevieve had her mouth open and eyes wide. 'Do you want the date and time?' There was a pause and silence. 'Now, will that be all, officers, or do you want more?'

Had Billy been running the interview, even she would've struggled with the next question. Jo was in the same boat. She kept calm.

'How do you know Madison, Maddie?'

'We were first-best friends. She was with me the night of the rape. She helped me back to Blairgowrie and cleaned up the blood. And by the way, I would never recommend any virgin starting out with three blokes. One rapist is shithouse; three?' She wagged a finger. 'Don't, it bloody hurts. And besides, there was no Barry White orchestra playing on the beach.'

Her speech was powerful and her performance riveting. Again Jo had to think on her feet. Where should she take Chelsea next?

'I'm so sorry. I can't imagine how awful it must have been.'

Chelsea looked at Billy. 'You ever been raped?' Billy shook her head. Chelsea turned to her solicitor. 'You?' Another head shake. 'What about you?' she said looking at Jo.

Her answer too was "no" although she once came close. And the person who saved her was a fellow officer with a French accent, the same man who asked her to marry him a few hours ago.

'Were the police involved?' asked Jo hoping to help Chelsea and possibly get more information about the two homicide victims.

'Have you met my parents?' glared Chelsea with her rhetorical question. 'The only thing worse than their daughter being brutalized, was the world being told about it. And you wonder why I haven't spoken to them since ...' She made a gesture of "who knows when".

'Do you want to talk about the attack?'

Chelsea fell back. She did and she didn't. It was like a festering sore. She could cover and forget it, try to, or talk about it by pouring acid on it. If using acid, she would suffer horrendous pain but see the sore suffer as she had. This wasn't Hobson's Choice but Hades' Choice. Whatever she did, she lost; with agony.

She chose to speak, what she'd never done before. 'I was pregnant with no idea who the father was—there were three rapists. I was sent to Horsham to live with an aunt. She made my mother look like Mrs Jolly from Happy Families. My baby was put up for adoption. I'm sure the law was broken. I got a full two minutes to cuddle my daughter, and never knew her name or location. For all I know, today she could be a doctor, druggie or dead.'

Chelsea looked at each of the three women in turn and spoke from the heart. 'But I do have something. I know the name *I* gave her—Katie—and I know the day she was born—I was present at the birth in case you're wondering. And every year on Katie's birthday, I bake a cake, I send her a card to her at my address, and I sing *Happy Birthday* to my little girl.' Her voice cracked. 'It would be nice to give her all those cards.'

Telling her life story for the first time hurt like hell. She wanted to continue but the pain began to crush her. Chelsea dug deep. 'Well, she'll be a grown woman now and maybe I'm a gran.' Now she recovered and sort of smiled. 'Wotcha reckon? Do I look like a gran?' She paused and her misery returned. 'I'd love to know Katie's okay. I'd hate to embarrass her but just to be told she's fine would be awesome.'

Chelsea's soul began to breathe. The pain found somewhere else to hide. She told the world, in the form of two detectives and a lawyer, a story which had lived on in silence, shame and despair. Chelsea didn't notice she was crying, or if she did, didn't care. The other women became teary, and Genevieve was the first to dab her eyes.

'So there's one highlight of my life thanks to those three dead men, gentlemen one and all.' She slapped the photo; 'these animals.' She spoke through her tears, not embarrassed, just proud enough to stop the saliva, snot and tears getting too messy. She recovered, sort of. Jo and Billy were in no hurry to continue mainly because they were so moved, and because they now had no interest in Chelsea as a witness.

'But in case you want to feel sorry for me, let me fill you in on another exciting chapter in my godforsaken life. I got married and pregnant—a little boy this time. Only he wandered inside a neighbour's yard when he was all of three and finished up in their swimming pool, and have a guess who never taught him to swim? So I've had two kids with one missing and one drowned. They say it's third time lucky but frankly after two false starts, I was never fucking interested.'

She looked at her stunned audience. Chelsea's life was buried under grief and cruelty. Jo struggled. Chelsea delivered her punch line.

'Surely that's enough of my sob story.' She looked at them. All three witnesses to Chelsea's tale were attending to their eyes with those little dabs designed to remove tears yet leave eyeliner and mascara pristine. Chelsea continued in a calm voice. 'Now I suppose you want to know how I killed those two bastards, Fischer and Bowman.'

Mouths opened, and jaws and floors became acquainted.

It took time for the detectives and the lawyer to return to planet Earth, and to get their heads around Chelsea's last statement. Without a single probing question, the witness went from being a person of interest to a confessor of two homicides.

Genevieve asked for time with her client. Chelsea brushed her off. 'Waste of time. I did what I did; too easy in the end, and I can't understand why the cops didn't pick up the clues I left along the way. Now let's wrap this up so I can get started on my new life inside.'

'Right, Chelsea,' said Billy who pulled rank on Jo, and wanted to dot the i's and cross the t's. She arrested Chelsea on suspicion of murder and cautioned her.

Chelsea appeared relaxed, and waved Billy and her speech-making away. 'Can we just get on with it?'

Billy led. 'Okay, please explain how each man was killed?'

Chelsea took pride in what she did, even delighted in her success. She'd suffered most of her life thanks to these men. Every year on her daughter's birthday, her pain increased. Now she wanted to tell all.

'I knew all about Brody Miller because of his fame with cars. The others I knew nothing about. When Miller was killed, I cursed I didn't have the chance to do the job myself. His funeral was big news. I went to it and saw Fischer and Bowman. They didn't know me. To them I was a slab of teenage meat. I followed them. Fischer had Heidelberg Rovers' stickers on his car. Bowman had a website address on his ute.

'But Bowman died hundreds of kays from his home,' said Jo.

Chelsea looked impatient. 'Do you want to hear what happened or are you going to interrupt? I'm doing both of us a favour here. For you it's a gift-wrapped confession. Okay?'

'Sorry,' whispered Jo, and Billy gave her a "back off" look.

'I had this fantasy of killing both of them together; seeing the look on their faces when they discovered who I was. So I hung around and listened. They talked about a journalist writing about Miller's many lovers including underage girls. I wanted to say "Hello boys". They decided to meet but Bowman said he couldn't for a few days because he was going camping near Licola. He boasted about his location on the Tamboritha Road two kays from the town. I found him easily.'

The detectives believed Chelsea. She spoke confidently giving so many details. But both knew how Bowman was killed, and looking at Chelsea's small frame and having seen her "sprint" in Coburg, and knowing Bowman's size and his lively canine pal, the cops had doubts she could have killed using a mighty gum.

'I saw Bowman had his dog at the funeral so went with a plan; drug the bastard and distract the dog. In the funeral parlour car park, on the seat of his ute was a thermos. I bought one the same. I mashed Valium tablets—I've lived on them for years—in some coffee, and had chunks of meat soaked in chamomile tea. I looked it up and it's a sort of sedative for animals; probably an old wives' tale.

'When I got near his camp site, I put on Jason's old boots which are miles bigger than my feet thinking I'd leave large footprints. I wore those flesh-coloured gloves. I bet your CSI guys find nothing.

'The idiot drank the coffee and felt sick. I approached and the dog went mad. I threw it meat. Bowman tried to threaten me. I smashed his face with a bar I had behind my back. He went down, and as he lay there, I told him who I was. Even groggy as hell, he knew.

'I had no method of killing until I saw the dead branch. I placed his tent under that tree. The hardest part was dragging him to the tent and shoving him inside all the time distracting the dog. Bowman never spoke to me while he raped me so I made a cut on his tongue. Then I stood on steps I found in his truck and grabbed the end of the branch. I jumped. The branch cracked and fell. Bullseye. I couldn't have lined it up better. I figured the mess of his face would cover the whack from the iron bar. I felt sorry for the dog but left it a ton of meat and water.'

She paused. The other three women thought she looked pathetic. Her deeds were terrible but her face and body language made one feel sorry for her. It was hard to know if she took greater pride in the killing or the confession.

'The only regret I had killing both of them was that I did not know who the father of my little Katie was. Did I kill her Dad?

When I came home, I put Jason's boots back on the verandah, made his tea and got on with life. But the pressure got to me.'

The detectives were impressed. It sounded plausible. 'But Bowman was your *second* victim,' said Billy.

'Fischer was easy. I went to the soccer club at night and crept around. I could hear arguing. There was a tradie's ute in the carpark. The toolbox wasn't locked and I pinched a knife. Then I let down the front passenger side tyre and hid in the dark. The shouting inside turned nasty, and then this bloke came out and swore because of his flat. I sneaked inside and found Fischer on the floor moaning. He tried to get up. I held out my free hand. He took it and stood. I reminded him of our previous meeting, and the look on his face was worth it. I stuck the knife in as hard as I could, and when he was on the floor, I knelt over him and nicked his eyebrow. He wouldn't look at me while he raped me; another clue I left for you guys.

'I crept outside and while the tradie was replacing his tyre, I slipped the knife in the toolbox and took off.'

She blew out a big breath. 'And that's it. Charge me. I'll plead guilty and be glad to tell the world what those animals did to me.'

Genevieve wanted a word with her client. The detectives retired. In the corridor, Billy looked at Jo. 'The DI's going to be spewing.'

Jo didn't understand. 'But we cracked it, Sarge.'

'*You* cracked it, Senior—again—and she tipped you'd get it wrong.'

Jo grimaced but felt fantastic. They waited till Genevieve came out.

'She's all yours, officers. I reckon there's a super strong case for leniency when her rape suffering comes out.'

'Assuming it can be proved,' said Billy and looked at the lawyer.

Chelsea was charged. It was time to tell the tribe.

DI Rose was busy in her office when Billy and Jo arrived. 'Come in,' said the boss. 'Was our witness of any help?'

'She was,' said Billy, 'and you owe our colleague here an apology.'

Rose wasn't exactly sure what that meant although a sneaking suspicion tickled her brain. She didn't want to ask for fear of looking foolish. Billy gave Jo an order.

'Speak up, Senior.'

Jo tried to keep a lid on it. 'Chelsea Lilliput confessed to the murder of both Fischer and Bowman. She gave a detailed and credible explanation of how she committed both homicides. We charged her.'

Rose sat there shaking her head. 'You are your bloody grandfather, Jo Best. DCI Robertson lives again.' She stood and extended her hand. 'Congratulations, Jo and you shall have the honour of telling the squad. Come on.'

'Ah, I need the ladies, ma'am, but I'll be right there,' said Jo.

She left with her boss yelling an order never before uttered in Homicide. 'Pee faster!'

Inside the loo, Jo checked she was alone then made a call.

'Tazmin Gallagher,' said the journalist, who had seen the name Jo Best on her phone.

'This is Deep Throat,' said Jo not trying to be funny.

Tazmin recognised the voice. 'Hello Deep Throat.'

Jo struggled. 'I'm having trouble with this,' she said and did indeed sound under pressure.

'I understand.' There was a long pause. 'Do you want to meet?'

Jo didn't want to meet, to talk on the phone or have anything to do with leaking. But she'd made a deal and blurted her response. 'One of your girls has been arrested for both homicides.' Jo ended the call and found herself shaking. She switched off her phone, removed the plaster from her right finger, placed her engagement ring on the correct finger on her left hand then headed for the meeting room. She held her notebook in her left hand giving a sort of cover for the sparkler.

The full squad gathered with Rose, Blunt and Hughes standing to one side chatting. Blunt had a face like a slapped arse. Nothing had been announced. Jo entered and copped a few remarks about being late. Blunt and Hughes sat and Rose began.

'Good news all round. Both homicides appear to be wrapped up. Well done everyone and especially to Billy and Jo.' The silence became loud. 'I'll let them break the good news.'

Billy stood and beckoned to Jo. 'Senior.' Jo joined Billy.

Charley Baldwin broke the silence. 'Oh she hasn't done it again. I don't bloody believe it.'

Billy spoke. 'As you know, Jo linked the victims. She found a woman who knew both Fischer and Bowman. I'll let Jo explain.'

She seemed reluctant and wasn't sure why. 'It all stemmed from the death of the racing car driver Brody Miller last month. In his youth, Miller was pals with both our homicide victims, and they had a reputation for womanising. All three allegedly raped a teenager and now, 30 years later, the alleged victim has murdered two of the three rapists. She claims the third was Brody Miller.'

'The one written about in the papers?' asked Stephen Payne, surprising everyone.

'The same,' said Jo. 'The witness turned confessor, explained the killings in precise detail, made a full confession with her solicitor present, and then stated she intends to plead guilty.'

The room remained silent. What should have become a celebration produced nothing. DI Rose stood and reprimanded the squad.

'Back when I was a Detective Senior Constable at Homicide, the announcement of a case being solved was met with spontaneous even riotous behaviour. This detective's grandfather cracked many homicide cases, and now his granddaughter is giving the old DCI a bloody good run for his money. What is the matter with you lot?'

The coach inspired, or rather shamed, her players. They clapped, they yelled, they went to Billy and Jo and shook hands, kissed and congratulated them. DI Blunt hid. The celebration went on and on until Rose yelled, and it took her yelling for order to be restored.

'Right,' said the boss, 'any questions?'

'What happened to the confession from Clunes?' asked DS Fletcher.

'Were we happy with it?' asked Rose. 'Why confess to so much? Why keep his knife? The man lost everything; wife, kids, home, livelihood. Attacking his ex was the last straw. If ever there was a man wanting to commit suicide by police, Barry Clunes was it.'

Rose's explanation had weight.

'And Bowman's wife and brother?' asked DS Melody. 'Were their confessions false as well?'

'No, we can allege they conspired to murder Max Bowman, and it was only our suspect getting there first which saved them. They'll be charged with conspiracy to murder.'

'And the other suspects, are they all clear?' asked Charley Baldwin.

'DI Blunt reckons he's close to nabbing Alex Hero on charges of fraud and extortion,' said Rose. Blunt's hatred simmered.

More silence until Charley Baldwin spoke again. 'Bloody Jo Best,' he said. 'How the hell does she do it? Surely no-one is *that* lucky.'

The room buzzed and Baldwin copped withering retorts.

'Enough,' cried DI Rose. 'I hereby order all members to Rafferty's for the longest lunch this year, with the first round on Jo Best.' Cheering exploded and Jo slipped her left hand into her pocket.

Callum looked foolish, particularly in his own eyes. He chickened out of sharing his video footage for fear of reprisal from Mickey Spillane. With a bus load of Soggies, yes, but on his own, this was Charge of the Light Brigade stuff. Yet doing nothing gained nothing. He had to try.

Ignoring the lunch, he headed for the Vino Encantador Wine Bar. It was crowded but there, alone at his table, sat the owner, one Miguel Spanielle. Blunt approached and the hubbub volume dropped. Who is the dude in the suit, a tailoring match for the mobster?

Mickey Spillane looked up from his Caesar Salad and smiled. 'Officer Blunt, please join me.'

Callum sat. 'Good afternoon Mr Spanielle.' The polite respect worked before. The hubbub from diners moved back to normal.

'Mickey, please. After all we're friends.' Callum hesitated. 'We *are* friends are we not?'

'Perhaps but I have something you may find ... unpleasant.'

'Not a stock market tip?' Mickey acted cool because he *was* cool.

Callum removed his phone, found the file, turned the phone for Mickey, and tapped start. The gangster watched in silence.

'Sound's not bad but the visual's crap.'

'This hasn't been seen by anyone else ... so far.'

Mickey looked at a nervous Callum. 'And your point is?'

'Have you anything you'd like to say?'

Mickey nodded. 'This Caesar Salad is seriously good. Have some.'

Callum couldn't match the gangster's coolness. 'Fair enough but I'll be back and when I return, I won't be as polite.'

He collected his phone, gave a stare he hoped was impressive and left. He was late to the Homicide luncheon but hoped like hell he would soon have terrific news to grab the attention of his colleagues.

Chapter 28

Every celebratory lunch tasted better when a case was solved, and cracking two cases at the same time meant the wine flowed freely and tongues wagged with ease. The detectives had a room to themselves in this popular eatery. Jo sat with Billy on her left and DI Rose on her right. Squad members called to Jo whenever a point needed clarification. Once all glasses were charged, DI Rose proposed a toast.

'Ladies and gentlemen, to Acting Detective Senior Sergeant Hughes and Detective Senior Constable Best; well done, ladies.'

Glasses were clinked and cries of congratulations heard. Food was collected and members tucked in. The usual buzz of chatter never ceased but came to an abrupt halt when Billy yelled.

'Oi.' She upped the volume. 'Oi!' Conversations stopped dead and everyone looked at Billy. It was as if she'd found something criminal or someone had pinched one of her chips which definitely was a crime in Homicide. Billy looked at Jo who knew she'd been sprung. 'What is that?' asked Billy, pointing. Billy was doubly surprised because she'd been sitting next to Jo for 60 odd minutes when interviewing Chelsea and seen nothing. Billy reckoned she'd been conned.

Others craned to see. DI Rose had a ringside seat. Billy lifted Jo's left hand. 'You been shoplifting, Senior?'

Others saw the reason for Billy's clamour. Officers carried on like school kids. 'Speech,' cried Charley Baldwin and soon the whole room joined the chant of "speech".

Reluctantly Jo stood and the chant subsided. 'This had better be good, Senior,' threatened Billy.

'Does DCI Robertson know about this?' asked DI Rose.

Jo cleared her throat. 'Yesterday I accepted a proposal of marriage from your colleague and mine, DI Pierre Richelieu.'

The room erupted. Ferocious clapping from everyone although latecomer DI Blunt showed fake enthusiasm. Everything about that man was fake.

'And?' asked Billy when the congratulations dimmed.

'You'll be pleased to know he's made wonderful progress moving from ICU to Critical Care, to his present position in a general ward.'

'I bet he's in a suite with hot and cold running nurses,' called Baldwin which prompted a laugh and wasn't all that far from the truth.

Jo looked at Billy. 'Sorry Sarge; I didn't want to distract you when we were close to cracking both cases so I hid the ring until we did.'

'*You* got the result,' said Billy, which set off the biggest roar.

'Thank you all for your kind remarks, and I'll tell the DI how you've been so supportive during this time when he very nearly lost his life.'

Her seriousness flattened the mood but it was apt and needed to be said. Silence followed until DS Fletcher broke the ice. 'At least you can use your own handcuffs, Jo.'

Laughter re-appeared and the eating and drinking resumed.

DI Rose squeezed Jo's arm. 'You won the double today, Detective—a murderess and a cop.'

Jo smiled and tried eating her fish. Billy attacked from Jo's other side. 'So where was the ring during the interview, or shouldn't I ask?'

'It was turned inside on my right hand and under a plaster.'

Billy smiled and nodded. 'You're right. The interview would have been a mess with you flashing that stone.'

The lunch continued when Charley Baldwin knelt beside Jo. 'Excuse me, ma'am and Sarge. Jo, I've gotta date with a dentist but listen, bloody good news and tell the DI he's the luckiest man in town.'

'I will and thanks, Charley.'

'So when's the big day?'

'When I know, mate, you'll be the last to find out.'

They laughed and he left. Conversations slowed as officers drifted back to work, calling their congratulations to Jo. Only three females remained; Jo with Hughes and Rose. They took their time over coffee.

'Have you told, Robbo?' asked the DI.

'About the double homicides?' said Jo.

'Don't be smart. That won't surprise him at all but having his little girl marry a copper might get him excited.'

Jo smiled thinking of her Pop. But her thoughts were elsewhere. 'I thought we might have done a Poirot today.' The other women looked at one another. 'Does that ever happen in real life?'

'She's talking about a modern ending to *Murder on the Orient Express*,' said Billy to DI Rose.

'What that girl, Chelsea, went through, first with the pack rape, then the treatment from her family, the child being adopted, the total lack of justice—and every year being reminded of her torment.'

'Not to mention her second kid drowning,' added Billy.

'If I'd been the boss and alone on duty, I would've been tempted to do a Poirot and forget all about charging her. Justice was done.'

Their reverie was interrupted when Jo's phone buzzed. She had it muted not wanting to hear from a certain journalist.

'It's your phone, Senior,' said Billy, 'from the first of your millions of fans.' Jo dragged her feet. 'Well answer it, woman.'

Jo dreaded the demands from the journalist. *Which girl? Both murders?* There were messages including two from the journalist. But the latest smacked Jo. She looked faint. Billy and Rose saw her shock.

'What's happened?' demanded Billy.

Jo struggled to speak. 'Pierre's collapsed. He's back in ICU.'

The other women stood pushing back their chairs and helping Jo. 'Go now,' said the DI. 'Take her, Billy.'

The three of them headed for the exit and into Bourke Street. Billy stayed beside Jo as DI Rose hailed a cab. She gave directions to the driver as Billy shoved Jo, piling in after her.

The driver took off. It was only a kilometre to the hospital but traffic in the CBD was always heavy.

'Who sent the text?' asked Billy trying to get Jo thinking about anything other than the obvious. She seemed nonplussed. 'Show me.'

Billy took Jo's phone and found the text from Dr Grant Buchanan. It read. *Hi Jo. Pierre's had a turn and been admitted to ICU. I suggest you come asap. Grant.* Billy also saw a text from a Tazmin Gallagher. *Need name of my girl you arrested. Please Jo.*

'It says he's had a turn, Jo. It may be they're simply being cautious.'

Jo nodded. She wanted to believe any piece of positive news no matter how trivial. Time dragged until the cab found a good run and pulled up outside the hospital.

'I'll pay, you go,' said Billy and Jo set off. She knew the way to ICU and was spotted by nurse Katrina. Her smile was warm but serious.

'Hi Jo,' she said. 'Wait here and I'll get Doctor Buchanan.'

Katrina left as Billy Hughes arrived. She asked with her face.

'The doctor's coming to see me.' He did and Jo introduced Billy.

'Pierre has a problem breathing. A collapsed lung is tricky but then we found he has a diaphragmatic rupture. As I told you, having his spleen removed increases other risks and he's picked up a bacterial infection too. All these things meant he was in pain so we've sedated him, and given support with his breathing. It sounds and looks bad but he's comfortable, pain free and getting the best care possible.'

Jo despaired. Billy hid her fear. 'Can I see him?' asked Jo.

'Of course but you need to be prepared.' Jo thought she now knew what a knife to your heart felt like. 'He can't respond, Jo.' He spoke softly. 'Do you understand?' Jo nodded. The doctor looked at Billy.

'I'll wait here,' she said, then to Jo. 'I'll wait, Jo. Chin up.'

In a daze, Jo left with the doctor who'd done the right thing. Warnings are important before a shocking and scary situation.

Pierre, what could be seen of him, was a marvel of modern medicine. Centuries ago, even decades, he'd be long dead. Science has given us seriously good equipment and when matched with knowledge, great results have been achieved; Pierre Richelieu's survival being one.

Two nurses and a doctor monitored screens showing results of different organs in Pierre's body. Jo surprised herself by not crying. She was devastated but found herself wanting to yell at her fiancé and tell him to wake up. They were a couple soon to wed.

You can't walk out on me, Pierre! Wake up. Look, it's me, your best girl, your favourite detective. Come on, get back to the general ward.

Dr Buchanan explained various pieces of equipment with most of the information going in one of Jo's ears and out the other. He watched her and decided it was time to leave. He knew even a tough homicide detective was no defence where the heart was involved, and too much time or information can be a bad thing.

He guided her back to where Billy joined them, studying Jo.

'Are you able to help Jo get home, Sergeant?' asked the medico.

'Of course,' said Billy.

He handed Billy his card. 'And please, if you or Jo have any questions, call me any time.' He squeezed Jo's arm. 'Pierre's a fighter, Jo, and now I believe he has something pretty wonderful to fight for.'

Oh dear. Talk about the Barnes Wallis moment as the dam wall burst. Jo lost it and Billy helped her to the street. Despite her trauma, Jo knew she had to be strong, and Billy took pride as the young woman fought her shock, steeling herself for what lay ahead.

'Where do you want to go?' asked Billy. 'Home? To your parents, sister, to Robbo?'

'North Fitzroy,' was all she said.

'Gabrielle Strange?' Jo nodded.

They found a cab and Billy walked with Jo to Gabrielle's front door. The pathologist did her usual complaining routine coming along the passage. She opened her door and reacted.

'Not one detective, but two.' Then she saw Jo's face. 'What's wrong?'

'Detective Best has had a shock, Doctor. Can you help please?'

Silly question as Gabrielle guided Jo in. 'Entrée Mademoiselle. Will you be joining us, Detective?'

Billy declined. 'Thank you but no.' She spoke to her colleague. 'I'll call you, Jo. Take care.'

She left and Gabrielle made coffee, keeping an eye on the woman who had often sat in this kitchen and shared secrets.

'What do I need to know, girlie, or what do you wish to say?' she asked hunting for chocolate.

'In the last 24 hours I've solved two homicides, accepted Pierre's marriage proposal, and just now, my fiancé's been rushed back to the ICU and placed in an induced coma.'

It took something special to shock the pathologist but right now, shocked she was. 'Jesus, Joseph and Mary, woman, why don't you tell me something important?'

Jo wept in silence. Gabrielle came around the kitchen island and gave the young woman a hug to please a bear. No words were needed. The hug remained until the kettle boiled. Jo grew stronger.

'*Two* homicides? Damn show-off. Why can't you settle for one?' Jo tried to smile. 'Well come on,' demanded Gabrielle, 'let's have a squiz at the rock.' Jo raised her left hand and Gabrielle examined the ring. 'Bloody hell, he didn't get that in the $2 shop.' There was another attempt at a smile by Jo silently observed by the pathologist.

Gabrielle sorted the coffee and shoved a half-empty box of Haigh's Assorted Creams across to Jo. When the doctor next spoke, she did so without emotion and certainly without any attempt at being funny.

'So what's happened to the dashing Frenchman?' With her mind and body a mess, Jo couldn't speak. 'Did you speak to the doctors? Jo nodded. 'And?' Jo remained silent. Gabrielle took a punt and got stuck into her. It would either help Jo grow stronger or see her collapse.

'Get a grip, woman. Your man needs you. *You* need you.'

Gabrielle's sigh was audible when Jo responded with strength. 'Yesterday he was fine. Out in a general ward, he was up and dressed, the best he'd been since the attack. And that's when he proposed.'

'Was it a surprise?'

'Total surprise. He had the nurses in on it of course.'

'Of course.'

'But he fooled me. I was doing something with the flowers, I can't remember, and when I turned he was down on one knee.'

'He's French. What would you expect?'

'And then he asked me.'

'To which you replied, "Can I get back to you on that?".'

Gabrielle was back to the wisecracks and again it helped Jo relax.

'I think I said "yes" then "oui" and kept saying oui over and over.'

Now it was Gabrielle's turn to smile. She selected a chocolate and urged Jo to do the same. *The girl needs to keep busy.*

'Then an hour ago he collapsed and was rushed back to ICU.' Jo fought to hold back the tears.

'Well girlie, look at the good news; he was in the right place when he had his turn, and most certainly is now.'

Jo took her time. 'Tell me about an induced coma, please.'

Gabrielle was reluctant to talk medical matters, mainly because recovery from Pierre's condition was difficult to predict with death a distinct possibility. Besides, she didn't know the specific details. She gave Jo the bare essentials.

'What are his chances, Gabrielle?'

'I don't know his exact condition, Missy.'

'Should I be prepared for Pierre to die?'

Gabrielle didn't hesitate. 'Yes, it's certainly a possibility.'

Neither spoke for a while. Gabrielle tried to be businesslike. 'I know from first-hand experience his family are lying, scheming murderers but is there anyone half decent who can be trusted with his affairs?'

Jo's face screamed shock. 'What do you mean?'

Gabrielle ploughed ahead not thinking. 'Do you know his lawyer? He or she will have Pierre's power of attorney.' Jo stared at Gabrielle who realised. 'Oh shit,' she muttered.

'I don't have to contact his lawyer if he dies!' Gabrielle didn't speak. Jo panicked. She put her hands on her head and screamed. Gabrielle went to her. 'It's me. I have to tell myself if he dies!'

Quality coffee and chocolate didn't help. Jo, who arrived in a mess, slumped into despair. The fact the man she loved was unconscious and being kept alive by mechanical means was terrifying. The fact she was the person who had to decide what to do with his affairs was all too much. Her mind suffered a meltdown. One thought involved her doing the actual deed, where she would physically, literally flick the switch. That idea, wrong though it was, crushed her.

Gabrielle briefly pondered alcohol or sedatives for her friend but decided against both. She ran a bath and ordered Jo to strip and soak. It was late afternoon but Gabrielle prescribed food. She ordered Jo to stay in the bath forever, and when she emerged, Jo was greeted with homemade creamy fettuccini carbonara with grated parmesan to make it sing. Jo was glad she'd not eaten all her lunch.

Gabrielle skilfully steered away from discussing Pierre. She asked about the tiny cuts on the eyebrow and tongue of the two men she examined. Jo tried hard to sound normal and explained everything. Half way through her meal, she dropped her fork and begged Gabriel.

'Please, will you ring Dr Buchanan and ask the right questions?'

Gabrielle knew that question was coming. 'Sure,' she said.

'I want to hear your questions but not his answers. You can tell me later. And I'm going to make notes.' Jo gave her the doctor's card.

Gabriel called and got straight through. The medicos knew one another from conferences, and had crossed paths at coronial inquests.

She alerted Buchanan to her situation. He asked if he should speak freely and was advised to do so. Jo took notes of the terms Gabrielle used. The medico maintained a professional manner. Then it was over.

'Dr Buchanan sends you his love.'

That was the worst thing Gabrielle could say. Once again Jo's stress levels were through the roof and being given love and kindness flicked her emotional switch. Gabrielle, with years of experience of death and misery, now struggled to control her visitor. She led Jo to the charming lounge, more like a snug, lit the fire even though it wasn't needed, and with the one soft light, as the setting sun signalled the end of another day, Gabrielle walked on eggshells and told it like it was.

She wasn't surprised at Jo's reaction. The young detective's response was short and to the point.

'So you're saying there's nothing they can do tonight and they'll review the situation in the morning?'

Gabrielle looked less serious. 'You hit it in one, kiddo. Now I'll give you a choice of movies and we can have a good laugh or cry together.'

'No, Gabrielle. I've used up enough of your hospitality.'

Gabrielle became the boss. 'You're going nowhere, Detective. As soon as I put a chocolate on your pillow, you'll be ready to retire whenever you like. Mind you, you're in the guest's bedchamber.'

Jo didn't argue. She knew she'd have a terrible time being alone in her flat. 'Can I recommend you for a damehood?' asked Jo.

Gabriel laughed. It was the first audible sound of glee in this house for some time. Both felt the better for it. 'Did you know Shakespeare left his wife his second best bed?'

'Did he tell you that?'

The medico cackled again. 'Cheeky; I'll get more coffee.'

'No you won't. I'll do it.' And she did.

Time stood still as they chatted about their more interesting cases together, and a few of their colleagues. Gabrielle didn't hold back. Then her phone rang. It was Billy Hughes.

'She's here, Detective, and we've just been talking about you. Are your ears burning?' Jo shook her head at the words being uttered by the pathetic pathologist—her description. 'She's right here. Hang on.'

Jo spoke to her senior sergeant. 'Good evening, Sarge.' Jo listened. 'Thanks but Dr Strange has offered to put me up.' Billy asked about Pierre, and Jo told her there was little change.

But what she said and her tone of voice disguised the agony inside her heart and mind. Her body literally ached from sadness.

Chapter 29

Once Cain abandoned the home renovations, he and Rosa laid down their weapons. It was hardly a loving reunion but at least they were talking, not shouting or fuming in silence. When Cain found a nursing home for both his parents, Rosa congratulated her husband. Her father-in-law would never come here again, and her next meeting with Nipper would be at his funeral.

Cain's parents settled in their new place and life seemed better although visits were a challenge. Cain couldn't forget his father's hospital mutterings. 'Sorry,' he kept saying, still suffering guilt at having accidentally killed his grandson.

Cain had no-one to talk to about his misery. How could he help the old man in Nipper's final days? Would anything help ease his guilt?

The only person he could discuss the matter with was his wife, and she was the last person to ask. But he did. He tried the roundabout way and lied with gay abandon. 'I met a retired cop last week; old guy at the pub. He was up for a yarn.'

'Bully for you.'

'I couldn't shut him up.'

'How did you know he was a retired cop?'

'He told me. He said he worked in Homicide way back when.' Rosa said nothing. 'I wanted to ask if he knew the bastard who came after Nipper that day.' Still his wife said nothing. 'I was buggered if I could remember the cop's name.'

Rosa left the room but uttered the words Cain wanted to hear.

'Robertson—Detective Chief Inspector John Robbo Robertson.'

The name was burned on her brain and now on Cain's too.

Jo was up and about with the birds. Gabrielle was never a morning person. From the kitchen, Jo heard her snoring. So what first—

breakfast, ring the hospital or jog home? She was scared to ring the hospital, thought it rude to cut and run, so made tea. With a hot brew in hand, she unlocked the back door and sat in the garden.

A dog barked, a train whistle sounded and Jo cried. Life was going on and the man she loved was only alive thanks to a machine. Was there a worse feeling? Who was on that train, what did the barking dog have for breakfast, and what is going to happen to Pierre? Her tears, gentle and sans sobs, rolled steadily down her face.

'Bloody hell,' squawked the homeowner, poking her head out the door, 'were you born in a tent, woman? It's freezing.'

Jo repaired her face, a little, and went back to the kitchen. Gabrielle was wearing what seemed to be a cut-down version of a circus tent with her hair just back from a party.

'Sorry about the door,' said Jo.

'Sit ye down, girl and get ready for a full English.' Jo went to protest but didn't.

'Sounds great,' she said, lying.

'Now I've sorted our day. After brekky, I'll run you home. I'll ring the hospital while you have a shower, shave, shampoo and shoeshine. Then we'll do whatever seems best.'

In her present predicament, Jo couldn't think of a better person to be with now. 'Thank you, Doc. I think you're officially my bestie.'

Across town in Mont Albert, the Carr family prepared for the day. Pop and young Harry were roaming the streets with Rags on his morning constitutional. Gran was setting out breakfast things and offering to help her granddaughter who kept telling her grandmother she was fine. The child wanted to take back control of her life.

GP Jack was dressed and ready for an early start planning to call on stuck-at-home patients before his busy surgery.

'Good morning,' said his mother.

'Morning Gran, morning Grace.' He drank his coffee and chewed a piece of toast.

'Dad, why do you call Gran, Gran? She's your mother.'

The grown-ups exchanged glances. 'Perfectly correct, daughter,' said Jack. 'I'll think of another name. What about "Mummy"?'

Grace wanted to growl at her father and tell him to stop being silly but before she could, the hound and its companions returned.

Harry had news. 'Rags did a big poo in the park by the swings.'

'Thank you, Harry. Please save the poo report until *after* breakfast,' said his grandmother.

Harry looked at his father to see if he too would reprimand the lad. Instead the boy copped a wink.

'Hand washing, Harry,' said his grandfather and the boy departed.

The mood in the kitchen seemed normal but was far from it. Jack had told his friend Grant Buchanan about his family's friendship with Jo Best, and the specialist kept Jack up to date with news on Pierre's situation. The public knew the gory details of the East Melbourne murder attempt by car.

Jack knew Pierre had progressed reasonably well, heard that he proposed marriage to one Detective Jo Best, and had then relapsed and been placed back in the ICU. Of course Harry and Grace knew nothing of these matters.

'Any news?' asked Peg. Her son shook his head.

'News about what?' asked the clever and with-it Grace. The adults loved her sharpness and rejoiced in her ability to bounce back after her shocking car accident. Walking was still her biggest challenge.

'One of Dad's patients,' said Peg, and Grace went back to her breakfast and book.

Gabrielle drove Jo the short distance to her Clifton Hill flat. Jo well remembered the time she borrowed Gabrielle's car. Anyone with experience driving tanks in the Army would have managed the elderly Humber with ease.

'I'll call the hospital. When you're ready, come out and we'll plan from there.'

Jo leant across, kissed the pathologist and scampered inside. Once there, her tears began again. She headed for the bathroom and her full English lurched into the toilet bowl. She showered, changed and went back to the car.

'No news,' said Gabrielle. 'He's comfortable and they said you're welcome at any time.'

'Thanks,' was all Jo could say fighting hard not to cry.

'Let's take a cab,' said Gabriel and opened her phone. 'I'm all right to park here?' Jo nodded and again any act of kindness, and especially from a friend, piled on the pressure.

The cab arrived and they set off for the hospital. En route, Gabrielle enquired. 'Have you checked your phone?' and Jo snapped back to a form of normality. Her phone was off and there were messages galore. A text from DI Rose was brief. *Thinking of you. Forget work. Keep in touch. Love Elly.*

In trying to think clearly, Jo had a thought which increased her worries. 'Gabrielle, I'm keeping you from your work.'

She chuckled. 'Alas, while I know I'm indispensable, sadly it ain't necessarily so. Rowdy Laudi is on hand to do the necessary.' Jo looked blank. 'Dr Petr Laudi, my new assistant.' Jo had forgotten him already.

Gabrielle grasped Jo's hand and held it tight. As they held hands, Jo read every word and meaning conveyed through her grip.

The cab reached the hospital and Jo produced her wallet. 'Wait for me inside,' ordered Gabrielle shoving Jo from the cab. Gabrielle paid and joined her friend. Both knew this might be tricky in the extreme.

In ICU reception they were spotted. Nurse Katrina was introduced then Grant Buchanan arrived and greeted both women warmly leading them to a quiet room. He was experienced in these matters and could pretty much guess what topics would be raised. Sometimes the loved ones were afraid to speak. Jo was terrified but determined to ask.

'Did you know, Grant, Pierre requested I hold his enduring power of attorney?'

The doctor nodded. 'He told me the day you brought him the paperwork and he was so proud.'

Jo didn't hesitate. She decided straight talking was the key to her sanity. She tried not to think of Pierre's survival.

'Doctor Strange has been a tower of strength and explained many issues. So please, Grant, what is your prognosis? And I want everything on the table please.' Grant looked at both women. Before he could reply, Jo continued. 'I will take your advice, Doctor. I want Pierre to recover so I can take him home and care for him as long as I'm able. We can both retire from the police, and live a new life together.' She hadn't rehearsed that speech and surprised herself but knew she spoke from the heart.

'Good for you, Detective. No wonder you're so damn good at solving homicides and finding lost kids. I admire your courage and can see why Pierre loves you so much.'

Oh God. Jo fought to stay "normal". 'Tell me, please,' she said and felt her eyes and nose begin to leak.

'Pierre is comfortable. He is sedated, and with the breathing apparatus, drips and tubes, and what we give him through that equipment, he's able to survive with the key word being *survive*. Doctors always like to say there's hope and with Pierre there is but with his latest problems of the collapsed lung and infection, I think Pierre has a really tough fight to recover. Of course another specialist may have a different opinion.'

Jo didn't realise but one of her fingernails pierced her palm. Gabrielle took Jo's hand slowing unpicking her scrunched fingers.

There was a long pause before Jo spoke in a calm and steady voice. 'May I see Pierre?'

'Of course you can; when you like and for as long as you like.'

This conversation was not rushed. 'I have two more questions.'

'Sure, fire away.'

'Does the hospital ask the family about allowing the patient to die or does the family ask the hospital?'

Gabrielle marvelled at the strength of her young friend, and Dr Buchanan too thought Jo was courage personified.

'There's no set procedure. We can talk about it whenever you like. There's no rush.' Jo nodded her thanks. More silence. 'You said you had two questions.'

Jo's brain began racing. This subject hammered her mind. 'Do you think Pierre tried too hard to get better in order to ask me to marry him, and as a result brought on this latest attack?'

Wow. Talk about the hardest one last. Both doctors struggled to think of an answer. Grant was in the firing line.

'I know he loved you, Jo, only because he told me so many times, I thought he had a smart phone on a loop under his pillow.'

Good answer Doc.

About ten minutes after Grant left the women alone, Jo decided to visit Pierre. Gabrielle waited, desperate for a snifter and, regretting her recent sobriety, dreading the return of her young friend. The trip home might be difficult to say the least.

Pierre's bed was tilted about 30 degrees and the amount of tubes inserted in various parts of his body was frightening. Being heavily sedated, he seemed at peace. The nurses apologised, whispering they would stay out of Jo's way. They explained how, if any of the machines made a noise, sometimes a loud noise, it was to tell them something about Pierre's condition, and was part of the routine of his care.

Jo moved close to Pierre. He slept with no idea of his predicament. His silk pyjamas—where *did* they come from?—were no more, and a hospital gown adorned the normally snappy dresser.

She remembered her first day at Homicide when this dashing detective with a strong French accent addressed the squad, his blue eyes flashing. The officers seemed to mock him as they finished Pierre's sentences with a choral version of "s'il vous plait". She would learn later that every member of the squad held the Gallic gendarme in the highest regard and their comments were a sign of respect.

She remembered their first kiss, and several others; their final night in Paris when Pierre was released and when their lives seemed primed to be together forever. She could never imagine the current situation.

And she could never forget his proposal of marriage. She towered over him as he knelt in his hospital room and again, his eyes were magnifique. Now they were shut, closed tight, and to Jo that was the saddest thing. He could not hear her, well probably not, but without his eyes and hers speaking and laughing, she felt alone.

Ignoring the medical staff coming and going, she kissed his forehead then whispered in his ear.

'You are the dearest man, Inspector Pierre Richelieu, the kindest and loveliest of men. And even though I have known you for only a few months, you have given me happiness beyond measure. I think I have always loved you but these last few weeks I *know* I love you. Not a doubt in the world.

'I want you to get well again, Pierre, so we can do all those things we love together. Caring for you would be a privilege, something I want to do, would love to do.' She paused, the emotion took over and she felt helpless knowing she couldn't last much longer.

'I will let you sleep now, my darling man. I will return soon and tell you all my news. Sweet dreams, Monsieur.'

She wanted to kiss his lips but a feeding tube placed in his nose proved an obstacle. A nurse's hand appeared and gently moved the tube a little allowing Jo to kiss his lips. Only then did she realise her tears were such to make her lover's face a mess. She didn't care and again kissed him before turning and leaving.

Once in Reception her tears turned to sobs. Gabrielle hugged her. Neither moved as life and death went on around them.

Right now, Jo didn't want to talk with Grant Buchanan or even arrange a time to meet again. The women found a cab and headed back to Clifton Hill. Gabrielle had forgotten her booklet, *Topics to discuss when travelling home from visiting a loved one in an ICU.* They muddled along and eventually arrived in Clifton Hill.

'Will you come in for coffee?' asked Jo forgetting the traumatic time the pathologist had experienced in this flat only a few weeks ago.

'Are there any more mad women inside?'

Jo nearly died. 'Oh, Gabrielle, I am *so* sorry. I didn't think.'

Gabrielle pushed her. 'Shut up and get moving.'

They ended up in the room where it all happened when Gabrielle gave a murderous woman instructions on how to shoot someone—in this case Detective Joanna Best—to make a murder look like a suicide; happy days. Jo's coffee was okay but not as good as Gabrielle's.

'I know I'm sounding like a cold-hearted bitch,' said Gabrielle, 'but you need to tell someone about your situation. What about family?'

'Not yet,' said Jo.

'What's wrong with your parents?'

'They're divorced. My father remarried—a child bride—giving me a step brother and sister about 20 years younger than me. My mother has an older, charming, wealthy and educated Italian boyfriend and nobody knows why he finds my miserable mother attractive.'

'This boyfriend,' said Gabrielle. 'He hasn't got a brother has he?'

Jo stopped. She didn't want to offend her guest by bursting into laughter but showed signs she would.

'What?' asked the pathologist with indignation. 'I'm a bloody good cook and the way to a man's stomach is through his oesophagus.' Jo started to laugh. 'Mind you, me in any form of lingerie is way too much information.' Jo's laughter increased—rapidly. 'But I'm brilliant in handling a stiff.' Jo shrieked and lost control.

Gabrielle, one cunning woman, steered Jo's misery to mirth coaxing her from the horrendously sad situation she faced. When the laughter subsided, and it took time, Gabrielle prepared to leave.

'Well if your family won't help, what about your friends?'

Jo felt sad. 'Girlfriends married or dropped off as I worked typical police shifts. I'm good friends with Michael Chan but there's a bit of unrequited love there. Look, Gabriel, yet again you've been a saint. I couldn't have gone there today without you.'

They hugged—hard. 'All right, but ring me at any time even to chat.' They kissed and Jo followed her to the door. Gabrielle stopped. 'You didn't tell me if your mother's boyfriend has a brother.' Jo laughed and Gabrielle left. From the street came a cry. 'Even a cousin would do, and preferably male!'

Alone, Jo sat and pondered. Should I tell people? I'm engaged and my fiancé's in a coma. She decided against calling family and friends because you can't announce those bits of news at the same time. She did what she did so often—ran. Her phone snuggled in her bum bag for emergency use only. Yarra Bend Park is 260 hectares of greenery filled with trees, paths, a golf course, a river and even a waterfall of sorts. Her pumping heart and straining muscles pushed her agonising thoughts to one side. It took a marathon effort to settle her despair.

At home, she showered and slipped into pyjamas in mid-afternoon. Billy Hughes and Charley Baldwin left text messages saying they were thinking of her. She watched the news which depressed her further so went to bed, early for her even with her shifts, and tried to sleep.

Stress is a real bugger. Even if you think you're on top of it, it creeps into your body and mind and does its best to make you crook. It was the thought she might have to decide if Pierre should be allowed to slip away that brought her undone. How can I order Pierre's death? It's not monstrous, it's worse, it's so bloody unfair.

With those thoughts dominating her brain, she fell asleep. Hours flew by. She slept through into the night, her phone on mute. It rang again and instinct kicked in. She woke but refused to answer.

In the darkness, her flat was lit only by her clock radio, phone and Fitbit. She saw the time and died—0127. She grabbed her phone and saw the caller ID, Dr Grant Buchanan. She felt sick and answered.

'Hello.'

'Hi, Jo, it's Grant.'

'Yes?'

'I'm awfully sorry, Jo, but Pierre has slipped away. Are you okay?'

Shock never plays by the rules. Jo struggled. 'Has Pierre died?'

'Yes, Jo. He had a massive heart attack about half an hour ago and, although we did everything to try and save him, the damage was too great. I'm so sorry, Jo. Is there someone with you?'

'Ah, no, but I'm okay.' She wasn't. 'Thanks.'

'You can come in later and we'll talk about everything. But there's no hurry. Is there anything I can do for you? Can I make some calls?'

'No, I'll do it later. But thank you and thanks for everything you and all the staff did. I'm ever so grateful.'

There was a pause. 'I know this may be of little comfort, Jo, but to me Pierre was the sort of man who wouldn't want to burden you with making a decision about his death. Who knows, he may have chosen to take the decision away from you.'

Jo cried. 'You're right,' she said as the tears flowed. 'He was exactly that type of gentleman.'

'I'm on duty, Jo, so please call me at any time and we'll talk later.'

'Thank you and goodnight.'

She cried those tears of loss, of rage, of sadness and grief. She thought of questions she wanted to ask. *Where is Pierre now? Is he safe? When can I see him? Did you tell him I love him?*

It was a long night; no, a very long night.

It was too for DI Callum Blunt. He pondered his next move with the clip he had of Spanielle and Hero. Should he show it to a prosecutor or to DI Rose? Frustration reigned. It's not easy being a selfish bastard.

He decided. He took a single frame of Mickey Spillane and Mr President, and sent it to the café owner's phone. The text with the photo was simple. *Last chance, Mr Spanielle. Time to talk.*

He hit Send and discovered he was shaking. He needed the criminal to do something to help the cop. Offer a bribe, agree to talk, make a plea, turn on Hero, anything. Blunt put down his phone and grabbed a beer from the fridge. His phone pinged and he raced to the lounge.

It was a text from Mickey Spillane. Quick reply meant the jury had made a decision. *Callum, you little ripper, you did it.*

There was a picture and a one word text. The word was *Snap* and the picture featured Callum strapped to a chair wearing what was obviously a brand new pair of concrete shoes. His groan said it all.

Chapter 30

Not many people get engaged, don't tell their friends or family about the happy event, and then have their fiancé die two days later. Jo went to the hospital later in the morning. She sent texts to DI Rose and Billy Hughes and rang Gabrielle Strange. She knew the social media grapevine would run wild. It did. Her phone prepared to crash.

Grant Buchanan was ending his shift when Jo arrived and took her in hand. Other staff members hugged Jo, and their sadness at her grief multiplied her pain.

She did well in tackling the many essential tasks. When her grandmother died recently, Jo took over, allowing her grandfather, Robbo, to grieve, not having to think about the funeral details.

In her situation, rather than rush, she followed Pierre's written instructions; he wished to be cremated, to not have a funeral but perhaps a remembrance service at the police chapel at some time in the future. DI Rose and Assistant Commissioner (Crime), John Cowley, gave her their full support. Taking Pierre's ashes back to Paris to be buried with his mother could wait.

Jo was sent on compassionate leave and ordered to stay away from Homicide. She thought getting back to work sooner might be good but then she simply didn't have the heart for it.

As the days went by, the number of calls, texts, emails and cards she received was overwhelming. Everyone knew Pierre was attacked by relatives from overseas, and that Jo was, at one stage, implicated in the attack. They knew too about the attempt to murder Jo, and the shooting death of the American drug runner in her flat. Finally they discovered that Pierre had died. The attempt murder charge against his estranged wife and step-sister was upgraded.

But few people knew Jo and Pierre were engaged.

She spent time with her parents and sister. It was all a bit strange. They were used to seeing her cases make headlines but when they discovered the man who died was engaged to Jo, real shock set in.

Pierre's private cremation was as he wished and Jo invited DI Rose, Billy Hughes and Gabrielle Strange. She was touched by their kind words. Everyone admired the Inspector, regarding him as a kind man and a bloody good detective. Jo loved him.

Michael Chan proved a great friend offering to help in any of the routine tasks associated with a death in the family. Gabrielle Strange prescribed a different type of drug, giving Jo the key to a cottage in a hamlet not far from Castlemaine. 'It belongs to a lady I once helped and she insisted if ever I needed to get away for a few days, I simply had to go there.'

Jo argued but Gabrielle wouldn't take no for an answer—threatened would be unkind—and Jo threw clothes in a gym bag and left town.

The cottage was perfect. The elderly neighbours, who had no idea of her fame, introduced themselves and Jo settled. Her running routine took on new heights. There were country roads to explore with animals curious to watch the fit young detective running free.

She had plenty of time to think. *Will I return to policing and to Homicide? Do I need to ever work again? Where will I live? What will I do with all this new-found wealth?*

She tried to avoid her phone and only replied to those she thought most important. One interesting consequence was the action of the journalist, Tazmin Gallagher. Jo had gone back on her word; well almost. When Tazmin discovered DI Richelieu was engaged to Jo and had died, she sent Jo a text expressing condolences and thanking her for being helpful. Clever. Billy Hughes left the leaking texts alone.

Gabrielle was right. Getting away from work, family and all those kindly souls was the best thing but after four days, she'd had enough. Pierre's legal affairs needed attention. His remembrance service needed planning. It was time to head home.

On her last night, she again checked her phone and saw a text from Dr Jack Carr. He was one friend she would always have time for—Jack and his family.

*Hi Jo. Our thoughts are with you
at this tough time. Stay well and
everyone sends their love. Jack*

It was the perfect message; enough but not too much. She replied to few of her callers and though tempted to say "thanks", chose not to respond. Next morning she said goodbye to the old folk next door and as she headed back to town, a kookaburra, sitting on a fence post, looked at her and laughed. Jo smiled for the first time in a while.

Close to home, she rang her grandfather. 'G'day Pop, how are you?'

'Where are you, Detective?' asked, or rather demanded the former DCI. 'I'm worried sick. You have terrible news and all I get is one fleeting phone call and then a text message telling me you're fine and going away for a few days.'

'Well I'm back and ready to tell you all my news. Is the kettle on?'

'It will be. When are you coming?'

'ETA twenty minutes. Over and out, Chief Inspector.' She parked outside Robbo's house and took no notice of a van parked fifty yards away. Why should she?

Pop was the first to hear about Jo's rollercoaster week, a time when she became engaged, lost her fiancé, arranged his cremation, left town for a few days of R 'n R, oh and not before she managed to crack two homicides.

Robbo was a mix of huge pride and huge sorrow. He wanted to know what she planned to do and when. He would normally give her advice but held back, now regarding his granddaughter as someone who had control of her life.

Jo was as interested in his future plans as he was in hers. 'I'm staying put for now,' said Robbo, 'but your mother is telling me to move into one of those retirement villages.'

'And?'

He looked at her. 'Mind your own business,' he said and winked.

They both found great comfort in chatting face to face but Jo wanted to get home to her own flat, now but one part of her real estate portfolio. She kissed her grandfather and headed for Clifton Hill. Driving through Mont Albert, she made a snap decision and parked outside the Carr home.

It was mid-afternoon and Jo had no idea who might be there. She rang the front doorbell and Peg opened it. Her smile and hug were both tending towards enormous. Jo explained she was passing and wanted to see how the family was going.

'Terrible,' said Peg and led Jo into the kitchen. Hugh sat on a chair with pain etched all over his face while Rags couldn't believe his luck. 'This silly old man has twisted his ankle and the kids need collecting in twenty minutes. Jack's in surgery and I can't raise the neighbour who fills in when there's an emergency.'

In-between patting Rags, Jo kissed Hugh and teased him about being drunk during the day. 'Problem solved, folks, Jo's taxi service is ready to roll.'

The Carrs were over the moon, gave Jo instructions and waved her away with Peg calling. 'You'll stay to tea.'

Hugh's sore ankle already felt better although Rags thought the visit far too short.

The plan was to collect young Harry first and then pick up Grace who was doing physio at a nearby clinic. Jo parked behind the school and wandered over to the gate. A few mothers and one stay-at-home dad were gathered. Jo nodded and smiled and a couple of the parents knew who she was. Soon the kids came out and Jo spotted Harry who was looking for his grandfather. When he spotted his favourite detective he ran towards her.

'Hello Harry Carr,' said Jo saluting. The lad's joy bubbled over as he returned the salute. 'I've come to collect you as Grandpa has hurt his ankle.'

Finally Harry found his voice. 'That is so brill, Detective Jo. Can I sit in the front?'

'Now we can't break the law if we're going to join the police.'

Holding hands, they walked, Harry skipped, to Jo's car with the boy never more serious. 'I promise I'll be good.'

They laughed and as they drew close to Jo's car, they passed a van when a man stepped out from in front of it, grabbed Jo's arm and spoke in a soft but threatening voice.

'Wait or else.' Jo stopped, prepared to fight but looked down. The man had what looked like a gun inside his overalls. 'No tricks.'

Jo looked at the boy. 'Wait a minute, Harry. I need to speak to this man.' The child did as he was told. Why not? The best person in the world to trust was Detective Jo Best.

The man released his grip and moved slowly backwards. When level with the handle on the side of his van, he stopped. His right hand held the hidden gun. He hissed. 'Behave or the kid gets it first.'

'Take it easy, we're not going anywhere,' replied Jo, looking for a way out. The parents and kids on the other side of the road couldn't see with the trio now hidden by the van.

Using his left hand, the man reached across his body to open the van door. He made the gun look bigger and Jo remained still. The van door was flung open. 'In,' he snapped and stepped back.

'I'll give you my credit card and PIN now. You can take it,' she said.

'In or the kid is gone. I'm serious.'

Jo turned to Harry. 'Come on young man. This is a police game and you can play it with me.' Harry's eyes widened. She guided Harry into the empty van. The door slammed shut. Jo checked the back doors. Locked. She heard the driver's door open and saw the man jump in and start the motor. 'Sit there, Harry.' The boy sat, a mix of excitement and concern.

'Phone,' snapped the driver who looked at Jo. He spoke louder. 'Phone, now!' She moved and handed her phone through to the cab. 'Now sit,' he snapped and if I see you move, the kid's first and then you.' Jo hesitated. 'Sit!' She sat next to Harry, shielding him from the driver. They held on to one another as the van accelerated.

Jo's mind worked overtime. *Is this a robbery? Does he know I'm a cop? Wealthy? Is this a kidnap and do the Carrs have the money?*

Jo wrapped her arm around the boy who felt safe with her. But even a young child can sense danger and Harry toyed with fear. Jo needed to keep him calm and get away without harm.

She kept up the lies. 'When we play these police games, Harry, we have to be quiet and follow the rules exactly as we're told. Okay?'

He looked up at her. 'Okay, Detective Jo.'

'Good boy,' she said with a nasty taste in her mouth.

The van was driven so as not to attract attention. It headed east towards Box Hill. The driver adjusted his interior mirror to watch his passengers. Without her phone, Jo felt helpless. *What is his motive and how the hell can I overcome this lunatic?*

About 20 minutes later, the van swung into a side road and then an industrial complex. Jo didn't like the setting. The van stopped in front of a large roller door which rose. The van drove into a factory, silent as a Quaker prayer meeting; the roller door descended. It was a storage facility with plant and boxes standing idle. The van stopped. The driver was around to the side and opened the door. He stood back.

'Out,' he said and Jo guided the boy. 'This way.' He walked backwards with Jo shielding Harry as the gun was obvious although still hidden.

Why won't he show the gun, to me, to the child? He's clearly disturbed. Is he a friend of a crim I once put away? Has he got the wrong victim? Is he working alone?

There was a small shed-cum-office in a corner of the factory. The man opened the door always looking at his prisoners. 'He goes in.' Jo worried Harry would have a terror experience he may never live down.

'Harry, I want you to wait in here for me. Soon the game will be over so be a good boy and I'll come and get you very soon. Okay?'

'Okay, Detective Jo,' said the child trusting implicitly in his friend.

Once Harry was inside, the door was closed and locked. The man pocketed the key. Then he produced the gun. It looked real. 'Over there,' he said. Jo sat on an old former cinema seat in a row of three.

'Look, whatever you want, let's talk,' she said. 'No-one needs to get hurt.'

'Oh yes they do,' he said. 'Someone definitely needs to get hurt.'

That comment stung. Jo wanted details, to know the motive for the man's behaviour. She ruled out robbery. *Revenge? But for what? Kidnap? Possibly but why Harry?* 'Okay,' said Jo. 'Tell me what you want and I'll help.'

'You have to get your father to come here right now.'

'My father?' asked Jo more confused than ever.

'He has to suffer and you have to see him do the business so the pain goes on and on for the rest of his miserable life. Your son is going to die.'

Panic hammered Jo's body. She knew upsetting the man was the worst thing to do. He was distressed. *He's a loose cannon. Has he made a mistake, got the wrong person? Will he listen to reason? What have I missed?* She decided to keep him talking and pretend she understood him.

'Okay but what has my son done to deserve this? He's a good kid.'

'My son died because of your prick of a father. Your father ruined my father's life. Now your father can get a taste of lifelong misery.'

'Well I'm sorry to hear about your son but please tell me when my father hurt your boy.'

The gunman scoffed. 'He hasn't told you? Typical, he's ashamed. Coppers are all cowards and animals.'

Jo's mind raced. She knew the wrong question might cause the desperate man to explode and kill them both. 'Okay, you want me to contact DCI Robertson? You know he's no longer a cop, he's retired?'

'Of course I know. I've been following that bastard for days. Thirty years ago he came after my old man causing him to accidentally kill my boy. So now it's payback time, justice for my Dad.' He slid Jo's phone along the concrete where it stopped in front of her feet. 'Call him.'

Now she knew the motive but did that help? She picked up her phone. 'Please give me a minute.'

Nipper Reid's son, Cain, had come this far and was not stopping now. His Dad would find peace. 'Do it or I'll shoot you and the kid with the kid first. You can watch him die.'

'Okay, how about I call my father? We can put him on Speaker, and you can let him know what he did, and how it has made you so angry.'

Cain erupted. He didn't want to chat. He wanted an eye for an eye, a small boy's life for another small boy's life.

'No, my son died, so your son dies. Get your old man here so he can do the business. Now call him.' He raised the gun. 'Or you both die.'

Jo threw caution to the wind. A reasoned argument was getting nowhere. She decided to risk causing the gunman to lose it and shoot. What choice did she have? She blurted her reply. 'He's not my son.' Cain felt confused and hesitated. 'And DCI Robertson is not my father.'

Cain screamed. 'Liar! I saw you go in his house. I saw you collect the kid. Now call him!'

Jo spoke calmly and quietly to try and pacify the gunman, and keep little Harry from hearing such terror. 'Listen, if you cause the death of a child who is not related to DCI Robertson, what will your father think? Will he be glad you killed the wrong kid? You'll only make your father's pain and misery worse. He'll die in total despair.'

'Shut up!' Cain lost control as spit and snot oozed from his face.

'How old is your father? He must be in his eighties. He can't have much longer to live. Why make his final years even more painful and distressing than they are already?'

Cain trembled making Jo start to panic. *I've pushed him over the edge,* she thought. Cain breathed quicker and looked wilder. His plan had to work, *must* work, but a skerrick of doubt arose. He pointed the gun at Jo. 'You're lying. You're lying to save your son's life. My boy died; your boy dies.'

Jo lost it and spoke with fear and anger. This was her final roll of the dice. 'He's not my son, and I'm not DCI Robertson's daughter.' She pointed, threatening without a weapon, and hissed. 'You grabbed the wrong kid, you fucking idiot!'

Now that was not a line from the manual for talking down crazed gunmen. Cain blew up. He pointed the gun at Jo and started to squeeze the trigger. He roared a scream of frustration and put his hands to his face making the gun point up. Jo took two steps and launched herself. It was a shirtfront, a superb front-on tackle.

Cain went backwards, his gun exploded as both adults attacked the concrete floor. Lying on top of her assailant, Jo went for his hand holding the gun. Enraged he fought like crazy. All the years of his father's suffering, all his wife's pent-up anger, and all his despair at the death of his son, ignited a temper. He exploded. He kicked at her and swung his left hand. Jo's elbow collided with his throat. He thought he would choke, broke free and thrust his head. A Liverpool kiss smacked Jo's forehead. That loosened her grip on his right hand allowing him to turn the gun towards her. She knew what was coming and rolled off him in desperation. Cain twisted to get the best shot possible and Jo lashed out with her left foot.

The gun exploded and the fight stopped dead. The gunshot in the acoustics of the concrete floor and tin roof factory produced a long, long echo. The silence took over. After what seemed like an age but was only ten seconds, a plaintive cry was heard from inside the office.

'Detective Jo? Can I come out now?'

The child was genuinely scared until he heard a reply.

'Hang on, Harry. I'll be right with you.'

To be continued.

The DCI Robertson Mysteries

Somebody Murdered Maggie is a crime fiction novella. A young mother is murdered in her kitchen. Her toddler son is crying in the next room. Whodunit? There's a laundry list of suspects. Then a motorcyclist crashes and dies. Some strange woman reckons it's murder. Really? DCI John 'Robbo' Robertson heads the Victoria Police Homicide Squad and is about to retire. Can he crack the cases before he leaves? Can you solve the murders before the police? Can Robbo's six-year-old granddaughter Joanna Best help her Pop crack the case? Surely not. Download *Somebody Murdered Maggie* now. It's free.

www.cenfoxbooks.com

It's the prequel to the Detective Joanna Best novels, and it's free.